A Father's Redemption

TRACY BLALOCK

LOVE INSPIRED

INSPIRATIONAL ROMANCE

LOVE INSPIRED®
INSPIRATIONAL ROMANCE

Recycling programs for this product may not exist in your area.

ISBN-13: 978-1-335-47474-2

A Father's Redemption

Copyright © 2021 by Tracy Blalock

This edition published by arrangement with Harlequin Books S.A.

For questions and comments about the quality of this book, please contact us at CustomerService@Harlequin.com.

Love Inspired
22 Adelaide St. West, 40th Floor
Toronto, Ontario M5H 4E3, Canada
www.LoveInspired.com

Printed in U.S.A.

I will be glad and rejoice in thy mercy:
for thou hast considered my trouble;
thou hast known my soul in adversities.
—*Psalm* 31:7

To my mom and dad, for your support
and encouragement during the long wait
between the release of my last book and this one.

And to the readers who were anxious to find out
what happened to Elias. Here is his story.

Chapter One

*Silver Springs, Willamette Valley, Oregon Country
Mid-July, 1846*

"You're her father, Elias. It's past time you start acting like it."

Elias Dawson's hands automatically wrapped around the sturdy frame of his eleven-month-old daughter as his sister-in-law, Mattie, unceremoniously deposited the infant on his lap.

His gaze rested on baby Emma for a brief moment before lifting to focus on his brother's wife. She stood with her hands on her hips, a resolute expression on her face.

Although he could hazard a guess, still he asked, "What exactly do you mean by that?"

"Don't pretend you don't know what I'm talking about." Frustration edged Mattie's voice as she impatiently brushed aside a strand of brown hair that had escaped from the knot at the back of her head. "Josiah and I have been taking care of Emma for almost a year now, and we love her dearly, but she's *your* daughter. She deserves so much more from you than the occasional snatched visit whenever we can get away from the ranch and drive into town. Her place is here with you." Though her expression didn't soften, her eyes silently beseeched him. "Surely, you must see that."

No. He didn't see that. He couldn't accept it.

But his behavior had been a bone of contention with his sister-in-law since the day Emma entered the world—just a handful of moments before her mother had left it.

In his grief, Elias had isolated himself from everyone, including his baby daughter, which Mattie had seen as breaking faith with both his late wife *and* their new child. Right from the start, Mattie had made it plain she disliked his actions.

There was no denying she had a kind heart, but Mattie also possessed a forthright nature that demanded every problem be faced head on. Elias's choice to retreat into himself, to pull away from his family and shut out the rest of the world, ran counter to Mattie's personal inclination. And she'd been left confused and upset by his behavior.

When it had fallen to her and his younger half brother, Josiah, to care for the newborn in Elias's stead, she'd protested the arrangement. But Josiah had persuaded her to make allowances given the tragic circumstances.

The days and weeks had turned into months, until nearly a year had passed without Elias noticing. And while he was content to let things stay the way they were for the foreseeable future, Mattie's tolerance had clearly reached an end.

She had never wavered from the belief that it was wrong to allow him to close himself off from his child. It was Josiah who had advocated patience. Convincing her to give Elias time and space to move beyond the loss of his wife and find some way to carry on with his life.

But how did a man move past a loss like that? Was it even possible? It certainly hadn't occurred yet. Perhaps the torment of dark thoughts and self-reproach would be with him always. Still, he'd held out a slim hope that day might eventually come.

But forgetting would prove impossible with Emma as a constant reminder of a life that was gone forever.

Not that he blamed his daughter for what had happened. He didn't.

The fault lay with him. He was the one who had failed Rebecca. Even with all his skills as a doctor, he hadn't been able to save his wife.

And he couldn't shake the thought—the stark fear— that he would fail again despite his best efforts. If he once more found himself in a situation where everything depended on him alone, would he fall short as he had before? Even if it didn't lead to another death, he could still inflict untold damage. The kind that left lasting wounds where no one could see.

That unsettling possibility sliced through him with the deadly precision of a scalpel, tearing open the heart he'd worked so hard to numb. Pain rushed in, and he quickly clamped down to stanch the flow.

Never again did he want to be responsible for another's well-being. Most especially not for the happiness and safety of a vulnerable child. His child. And Rebecca's. He couldn't be what Emma needed.

He looked to his brother for help.

But for the first time, Josiah positioned himself on his wife's side instead of his usual stance bridging the divide. "Now that Mattie's growing large with child," he explained, "I don't want her making the drive into town by herself a couple times a week as she's been doing. And I can't get away from my work with the horses to accompany her, except on Sundays." He folded his arms across his chest, his expression set in unyielding lines.

Elias's focus slid down to Mattie's middle. The other man was overstating things a bit. His wife wasn't due to deliver their baby until December, and it was only in the last couple of weeks that her condition had become discernable to a casual observer. But there was no arguing with the fact that she'd soon grow bigger as summer gave way to autumn.

Mattie placed her hand over the slight curve of her stomach. "Josiah's worried about me and this little one running into trouble while on the road alone."

Elias could understand his brother's feelings all too well. Although he hadn't known it when they set out from Tennessee all those months ago to join the wagon train, Rebecca had been in the family way before the start of their journey to Oregon Country. And she hadn't lived to reach their destination.

Even though the five miles between the town of Silver Springs and Josiah and Mattie's ranch was in no way comparable to that arduous five-month trek, which had caused Rebecca to deliver the baby too soon and with grave complications, it was little wonder that now the couple was expecting a child of their own, they were inclined toward caution.

It was during the journey west that Josiah and Mattie had met and married. She and Rebecca had become friends—and she had been by Rebecca's side on that awful day that proved to be her last on earth.

Anyone who had witnessed the tragic end of Elias's wife would surely experience a measure of fear that they might suffer the same fate.

He couldn't fault his brother for doing everything in his power to prevent it. Josiah was a wise man, refusing to take any chances with the health and welfare of his wife and unborn child.

Emma patted Elias's cheek, drawing his attention back to her. Her tiny fist latched on to his beard and tugged. He winced at the sharp sting and gently disengaged her fingers, then shifted her in his arms so she could no longer reach the coarse hairs.

She stared up at him with trusting blue eyes so like her mother's. If she only knew, he was the last person she should put her faith in. He hadn't been able to keep Rebecca safe. What hope did he have of doing any better with their daughter?

He broke out in a cold sweat simply thinking about all the bad things that could befall this innocent child if left in his inept care.

His gaze returned to Josiah and Mattie, searching for an alternative. Grasping at a way out. "If you don't want Mattie traveling alone, then by all means that should stop. But I see no reason why Emma can't stay with you, regardless. I have no issue with her only coming to visit on Sundays."

"Well, of course *you* wouldn't." Frustration filled Mattie's tone. "You didn't care when heavy snowfall kept us from visiting at all during long stretches this past winter. I'm only glad poor little Emma can't understand what her feckless father is saying!"

Josiah placed a hand on his wife's back. "Calm down, sweetheart. It's not good for our baby for you to get so upset." When she turned to him to reply, he forestalled her. "I'll deal with my brother."

After she gave a stiff nod in acknowledgement, he shot a look at Elias, in which resolve overrode compassion. "I'm sorry, but this is the only way Mattie will agree to refrain from making trips into town by herself."

"Your wife has an unfortunate stubborn streak a mile wide."

The corner of Josiah's mouth crooked up. "I'm acquainted with it."

"My delicate condition hasn't affected my hearing," Mattie interposed.

Josiah patted her shoulder. "Of course not, sweetheart."

Her eyes narrowed at his placating tone, but she didn't take him to task over it. Instead she skewered Elias with a steely stare. "You've missed enough of Emma's life already. She deserves better from you. She's already lost her mother—I won't allow her to grow up without her father, as well. It's only sensible that she lives here with you from now on."

He resented his sister-in-law's mulish insistence on this course, but how could he hold it against her when he knew she was merely doing what she believed was best for his daughter? The trouble was he and Mattie didn't see eye to eye on what exactly that entailed.

And now that Josiah had taken a stand, siding firmly with her, what chance was there that Elias could prevail?

There had been a time when he would have looked to the Lord for guidance, but not anymore. He'd stopped talking to God after Rebecca was taken from him. If He hadn't heeded Elias's prayers then, why would He care about his troubles now?

Emma squirmed in his arms, pulling him from his dark thoughts, and he tightened his grip to keep her from toppling to the hard wooden floor. But she squawked a protest as he squeezed her a bit too tightly. He hastily loosened his hold. Her wiggling didn't cease, and his heart filled with dread at the thought of her slipping from his lax grasp.

Wasn't this proof that he didn't know what he was doing—that he wasn't fit to be a parent? He needed more time before stepping in to be a true father to Emma. Not only for his sake but also for hers.

He didn't trust himself alone with her for five minutes, never mind several days at a time. So, how could Mattie imagine that this was a suitable arrangement?

His thoughts circled, frantically seeking a way clear of this. For himself.

And for his baby girl.

On the way home from an excursion to the edge of town, Abigail Warner spotted a wagon parked in front of the two-story building that had been constructed as a doctor's clinic and residence for Elias Dawson. She recognized the horse and buckboard as belonging to Elias's sister-in-law, Mattie. Over the past few months, it had become a common sight. And a welcome one, as it indicated the presence of not only Mattie but Abby's niece, Emma, as well.

Spending time with her sister's child helped soothe the pain of Rebecca's passing, each visit bringing another bit of healing. Abby thanked the Lord that she now saw the baby a couple times a week. The winter months had been especially hard with news of Rebecca's death still fresh and Emma cut off from Abby and her parents by inclement weather.

She'd accepted the situation for what it was, however. Her brother-in-law had needed time to heal, too, and while she was saddened that Elias didn't seem to find the same comfort in Rebecca's daughter as Abby did, it wasn't her place to judge him for the way he dealt with his grief.

No matter how his actions affected her personally.

Because even though the visits had become more frequent with the advent of warmer weather, they still seemed far too short. Abby missed her niece when they were apart. Missed seeing her bright eyes, alive with curiosity, and her tiny mouth curved in a sweet smile. Missed hearing her giggles of pure joy.

The time spent with Emma wasn't nearly enough to satisfy Abby. Or her mother. On that—if on nothing else—they could agree. But even in this, their underlying reasons differed greatly.

If Abby had known Mattie was bringing the little one into town today, she wouldn't have whiled away so much of the afternoon sitting in a grassy meadow and sketching. But their visits didn't occur on a precise schedule that one could anticipate. And the wonders of the countryside in full summer splendor had acted as inspiration for Abby's artistic nature.

Now the sun was edging toward the horizon and would soon disappear below the tops of the trees growing thick on the hills surrounding town. Doubtlessly, Mattie would want to return home to her ranch before dark. Abby picked up her pace, concerned that the other woman might even at this moment be preparing to depart.

She crossed the street, holding the hem of her skirt above the dust as she dodged the wagons and horses making their way down the main thoroughfare of town. The clip-clop of hooves accompanied the jangle of harnesses and the sound of wheels rolling over the hard-packed dirt.

Abby stepped up onto the wooden walkway that fronted what should have been the doctor's clinic. Her gaze landed on the image reflected in the large plate-glass window. She stopped short, silently groaning at the sight she made with flyaway strands of light brown hair sticking up in a fuzzy ring around her head.

She reached up to smooth the wisps back into place and tucked the ends into the bun secured at her nape. But no sooner had she completed her tidying efforts than a slight breeze teased several curls loose again.

Heaving a sigh, she lowered her gaze from the reflection, only to note her yellow gown looked decidedly the worse for wear, as well. The gathered skirt was creased and stained from hours spent seated on the ground with her legs curled beneath her.

She gripped the fabric and gave it a vigorous shake in an attempt to remove the worst of the wrinkles. Unfortunately, putting things properly to rights would require more than that paltry effort. She needed a hot iron, not to mention some strong lye soap to take out the grass stains. Another sigh escaped as she brushed ineffectually at the green streaks marring the pale cotton.

She should go home and change into a clean gown before paying a visit to Elias and Mattie. Her mother would have insisted on it, had the older woman chanced to see Abby in her present state. However, Abby was disinclined to miss even one minute with Emma. She only hoped that neither Mattie nor Elias would take any notice of her disheveled appearance.

The heels of her high-button shoes tapped against the wooden boardwalk as she moved toward the front door that stood open invitingly. She entered the foyer, which was meant to serve as a waiting area for patients, with a bench against the staircase and several ladder-back chairs along one wall. Two doors opened off the front hall, leading to the unused examination room and doctor's private office.

The spaces had been furnished by the town leaders in anticipation of Elias's arrival in Oregon Country last fall, when it was expected that he would take up the position as town doctor. But after tragedy had struck along the wagon trail, leaving him a grieving widower, he hadn't opened his medical practice as planned. Everything that had been so carefully laid out and prepared in the clinic remained untouched, gathering dust.

Not surprisingly, the townspeople—who had been so sympathetic and obliging in the beginning—had long since lost patience with the situation and started looking for another doctor to do the job that Elias couldn't.

And when they found one…then what?

Would Elias have to move out to his brother's ranch? Mattie would have no reason to bring Emma to town for visits after that. And Abby would go back to seeing her niece only on Sundays, when the Dawsons came into Silver Springs to attend church and buy supplies.

She pushed the worrisome thought from her mind for the time being. Setting down the large canvas bag containing her sketchbook and charcoal pencils, she moved toward the stairs leading to the private quarters on the second floor, where she could hear movement and voices.

"Hello," she called out, announcing her arrival.

Mattie came into view on the top landing, a welcoming expression on her face. "Good afternoon, Abby."

The corners of Abby's mouth curved up. "You're looking exceptionally well today."

Mattie's skin glowed with good health as she rested her palm on the slight mound of her child nestled beneath her heart. "Thank you for the kind compliment. And if I may offer one of my own—that yellow gown is lovely on you."

"Thanks." Abby's grin felt more like a grimace, and she fought against the urge to smooth the skirt or attempt to hide the stains. Though she longed to cover them with her hands, they were far too large. "I'm glad you decided to come to town, Mattie." Her smile came easier now. "As soon as I saw your wagon out front, I came right over to visit with you and Emma."

She placed her fingers on the wooden banister but

paused in surprise at the foot of the staircase as Josiah Dawson appeared by his wife's side. Since Mattie usually came alone, his presence was unexpected, but Abby didn't think about it too closely. Not when he looked ready to depart, edging past Mattie to start down the stairs.

"Afternoon, Abby. It's a pleasure to see you, as always," he said.

Forgetting her manners, she ignored his greeting. "You're not leaving already, are you?"

Not yet, please, Lord.

Had she missed her chance for more than an abbreviated cuddle with Emma followed by a hasty farewell?

"No," Josiah answered, seeming startled by the way she stood squarely in his path, barring his way.

He came to a halt three steps above her, waiting patiently for her to shift aside. One light red eyebrow arched in inquiry when she didn't budge from her spot, and a slight smile turned up the corner of his mouth.

Abby paid it no mind. "Then, where *are* you going?" she demanded.

"Josiah's simply bringing in a few things from the wagon," Mattie explained.

Abby glanced back up at her. Despite Mattie's light tone of voice, it seemed as though shadows lurked in the other woman's golden-brown gaze. Which raised unsettling questions in Abby's head. Was Mattie plagued merely by her usual concern over Elias's current frame of mind? Or was she troubled by something more?

Those thoughts were quickly pushed aside, however, when Mattie continued, "Come on up and visit with Emma for a bit."

Eager to accept the invitation, Abby moved back to let Josiah pass. Then she gathered her skirts and mounted the stairs that opened directly onto a parlor.

The second floor was comprised of the large sitting room and two bedrooms. The upper story along with the kitchen downstairs made up the doctor's residence.

Abby turned her focus to her brother-in-law, sitting in an armchair by the window, with Emma perched on his lap. "Hello, Elias."

He offered her a brief nod in return but didn't speak.

His chestnut hair was in need of a trim, hanging loose past his collar, and a thick beard covered the lower half of his face. It had been so long since she'd seen him clean-shaven that she could barely recall what he'd looked like before. One thing she hadn't forgotten, however, was her feelings of guilt that she'd always found her sister's husband devastatingly handsome—and not just from a purely aesthetic point of view.

Back when he and Rebecca had been courting, Abby couldn't help but stare at him with longing. She'd even entertained wild fantasies about him choosing her over Rebecca. Never mind that he had been much too mature for a young girl of fifteen or that, even if age hadn't been a factor, she'd had no hope of competing with her older sister's beauty.

They'd been silly childish imaginings, hidden in her heart and shared with no one. And if they hadn't quite been forgotten… Well, no one needed to know that, either.

But it seemed as if the man of her youthful daydreams had vanished without a trace.

No longer was he the jovial and carefree individual

she'd known back in Tennessee. He had always seemed rather self-contained, but he'd been more easygoing and undeniably happier then. This quiet, morose man sitting before her now appeared to have aged decades, though he was only in his early thirties. Deep lines of strain grooved his skin, fanning out from the corners of his dark brown eyes. Gone was his infectious smile and boundless joy in life.

She'd had months to grow accustomed to his altered disposition, but the first view of it during every visit still shocked and saddened her. At one time, he'd treated Abby like a little sister. Now he didn't let anyone close. Not his brother or Mattie. Not even his own daughter.

And certainly not Abby.

She didn't spare him another glance, as she focused her attention on her niece instead, assured of her welcome from the little one. "Hello, my sweet Emma. How are you this fine afternoon?"

A stream of indecipherable baby talk was her answer, accompanied by a happy grin that displayed a matched set of dimples in Emma's round, rosy cheeks. The little girl reached out her arms to Abby.

She moved forward and lifted the child from her father's lap. He relinquished Emma without protest, his expression showing not a moment's regret that his daughter had been taken away from him.

Abby was all too familiar with his apathy by now. She hadn't accepted it—but she was at a loss as to what she could do to change the situation.

Stepping back a few paces from Elias, she settled the baby on her hip. She tapped Emma's button nose, eliciting a chortle. "Have you been good for your Aunt

Mattie and Uncle Josiah, like we agreed? No crying fits or screaming tantrums?" Her fingers smoothed over her niece's cap of silky, dark red curls.

"She's behaved like a perfect little lady," Mattie answered, then moved hastily to their side as the little girl latched on to Abby's collar and brought the fabric to her mouth. "None of that now, precious, or Aunt Abby will think I'm a liar." Extricating the damp material from Emma's fingers, Mattie replaced it with a rag doll, which Emma immediately stuck in her mouth. Mattie pressed a kiss on the baby's temple before straightening, her expression rueful. "I'm sorry about your dress, Abby. I should've warned you that she has a new tooth coming in."

"It's fine. I don't mind." Given the already wretched state of her clothing, a bit of baby drool wasn't likely to make it look any worse.

Wood creaked as Elias shifted in the armchair, drawing Abby's attention to him. His face was curiously blank. There were no signs of a lingering smile on his lips or affection for his child warming his dark eyes. Not even a look of mild distaste at the sight of baby slobber dampening Abby's collar. How could he have absolutely no reaction at all to his daughter?

Abby doubted it was something she'd ever get used to. And she hoped she wouldn't have to—prayed that he wouldn't spend the rest of his life with a heart covered by a thick layer of killing frost.

Turning her gaze back to Emma, Abby watched the little one contentedly gnawing on the arm of her rag doll.

Emma was generally a happy child, but how long

would that last once she was old enough to become aware of her father's apparent indifference? Would she trust that he loved her when—for reasons she may never know or understand—he was unable to show it? Though he hid behind a great, emotionless wall, he must feel something for his daughter. He had to love her.

Abby had to believe that—even though his actions appeared to indicate otherwise. It would break Abby's heart if Elias truly felt nothing for Emma. Not to mention what it would do to a young girl to be utterly devoid of her father's love. Abby was all too familiar with the pain of a parent's rejection, had spent too many years trying to gain her mother's unconditional affection to no avail. She prayed for a different sort of childhood for her niece.

Father and daughter were in Abby's daily prayers, and would continue to be. But surely there must be something more she could do to help her niece. Some way for her to reach Elias despite the distance he seemed at pains to maintain between himself and others.

The tread of boot heels on the stairs pulled Abby from her musing. She glanced up and watched as Josiah gained the second floor, carrying a cumbersome trunk balanced on one shoulder. He crossed the room without a word and disappeared into the spare bedroom. A grunt sounded from within, followed by the thump of a heavy object—presumably the trunk—hitting the floor, then a scraping noise as it was shifted across the hardwood. A moment later, Josiah reemerged, his eyes going straight to his brother, who had remained sitting motionless throughout the whole proceeding.

"No, no, Elias, don't bother to get up and help. Let me do all the heavy lifting. I can carry in everything by myself." Josiah's words dripped with sarcasm.

Even that wasn't enough to prod Elias from his chair. Heaving a resigned sigh, Josiah headed back downstairs to retrieve more items.

From her vantage point, Abby could look out the window to the wagon parked below. It was only now that she noticed the buckboard was piled high with furniture and crates. That explained why Josiah had accompanied Mattie and Emma today. But it also presented more questions than answers.

Just then, Josiah appeared in view outside and slid a wooden cradle to the edge of the lowered tailgate. Hefting the unwieldy object, he pivoted on his heels and headed back inside.

Abby turned away from the window to address Mattie and Elias. "What's going on?"

Mattie was the one who provided an explanation. "Emma's coming to live with her father at last."

The news stunned Abby. "Truly?" She looked to Elias for confirmation.

He cleared his throat before replying. "It's true enough."

"That's wonderful!" It was a blessing—an answered prayer. Much more than she'd dared to hope for at this juncture, in fact.

Josiah trooped past, weighted down by the cradle. A few seconds later, he exited the bedroom empty-handed and retraced his steps downstairs.

Abby's focus stayed on Elias. While his continued remoteness concerned her, she decided she could be more forgiving of that, since it seemed as though he'd finally decided to make an effort. No matter that he obviously still struggled with it.

His willingness to effect a change could only be viewed as a sign of his heart healing. The first shoots of bright green indicating a thaw after months of cold and gloom. A renewal of faith, guided by the Lord's hand.

Warmth spread through Abby at the thought, and she felt a softening toward her brother-in-law. "I'm very happy for you and Emma." She graced him with a smile of approval. "This is a good thing you're doing."

He shifted in his chair and sighed. "Mattie's determined I not shirk my responsibilities any longer."

Abby's joy dimmed a bit and confusion filled her at his emotionless words. "But Emma's more to you than merely a duty." It felt as if an iron band was squeezing around her heart when he didn't offer an immediate agreement. "Isn't she?"

Chapter Two

Elias's mind was a seething mass of emotions too tangled up and jumbled together for him to separate or make any sense of them.

For so long, he'd numbed himself against feeling much of anything, keeping thoughts of the past locked behind an impenetrable door. Emma acted as a key, however, bringing back memories he didn't wish to recall.

His daughter was a physical reminder of everything he'd lost. With each passing day, she looked more and more like her mama.

Elias wasn't ready for this, didn't know if he would ever be ready for it. But he hadn't been given a choice.

Clearly, he wasn't meant to forget what his actions had cost him, how he had failed to keep Rebecca safe.

Unable to put any of his chaotic thoughts into words, Elias remained silent—and watched as the last traces of light in Abby's expression winked out like a snuffed candle.

He tried not to let her palpable disappointment

bother him. It was nothing to him if her impossible, out-of-reach optimism had been dashed. Still, he felt a distinct pang in the region of his heart that he'd obviously let her down.

He refrained from rushing in with the *I'm sorry*s. Though he wasn't proud of what grief and regret had done to him, he wouldn't apologize for the man he'd become. No more than a storm-tossed sea would apologize for its roiling.

Apparently, Abby had been laboring under the misconception that Emma's move here had been Elias's choice. He didn't know what could've given her that idea. It certainly wouldn't have been his enthusiasm, since he'd displayed none.

"Of course Emma is more to Elias than a mere obligation," Mattie leaped into the void.

Abby offered her a wan, unconvinced smile.

Despite her dampened spirits, Abby dredged up a bright expression for her niece. "I'm so very glad you've come to live with your father at last. It's an answer to my prayers, and we have the Lord to thank for it."

If that was the case, Elias wasn't feeling particularly appreciative toward the Almighty just now. Rather than a blessing, he looked on this situation more in the way of punishment for his wrongs. A constant reminder of his failings, so that he would never forget what he'd done. And the Good Lord strike him down if he ever failed again.

Immediately, guilt assailed Elias for his unworthy thoughts. What a truly reprehensible sentiment for a father to feel toward his own child. Yet Elias *had* thought it. Which just went to prove he wasn't fit to care for Emma. But try telling anyone else that.

Clearly, his opinions on the matter weren't wanted.

Had he truly expected Mattie and Josiah to keep his daughter and raise her as their own for the next twenty years? Elias was ashamed to admit that he hadn't thought that far ahead, had never considered the future at all this past year, merely taking each day as it came.

But now, he was faced with an immovable obstacle that he couldn't push aside or ignore.

Instead of feeling sorry for himself, however, he should be feeling sorry for his poor daughter, that she had *him* for a father. She was stuck with a man who could never be what she needed.

Elias couldn't even be a proper father to her, never mind mother and father both.

He looked at his baby girl, snuggled in Abby's arms, both females blissfully ignorant of his all-consuming fears and doubts. Abby was chattering away to the child, and Emma seemed completely absorbed in the one-sided conversation.

"You and I are going to have such fun together, now that you're living close by, aren't we?" It didn't seem to matter in the least to Abby that Emma couldn't respond with anything more than indecipherable babbles—she simply took the baby's agreement as a given. "I'll take you to my favorite sketching spot. It's a grassy meadow just outside of town. You can draw pictures of your own there if you'd like. The colors of nature are truly wondrous. We're sure to see birds in the trees and squirrels scampering to and fro, collecting nuts. If we sit very still and quiet, we might even sight a mama deer with her fawn or fuzzy cotton-tailed rabbits. Wouldn't that be exciting?"

Mattie made agreeable noises and offered encouraging remarks throughout Abby's commentary. Elias paid scant attention to the words as Josiah continued to trek through the parlor, loaded down with Emma's possessions.

Elias's feet remained rooted to the spot. Perhaps he was acting petty and callous to not lend his younger brother a hand, but he was against this course. He refused to do anything to help hasten it along. If Josiah was determined to see it through, he would do so on his own. Though Elias knew better than to think Josiah might change his mind.

Elias didn't glance directly at his brother. There was no need when he could feel the other man's censure burning a hole through him from across the room. Instead, Elias kept his gaze focused on Abby.

Though he didn't share her enthusiasm with Emma's relocation to town, he could understand why this arrangement would be to her liking. With Emma taking up residence just down the street from the house Abby shared with her parents, the Warner family could visit the baby any time they chose. Doubtlessly a welcome change not only for Abby but for her mother and father, as well. Emma was a joy to Rebecca's family. A link to their dearly departed daughter and sibling.

Abby's animated face attested to the happiness she found in her niece as she carried on chatting to the child in her arms. Elias propped his chin on his fist and considered her expressive features. He supposed she was pretty in an understated sort of way. She had a lovely smile, delicately arched eyebrows and a dainty nose that tilted up ever so slightly at the end. He'd known her for years, and yet he'd never taken much notice of her appearance before. In the past, he'd had eyes for only Rebecca, who had been a striking beauty. Still, he could remember how Abby had often seemed to fade into the background, especially when placed beside her older sister.

She lacked the vibrant coloring Rebecca had possessed. Instead of bright honey-blond hair, Abby's was a light brown. And her eyes were the pale blue-gray of a winter sky rather than brilliant sapphire.

There were few physical similarities between Elias's late wife and Abby, for which he could only be grateful. It made it easier to be around her. The same couldn't be said about Emma. Though she'd inherited his hair color, he saw Rebecca all too clearly in her eyes and her features. A fact that made it nearly impossible for him to look at his daughter without feeling the crushing weight of misery and guilt for his many shortcomings.

Cutting off the useless emotions, he turned his attention to what Abby was saying and concentrated on her words to ground him in the present.

She was still going on about the many activities she and Emma would do together. "We'll take walks through the forest and have picnics in the fresh air."

"Two such lovely ladies as you and Emma should have an escort for your outings," Mattie inserted.

Abby's eyebrows pulled together at the interruption, and she chewed the corner of her lip for a moment. "Perhaps if we ask nicely, your father will come along, too."

Though she directed her remark to Emma, her eyes were on Elias as she spoke.

But what did she truly want from him? Was she looking for his agreement? Or did she hope he'd refuse so she could have Emma all to herself? He hesitated to open his mouth for fear of saying the wrong thing. Already, he was at odds with Josiah and Mattie, and he didn't care to add to their number.

Seeming to understand his predicament, Abby gave him a slight smile and voiced another comment aimed at him by way of Emma. "I'm certain he'd love to join us." She nudged Elias subtly toward an affirmative response.

Love might be a bit strong. *Tolerate* would be more like it. That was about as much as he felt able to commit himself to at this point.

If he had to be fully involved in Emma's upbringing, as it appeared he must, how could he do any less than to give it—to give *her*—his all? No matter that he could never be anywhere near enough, that didn't mean he shouldn't strive to provide for his child as best as he knew how.

She required more than a roof over her head and food in her belly. She needed attention and affection, caring. Love. Sure, she got a fair bit of that from her aunts and uncle, and her maternal grandparents, too. But Elias didn't want the time Emma spent alone with him to be a wasteland devoid of emotion.

Even at the risk of pain to himself.

He couldn't continue to keep himself closed off from his daughter, though that had been his method of coping for almost a year now. Suddenly, he was faced with ripping away the thick scab that had formed over his heart, an action that would set him bleeding again. He felt like a coward for wanting to put off the inevitable task. He used to be a doctor, so the thought of necessary bloodletting, even his own, shouldn't bother him. But knowing full well the reopened wound he would yet be made to endure left him feeling decidedly ill.

Abby glanced up as Josiah exited the second bedroom once again. His breathing was slightly labored and perspiration glistened along his hairline, turning the light red-gold strands several shades darker.

She longed to lend her assistance to him. To set Emma squarely in her father's lap and trail behind Josiah, providing whatever aid she could. But she didn't want to give Elias cause to think she was provoking him deliberately by taking on a job he hadn't stirred himself to do.

She shouldn't feel so worried over the state of his emotions. Especially as he likely didn't care about her opinion of him in any case—and had shown no consideration for his brother, besides. Still, she found that she couldn't dismiss her concern for Elias's feelings so easily.

More to the point, there was no sense in adding fuel to the fire of an already volatile situation. Even if she didn't see how things could possibly get any worse.

Mattie moved to her husband's side and placed a hand on his arm, drawing him to a halt. "I hate that I can't help you carry any of the heavy items in from the wagon. Let me get you a drink of water before you head back outside."

Josiah leaned down and pressed a quick kiss on her forehead. "Thanks for the offer, sweetheart, but that can wait until after I've finished bringing in the rest of Emma's belongings."

"Then, I'll see to their proper placement in the meantime." Mattie released her hold on Josiah and headed toward the bedroom.

"Don't lift anything that weighs more than a five-pound sack of flour," he admonished.

"Of course not," she placated him before issuing a directive of her own. "Now off you go. The wagon's not going to unload itself."

Mirth bubbled up inside Abby as she observed the couple. It was sweet to witness a man acting so tenderly toward his expectant wife, even though Mattie seemed to think Josiah was being overprotective.

It was only after the other woman had disappeared from sight that Josiah turned and descended the staircase. A few short minutes later, he returned with two wooden crates stacked one on top of the other and crossed the sitting room to join his wife in the bedroom.

"I never realized that such a tiny child would require so much stuff," Abby remarked to Elias.

When he simply grunted in response, she again addressed her comments to Emma—a much more receptive audience, even though her verbal replies were no more intelligible than her father's.

While Abby talked, she moved to the open bedroom door and glanced inside to view the progress underway. It looked as if a mini twister had hit, but Mattie was swiftly putting things to rights. Soon it would be a wonderful room for Emma.

"Would you like some help organizing all of this?" Abby questioned, as she shifted the baby on her hip.

"Thank you, but no. You'll be much more helpful if you stay just as you are."

Standing around doing nothing while Mattie did all the work? "How's that helpful?"

"Well, you're keeping ahold of Emma." Mattie knelt in front of an open trunk. "This will go much quicker without her underfoot."

Abby had never given it much thought, but now she could see how it might be difficult to get any chores done in a timely fashion with a small child in the house. "I suppose that's one thing you can look forward to no longer being an issue, now that Emma's going to be living here."

Mattie rubbed her nose and made a noise that sounded like a sniffle.

"Are you feeling all right?" Abby queried, worry for Mattie and her unborn child filling her heart. "You're not ailing, are you?"

"Of course not," the other woman reassured her. "I'm perfectly healthy."

"I'm glad to hear it. But…" Reminded of Mattie's delicate condition, the current division of labor seemed skewed in the wrong direction. "Perhaps I should handle the unpacking while you hold Emma on your lap."

Mattie was already shaking her head. "You came here to visit with your niece, not to be put to work."

"I don't mind, truly."

When Mattie waved aside the offer once more, Abby didn't press the issue.

Mindful to stay out of Josiah's path, Abby enter-

tained the baby by pointing out bits and pieces here
and there. Such as a quilt made up of pastel squares
of fabric, which Mattie had draped over the side of the
cradle, and various other items she removed from the
crates and trunks placed haphazardly around the room.
It was immediately apparent when a favorite toy appeared because Emma's eyes lit up as she clapped her
hands together and bounced in Abby's arms to the ac-
companiment of happy babble.

Though Mattie smiled slightly in response, she kept
her head bent to her task, leaving it to Abby to enter-
tain Emma.

After several more trips to and from the wagon, Josiah dusted off his hands and surveyed the room. "It
looks like you're about done in here, Mattie. There are
just a few odds and ends left to unload, including the
basket of food you packed. Why don't you come downstairs with me now and get everything organized to
your satisfaction in the kitchen while I bring the rest
of it up?"

Nodding, she joined her husband, and the pair exited the bedroom.

Following them into the parlor, Abby noted that Elias
had leaned his head against the chair back and closed
his eyes, but now they popped open.

"I guess you'll be leaving soon, then?" he asked, indicating he'd overheard his brother's words.

"Yep." Josiah placed an arm around his wife's waist.
"Mattie and I need to head back to our ranch. I have
horses to tend and chores to see to before dark."

Elias clenched the arms of the chair, his knuckles

showing white. "Emma will be getting hungry before too long. What do you intend I should do?"

Josiah's eyebrow arched. "I suggest you feed her." He rubbed his palm up and down Mattie's back. "It wouldn't do to let your daughter go hungry."

The corners of Elias's mouth turned downward at the rebuke, and he glowered at his brother. "Obviously not." Then his expression changed, his Adam's apple bobbing up and down as he swallowed audibly. "I was merely inquiring as to *what* I should feed her."

Mattie opened her mouth to reply, but Josiah beat her to it. "Well, Mattie packed some food for Emma in the basket, besides her usual offerings for you." He crossed his arms over his chest. "If it wasn't for my wife making sure you had something to eat, I do believe you would've starved by now."

Abby noticed that Elias didn't disagree with his brother's assessment. It was all too easy for her to imagine him ignoring that basic need if too much effort was required to get food. To her knowledge, he hadn't left his home to go anywhere farther than his back fence since arriving in Oregon Country last autumn.

It was Mattie or Josiah who visited the mercantile owned by Abby's father, Thomas, and arranged the delivery of supplies to Elias's residence. And according to her father, Josiah was the one paying for the goods. Which made sense, she supposed. Given that Elias hadn't attended to a single patient in all the months he'd lived in Silver Springs, he was certain to be short of funds.

Would he get out more, now that he had a child to provide for? Would Emma bring him out of his self-imposed isolation and back into the world again? Surely, he couldn't continue to hold himself at a distance from her—and everyone else—when she was with him day and night.

Mattie moved toward Elias and rested her fingers lightly on his shoulder. "I realize this happened rather unexpectedly and you're somewhat ill prepared because we didn't give you any advance notice. That's why I fixed a few days' worth of food for Emma."

"Thank you." Elias laid his hand over his sister-in-law's and gave it a quick squeeze. "I do appreciate it."

Mattie smiled, but it seemed to wobble a bit. "It should be enough to tide over you and Emma until Sunday, when Josiah and I come into town for church. And to visit with you and our precious little one again." There was a distinct catch in her voice at the end.

Elias seemed unaware of anything amiss.

Abby, however, looked more closely at the other woman and noticed the sheen of tears misting her light brown eyes.

It suddenly dawned on Abby how difficult this must be for Mattie, to face saying goodbye to Emma and leaving her behind. To be parted from the baby for the first time since her birth.

Abby hadn't been on the wagon train with them— she and her parents had come to Oregon Country several years earlier—but she had heard how the newly delivered baby had been put in Mattie's arms to tend to while Elias tried to save his wife. After losing Rebecca, Elias had shut down—and Emma had stayed in Mattie's care ever since.

Josiah took his wife's arm to guide her across the sitting room. "Come on. Let's go downstairs."

Mattie captured her bottom lip between her teeth to still its trembling, then nodded. When a single tear slipped over her lashes, she hastily wiped away the droplet. Accepting her husband's assistance, she descended the steep staircase.

Abby's heart ached for the other woman. Poor Mattie. Plainly upset, hurting. And with good reason.

Abby's incessant prattle wouldn't have helped matters any, either. Oh, what a featherbrain she'd been to not realize it sooner! She cringed when she remembered her thoughtless remark to the other woman a short time ago. How could she have imagined for even a moment that Mattie would look forward to Emma being gone from her home? And, as if that wasn't bad enough, Abby had blithely expressed her own joy with the changed situation, detailing all her plans to spend time with her niece—plans Mattie could have no part in.

"I shouldn't have nattered on and on to Emma like that," she spoke her regret aloud.

Confusion filled Elias's dark eyes at her abrupt shift in topic. He crossed one boot-clad foot over the opposite knee and rested his hand on his bent leg. "Don't worry on my account. I know as well as the next man how women are prone to chatter without pausing to draw breath."

Sucking in a breath at his casually-voiced insult, she unintentionally proved his statement false. "For a man who doesn't say more than two words together if he can manage it, perhaps it seems as though I talk overmuch.

However, I was merely making conversation—something you seem incapable of most days."

"It isn't a conversation when one person's doing all the talking," he refuted, a hint of amusement in his expression.

"I beg to differ in this instance. Emma and I understand each other." She turned her focus to the baby and asked, "Don't we, sweetness?" When Emma grinned in response, Abby shifted her gaze back to Elias. "There, you see?" She didn't wait for his agreement, since it was in no way assured. "It's only because she hadn't yet mastered the skill that I must speak for both of us. But you've gotten me sidetracked."

His boot heel thumped to the hardwood floor as he straightened in the chair. "*I* have?"

"Certainly. You're the one who made an unkind remark about yammering women." Retrieving a small flannel cloth from the side table positioned next to Elias's chair, Abby used it to wipe away a bit of baby drool dribbling down Emma's chin.

Elias ran a hand through the overlong strands of his dark hair. "I never called them that. Besides, *you're* the one who—" His words cut off midsentence when the damp cloth landed in his lap.

He narrowed his eyes at Abby, likely trying to determine whether she'd done it on purpose.

She maintained a perfectly straight face. "If I could get back to my original point."

"By all means." Picking up the cotton square, he tossed it on the tabletop and waved for her to continue.

"I think it upset Mattie."

His eyebrows bunched together above the bridge

of his nose. "By *it*, I'm assuming you mean your so-called conversation. I don't see what Mattie has to be upset about." Then under his breath he added, "She got what she wanted."

Clearly, his thoughts hadn't run along the same lines as Abby's. How could he not have realized the reasons behind Mattie's distress? Was he truly so wrapped up in his own concerns that he couldn't comprehend how painful this decision must be for his sister-in-law?

"Yes, Mattie wanted this," Abby acknowledged. "She wanted you to take over raising your child. But not for herself. She's doing it for Emma's sake." And for Elias's, too, though he wouldn't care to hear that. Refusing to see that Mattie was trying to pull him out of his depression and force him to live again. "Making this choice couldn't have been easy for Mattie. It means she'll be spending considerably less time with the baby she's raised as a daughter for almost a year now."

Perhaps that wouldn't seem significant to Elias, given the miniscule amount of time *he'd* spent with his daughter over the past eleven months. But Abby could sympathize with the other woman because she'd been praying for more time with Emma herself, ever since the baby had arrived in Oregon Country last autumn.

She smoothed a lock of her niece's silky hair. "Mattie's been like a mother to Emma. She couldn't love her more if Emma was her own child. It must be breaking her heart to do this."

A short time later, Elias mulled over Abby's words as Josiah and Mattie prepared to leave. He stood on the covered wooden walkway that fronted the two-story clapboard building where he currently resided, watching Mattie delay the moment of parting. Now that he was really observing her, it was plain to see that Abby had been right about Mattie's state of mind. Her sadness was apparent, even to an unfeeling cur like Elias.

Mattie hugged Emma close, her eyes awash with tears. She rested her cheek against the top of the baby's head and rocked from side to side. Elias suspected it was more to comfort herself than the child. Emma was too young to understand what was going on. But perhaps she sensed something wrong, because she squirmed in Mattie's embrace.

For a brief instant, Elias contemplated using this moment for his own ends. Perhaps if he pressed his advantage now, when Mattie's anguish was greatest, he could convince her to change her mind about leaving Emma with him.

He rejected the notion almost as soon as it had formed in his mind. Manipulating her in that manner would be a poor way to repay her for all the help she and Josiah had given Elias over the past year. He couldn't use Mattie's emotions against her to serve his own selfish purpose. To do so would be truly reprehensible, and though there was no denying he'd sunk low since his wife's passing, even he had his limits.

He had to face the fact that Emma wasn't here merely for a short visit before he handed her back to Josiah and Mattie to take home. They truly meant to leave her here with him. He had to accept that he couldn't talk or bargain his way out of this. He'd managed to put off this moment for nearly a year, but his respite had come to an end.

He couldn't avoid being a father any longer, whether he felt up to the task or not.

Josiah moved to his wife's side and laid a hand on her back. "It's time for us to go, Mattie."

"I know." She placed several kisses on the baby's head. "I love you, my precious little one." Loosening her hold, she allowed Josiah to take Emma from her arms.

Abby reached for Mattie's hand, silently offering her support.

Josiah tucked the baby against his chest as he walked toward Elias. "Be good for your papa now, you hear? Go easy on him. Love you, sweet pea." He kissed Emma's cheek then passed her to Elias. "We'll be seeing you on Sunday."

"Have a safe journey home." He shifted his daughter to his left arm and clasped his brother's hand in farewell.

"God be with you and Emma." Josiah pivoted and retraced his steps, returning to Mattie's side. "Are you ready?"

After a slight hesitation, she nodded. Abby squeezed her fingers, then let her go.

Josiah assisted Mattie up onto the high wagon seat before climbing in himself. Retrieving a handkerchief from his pocket, he passed it to Mattie. She dabbed at the tears that continued to well up in her eyes. Josiah wrapped his arm around her waist and pulled her close to kiss her temple.

Witnessing the tender care and steadfast support the other man gave his wife reminded Elias of how it used to be between him and Rebecca. It would never be that way again. Not for Elias.

Rebecca was gone, and he never intended to remarry. He couldn't risk the possibility that he might fail to protect his wife a second time. Couldn't live with the weight of another death on his conscience. And couldn't bear the thought of going through this agony of grief and loss again.

Chapter Three

❧

Elias turned sideways so that Emma was facing the couple sitting on the wagon seat. "Say goodbye to your Uncle Josiah and Aunt Mattie," he instructed his daughter, though he wasn't certain whether that word was one of the few in her limited vocabulary.

Josiah smiled at his niece. "Bye-bye, sweet pea." Tipping his hat to Abby, he bid her good day, then nodded to Elias and tapped the reins against the horse's back. "Get up."

The buckboard lurched into motion amid the creak of wood and the rattle of harness chains. Mattie waved to Emma as they rolled past. She twisted on the wooden bench seat in order to keep the baby in sight, waving all the while, with her lips curved up despite the tears that now streamed down her cheeks unchecked.

Emma raised her arm and bobbed her tiny fist through the air, in what could only be an attempt to imitate her Aunt Mattie. The little girl seemed to think it was some sort of game, and she giggled with glee as the wagon moved farther away down the street. When it rounded a corner and vanished from view, Elias turned toward the open front door.

Emma's laughter ceased abruptly, and she swiveled her head in the direction Mattie and Josiah had gone. "Maa-Maa?" Stretching her arms out, she lunged toward the spot where she'd last glimpsed Mattie.

Elias had to react lightning fast to keep her from tumbling out of his arms to the hard ground. His pulse raced at the close call.

It was almost more than he could take when Emma started screeching. Mixed in with the earsplitting shrieks were cries for her Maa-Maa. Her ceaseless wails sliced through Elias's heart like a dagger. The sound was loud enough that he imagined it could be heard several streets over. He had no doubt Mattie and Josiah could hear it, and it must cut into them just as deeply as it did him. Perhaps even more so. Surely, they wouldn't be able to turn a deaf ear to his baby girl's misery and they'd come back, saying they had changed their minds about leaving Emma with him.

He waited, but though long seconds passed, his brother and sister-in-law didn't return. The dusty road remained empty save for Elias and his daughter.

And Abby, standing slightly apart from them.

She moved closer and raised her voice to speak above the baby's howling. "Come on. Let's take her inside."

Elias patted Emma's back somewhat awkwardly as he entered the front foyer, noting that Abby followed him. Once the door was closed behind them, he flicked one final glance through the glass window looking out to the street. Hoping against hope. But it was no use. Josiah and Mattie weren't coming back.

Turning, he started up the stairs, with Abby right on his heels. As soon as he reached the second-floor parlor, he set to pacing the hardwood with his inconsolable daughter.

With his experience as a doctor, she was far from the first baby he'd ever held—but never had he felt so completely at sea as to what to do to make things better. Though he'd tended to plenty of physical ailments and injuries in the past, he had no notion how to mend Emma's emotional hurts.

He couldn't even heal his own.

"Perhaps her favorite toy will help cheer her," Abby suggested, forced to practically shout in order to be heard over Emma.

She hurried into the bedroom and returned a few moments later with a colorful rag doll in her hand. She held it out to the baby. "Do you want this, sweetness?" she asked in a loud voice.

Emma swatted the toy away, knocking it from Abby's hand and onto the floor. Abby bent to pick up the doll and placed it on the side table.

The longer Emma cried, the tenser Elias became. As if sensing that, she cried all the harder, causing his tension to ratchet up several more notches. And on and on it went, in a vicious cycle with no end that he could see.

Her little body arched away from him, and he feared she might hurt herself struggling against his hold. If she kept up like this, she could suffer serious injury. The thought scared him out of his wits. His heart couldn't bear much more of this.

"Here, you take her. I'm no good at this." He tried to pass the baby to Abby.

But she crossed her arms over her stomach and refused to allow it. "She doesn't want me. This is something the two of you have to face together. Besides, you *can* do this, Elias. I have faith in you."

Did she truly mean that? Even though he hadn't done a single thing to inspire it? Her expression appeared entirely sincere.

He only wished he felt the same confidence in his abilities. But unlike Abby, *he* could see inside himself—and there was nothing there to justify her belief in him.

Perhaps he simply hadn't heard her correctly over Emma's caterwauling.

He was helpless to soothe his own child, which made him worse than useless as a father. The question was, could he do anything to change it? Was he capable of raising Emma despite his deficiencies? Because he could never be the openhearted and joyful father she truly deserved. He didn't have it in him anymore. That part of him was gone, buried with his wife on a desolate prairie hilltop.

With no clue what else to do, Elias continued to pace, even though it seemed to have little effect on Emma's distraught state. Her face was flushed a bright red, and fat tears rolled down her cheeks, while her wailing was near deafening.

Abby was plainly affected by the baby's cries, too. Pain shone in her pale blue eyes, and her arms were crossed tight across her body as if she had to physically hold herself back from snatching her niece away from him. Yet she didn't relent and take Emma into her comforting embrace.

Finally, Emma's screams lessened by degrees until

she quieted completely. Exhausted by her crying fit, she slumped against him and laid her damp cheek on his shoulder. Her tears seeped through his cotton shirt, burning him like acid.

He sank down onto the armchair, his head flopping against the high back. He felt as emotionally wrung out as his daughter, draped across his chest like a limp dishcloth.

"Maa-Maa," she repeated yet again, though it was nothing more than a pitiable moan this time.

His innards twisted up in agony for his little girl, that her surrogate mother had been ripped away from her so abruptly, in a way she couldn't possibly understand.

He remembered being separated from his own mother—and his baby brother—when he was a young boy of six. Pleading with her to let him stay with her, too. He'd believed it was somehow his fault that she didn't want him, only Josiah. Elias hadn't understood until much later that his father had given her no say in the matter, choosing to take his legitimate son and leave after he'd discovered Josiah wasn't his child.

Thankfully, Emma was much younger than he'd been, and the events of this day would soon fade from her mind. The memory of Mattie leaving wouldn't overshadow her through childhood and into adulthood. Though Emma was still little more than a babe, he didn't discount her current sorrow. Because he knew exactly how she was feeling right now, after crying and crying for her mama to no avail. Unable to understand what had happened.

"How could Mattie go through with leaving her behind, when Emma calls her 'Mama'?" he spoke the thought out loud.

Surprise flashed across Abby's face. "She doesn't call Mattie 'Mama.'"

Why was Abby trying to pretend she hadn't heard it?

"Emma has said it repeatedly." Several times at a fearsome decibel. It would've been impossible for even the neighbors to miss it, the way she'd been carrying on a short while ago.

Abby reached out her hand to rub Emma's back as the baby snuffled. "She said 'Maa-Maa,' not 'Mama.'"

He shook his head in confusion. "What's the difference?"

"Maa-Maa is Emma's attempt at saying Mattie's name." Her gaze dropped to the baby. "You miss Aunt Mattie, don't you?"

"Maa-Maa," Emma murmured, seeming to prove Abby's point.

Abby's eyes came back up to meet his.

"Even if that's true, how could Mattie and Josiah just up and leave when it caused Emma to react like that?" he demanded. "Didn't they care that she was screaming?"

"Of course they cared. But coming back would only have made the eventual, inevitable separation harder on Emma."

He found that difficult to believe. The situation already seemed as bad as it could possibly be.

"It's better that they got it over with quickly," Abby continued, as she took a seat on the settee positioned before the unlit fireplace. "Like pulling off a bandage that's become stuck with dried blood."

"You do that, and you run the risk of tearing open the scab and starting the wound bleeding again," he warned. "The bandage should be soaked and then removed gently." He shot a look at her. "Remind me to never let you anywhere near me if I'm injured. You're liable to do me more harm than good."

She sputtered for a moment and then wrinkled her nose. "I'll admit that might've been a poor comparison, but I stand by my initial assertion that a swift departure was the best way for Mattie and Josiah to handle this situation."

Elias didn't see things that way, couldn't view this in the same light as Abby. "I can't believe they didn't come back to check on her at least, once she'd started in. For all they knew, I could have hurt her somehow."

"Don't be ridiculous. You'd never hurt her."

"Not on purpose. But accidents happen. How could they be sure she hadn't been injured in some way?"

They had stronger nerves than Elias. That was for certain. Either that, or Mattie was so set on Elias caring for Emma that nothing on this earth could shake her from her course.

"They had no reason to think anything bad had occurred, because they trust you will protect Emma from harm. And if by some misfortune, she were to suffer an injury, there's nothing they could do for her that you couldn't do yourself. You *are* a doctor." She spoke as though she thought it might've slipped his mind.

He wished he *could* forget that he was as dismal a failure as a doctor as he was at being a proper father to Emma. After what had happened with Rebecca, he was frankly surprised that Abby had any faith left in his doctoring abilities. All his knowledge and experience hadn't been enough to save his wife.

Perhaps for Abby, it was merely a case of the lesser of two evils—a poor doctor being preferable to no doctor at all. It wasn't as though there was anyone else within a twenty-mile radius that had even a modicum of medical training.

Abby shifted, drawing him from his grim thoughts. "I didn't realize the hour had grown so late." She turned her gaze from the clock on the mantel and focused on Elias once more. "I should have returned home before this."

She stood up from the settee and leaned forward to place a kiss on Emma's head. The movement brought her close to Elias. Close enough for him to see the light dusting of freckles across the bridge of her nose and along her cheekbones. Close enough for the scent of her hair to wrap around him, teasing his senses. She smelled of sunshine and wildflowers, likely from time spent outdoors.

When she drew back, he felt oddly bereft. But he convinced himself it was merely due to his apprehension at the prospect of being left on his own with Emma.

He didn't want Abby to go.

Without conscious thought, his arm came up and he caught her hand before she could shift out of reach. Her fingers were soft and warm in his clasp. Her touch was as soothing to him as he suspected it had been for his daughter several moments ago when Abby had stroked Emma's back.

Abby's gaze dropped to their joined hands for an instant before returning to meet his. Her eyebrows arched in silent question.

He released her abruptly, his face heating at his knee-jerk reaction, and he rushed into speech. "Can't you stay a bit longer? At least until Emma's fed and settled for the night? Please."

She hesitated a brief moment, then shook her head. "There's no need for me to do that." Her lips curved in a gentle smile as she glanced at the baby nestled against his chest. "You and Emma appear to be coping well enough now."

Now being the operative word. Emma didn't seem happy, but at least she was quiet and still. He feared that could—and would—change in a flash, however. Just as soon as Abby walked out the front door.

"Please, Abby. Don't go yet."

The note of panicked pleading in Elias's voice almost had Abby reconsidering. Almost. But despite his apparent misgivings, she believed in him. Besides, she wasn't sure what benefit she could provide, other than moral support. It wasn't as if she had any experience putting Emma to bed. Still, it was nearly impossible for her to withstand the look of desperate entreaty in his dark eyes, and she lowered her gaze from his.

The grass stains on her skirt snagged her attention once more. They served as a stark reminder that she should return home to change without delay if she hoped to avoid a tongue-lashing from her mother about her appearance, liberally peppered with unfavorable comparisons to Rebecca. Though Abby was accustomed to it, that didn't mean hearing it yet again wouldn't hurt.

Unfortunately, she seemed to have a talent for doing things that displeased the older woman. Even when Abby tried her best to restrain her natural tendencies, in order to make her mother proud, she somehow ended up in a mire, regardless. Eventually, she'd reached the point where she'd stopped seeking Emmaline Warner's elusive approval.

But that wasn't to say that Abby was foolish enough to deliberately court another round of criticism.

Her mother had planned to spend the afternoon making social calls and attending the weekly meeting of the Silver Springs Ladies' Benevolence Society. But she'd be finished with that by now and making her way homeward.

Abby feared she was already cutting it rather too close for comfort. If she were to have any hope at all of beating the older woman back to their house, she had to leave here immediately.

She didn't admit as much to Elias, however. She doubted her familial issues were of any interest to him. "I'm sorry, but I can't stay. Papa will be closing up the mercantile for the day and arriving home soon. I have to help Mother get supper on the table beforehand."

"What about Emma's supper?" Doubts chased across his features and shadowed his expression. "You're just going to leave me to flounder on my own and make her suffer the penalty?"

Abby's resolve didn't waver. No matter his self-doubt, Elias didn't need to use her as a crutch. "I'm certain you and Emma will do fine without me. So, I'll bid farewell to you both." She refrained from her usual goodbye hugs and cuddles with Emma—which might inadvertently set the baby off again—and started toward the stairs.

"Abby, wait!"

The urgent demand brought her up short, and she turned back to face him. "Yes?"

He opened his mouth, but no sound came out. When he finally did speak, she sensed that it wasn't what he'd originally intended to say. "I'll walk downstairs with you."

Elias maneuvered himself out of the chair and into a standing position, with his daughter clasped securely in his arms. "I suppose I better get some food inside Emma before she starts howling again."

Deeming his words a positive sign, Abby's heart felt suddenly lighter. "That's a splendid idea."

At the bottom of the stairs, he came to a halt while Abby collected her bag and continued on to the front door.

"When will you be back?" he called out behind her.

She glanced at him over her shoulder. "I can return tomorrow morning if you'd like." Although she didn't believe it was a matter of practical necessity, she'd never decline an opportunity to visit with her niece.

This was what she'd prayed for—a chance to spend more time with Emma on a regular basis.

And if Abby's presence eased Elias's mind besides, that was so much the better.

His eyebrows pulled together in a straight line across his forehead. "Can you come first thing in the morning?"

The poor man looked as though he was coiled tighter than a rattlesnake that was feeling threatened.

"I'll come by directly after breakfast," she promised, as she placed her hand on the doorknob.

The assurance appeared to relieve a bit of Elias's tension.

Relaxing his rigid stance, he shifted his hold on Emma and hitched her higher against his cotton shirt-front. "We'll see you tomorrow, then."

Once Abby exited the house and crossed the street, she hurried along toward home.

"Hello, Abigail," Clara Wheeler hailed from the front stoop of her boardinghouse.

The stout middle-aged matron lived less than half a block from the Warners and was known to be an interminable gossip.

Not caring to appear rude, as the whole town was certain to hear exaggerated tales about any imagined slight, Abby reluctantly slowed her pace. "Good afternoon, Mrs. Wheeler."

Despite the greeting, her steps didn't halt completely, and she hoped the older woman would take that to mean Abby didn't have time for a lengthy chitchat.

Either Mrs. Wheeler failed to recognize the obvious hint or she chose to ignore it. "Has your father gotten in that bolt of fabric I've been waiting on? I'm sewing a wedding dress for my youngest daughter, and I ordered a lovely pale lilac organdy from New York."

Of course Abby had been well aware of that fact already, since the older woman made mention of it at every available opportunity. She bit back a discourteous comment prompted by frustration at being delayed. "It hasn't arrived yet, but he expects it by the end of next week."

"Oh, I do hope it comes soon. My Helen's wedding is only a little over a month and a half away, in the second week of September, and she's anxious to have all the details sorted. Why, just the other day she—"

Past experience had taught Abby that the older woman was likely winding up for a story that could take half an hour or more, so she saw little choice but to interrupt—even if it meant that her neighbor would spend the next week gossiping about her rudeness to anyone who would listen. "I'm sorry, Mrs. Wheeler, but I can't stay and chat any longer today," Abby broke in before the other woman could gain a full head of steam. "Perhaps you could tell me about it some other time. Good day to you."

The older woman didn't take kindly to being cut off so abruptly. "Well, really! You young people these days have no manners." She was speaking to Abby's back by this point. "I'll be informing your mother about this, you can be sure!" she called out, her voice carrying down the street.

Abby cringed but didn't stop or turn around.

Now she'd have one more thing to fear her mother lecturing her about.

Pushing the disheartening thought from her mind as she reached the white picket fence that encircled the Warners' small plot of land, she lifted the latch and let herself in through the gate.

The house was a modest two-story with a wide front porch. Pale cream trim complemented the sky blue paint used on the wooden siding, giving the dwelling a cheerful, homey feel.

Once she'd mounted the porch steps, she stole a swift glance back toward Elias's home, wondering how he and Emma were faring. The whitewashed clapboard facade gave no clues as to what was happening within its walls, but Abby could picture the pair seated at the kitchen table, enjoying the basket of food Mattie had prepared. The image brought a smile to her face.

Her lighthearted mood vanished quickly as thoughts of her mother's ire intruded. But the older woman would be angry only if she was here to see Abby's mussed hair and stained dress. Perhaps she wasn't yet home.

Abby twisted the doorknob, and the front door swung inward silently on well-oiled hinges. Ducking her head around the solid oak panel, she could hear movement coming from the kitchen located at the rear of the house. But all was not lost. She merely had to sneak upstairs to her bedroom on the second floor and change her dress without her mother any the wiser. *Please, Lord.*

The door clicked shut behind her as she sped across the front hall and toward the staircase.

"Who's there? Abigail, is that you?"

The sound of her mother's voice had her skidding to an undignified halt on the polished wood floor. She grabbed on to the newel post to catch her balance and hastily righted herself.

Oh, why couldn't the Lord have heeded her prayer? Instantly, shame pricked her conscience that she'd bothered Him with such a trifling matter in the first place. He had much more pressing concerns—famine, floods, disease, to name just a few. Abby's desire to avoid a confrontation with her mother rated extremely low in comparison.

"Yes, it's me, Mother," she answered.

"Well, for pity's sake, don't dawdle in the front hall. Come here so I need not shout at you in order to be heard."

Taking a deep breath, Abby straightened her spine and then did as she'd been bidden. When she entered the kitchen, she found her mother at the counter, cutting chunks of meat into cubes to add to a pot on the cast-iron cook stove.

"Where have you been?" the older woman demanded, but then continued without pausing to allow Abby to answer. "You spent all afternoon outside again, wasting time on those silly drawings instead of doing something useful, didn't you?" Her lips pursed as she aimed a pointed look toward the canvas bag Abby had completely forgotten she still carried over her shoulder.

"No, I—"

Her mother didn't give her a chance to explain where she'd spent the last hour. An eagle-eyed gaze swept Abby from head to toe—and missed nothing. "Your dress is ruined, and I do believe that being out in the bright sun without a hat again has further darkened your skin and caused the appearance of several more unsightly freckles. It will take liberal applications of lemon juice to repair the damage. You'll never catch a husband looking like that. How many times must I remind you to comport yourself as a lady?" Starting into her oft-used refrain, she bemoaned why Abby couldn't be more like Rebecca.

After twenty years of being compared unfavorably to her older sister—even when Rebecca was more than two thousand miles away, during the two years she'd remained in Tennessee with her husband after the rest of the family moved out west to Oregon Country—one might think that Abby would have become inured to it by now. But try as she might to not let it bother her, her mother's disdain still hurt deep down.

However, she'd stopped trying to suppress her true self in an attempt to please her mother once she had realized it was an impossible task. Abby wasn't a carbon copy of her sibling, and she could never be one. She didn't *want* to be one.

Besides, Rebecca hadn't been a perfect paragon, as their mother liked to pretend. No one could be that, in truth. For all that Abby had loved her sister for her innumerable good qualities, Rebecca had not been without faults, the same as anybody else. Others could be forgiven for thinking otherwise, however, after listening to Emmaline Warner.

There was a time when Abby had imagined that moving somewhere new, where no one outside their family had known Rebecca, would make a difference. Although the citizens of Silver Springs had never even met her older sibling, Abby still felt as if she lived in Rebecca's shadow since her mother never missed an opportunity to point out how Abby failed to measure up.

Even Rebecca's passing hadn't altered that. Instead of embracing the daughter who remained, Emmaline Warner seemed bound and determined to mold Abby into her sister's image. Trying to turn Abby into the daughter she'd lost.

Abby didn't want to be at odds with her mother, but she couldn't live her life to please her parent. It never worked anyway—not even when Abby had tried her utmost. She'd come to accept that she would never be the daughter her mother yearned for.

It wasn't until Abby sat down with her parents for supper around the table in the dining room that she had an opening to tell her mother and father about her visit with Emma.

Relaying what had transpired that afternoon while she was at Elias's house, she finished with, "We'll all be able to see Emma more often from now on."

Abby's father patted his mouth with a napkin, crinkles appearing around his eyes as he smiled. "That is indeed happy news."

His wife speared a chunk of meat with her fork. "It's high time things changed, if you ask me. But I don't like *that* man having the care of Rebecca's little girl."

Abby paused with a bite of food suspended in midair, halfway between her plate and her mouth. Her stomach knotted and her appetite fled.

Her mother hadn't been happy when Emma was staying with Mattie and Josiah on the ranch, a fair distance from town, and now she wasn't happy to discover that Emma would live with Elias. While she'd never made any secret of her ill feelings toward Elias since learning of Rebecca's passing, surely she must see that Emma's place was with her father.

"Where would you prefer she reside, if not with Elias?" Abby asked, praying the older woman would acknowledge that Emma's new situation was for the best.

"Most anywhere else would be better," she declared

in no uncertain terms, her words crushing the life out of Abby's overly optimistic hopes. "He's not fit to raise my granddaughter! Why, when I think about what that man did to my darling Rebecca, how he as good as killed her—"

"Mother! Please, don't say such things." Abby set down her food-laden fork on her barely touched supper plate. "You'll only upset yourself further." And it wasn't true, besides.

Emmaline Warner held Elias responsible for her daughter's death, not because of any firsthand knowledge of the events or true reason to think Elias had been negligent, but simply because she needed someone to blame. The horrible tragedy was nobody's fault, but grief had a terrible effect on people sometimes. Her mother wanted someone to rail at and revile. Elias had the misfortune to be a convenient target. It didn't help matters that he'd never defended himself against her outrageous accusations, which she repeated often.

Now she continued on with her heated tirade as if Abby hadn't spoken. "I have half a mind to go over there this very instant and snatch Emma away from him."

Abby's father laid a staying hand on his wife's arm. "Calm yourself, my dear. That young man doesn't need you barging in and interrupting his supper."

She subsided back into her chair. "Yes, of course. You're quite right, Thomas." She smoothed the gray-streaked blond hairs pinned into a chignon at her nape, then straightened the amethyst broach tucked into the ruffled collar of her dark navy gown.

Abby folded her hands in her lap. "We ought to

allow Elias time with his daughter," she inserted into the heavy silence. "They've been apart for too long already."

"Humph. And whose fault is that, I ask you?" Abby's mother sniffed her disdain. "He's done nothing but foist his responsibilities onto others since the day Emma was born. It was his choice to ignore his child for the better part of a year. He seemed more than willing to leave it to his brother and sister-in-law until they put an end to that. He would probably thank us for taking the baby off his hands."

"I don't think having Mattie and Josiah look after Emma was something he chose, not deliberately," Abby refuted. "He didn't *want* to ignore Emma, but he needed to be on his own for a while, in order to heal." At least, she assumed that was the case.

Though Elias didn't talk about it to her—didn't share his pain with anyone, not even his brother, as far as she could tell—he must've been hurting, the same as anyone who had lost a beloved spouse. His grief had been all too plain to see in the sadness that seemed to cloud his dark eyes, even when surrounded by the family who loved him.

Her fingers pleated the linen napkin draped over her lap. "Shouldn't we have compassion and show consideration for his suffering?"

"And what of *my* suffering?" her mother challenged. "He's shown no consideration for me. A man with so little compassion has no business raising an innocent child. Mark my words. This will come to grief if we allow the situation to stand."

Abby didn't believe things were nearly so dire as

the older woman made them out to be. It was a source of endless frustration to her that they couldn't have a conversation without her mother's tightly held prejudices intruding.

Elias was not a bad person or unfit as a parent just because his means of grieving didn't meet with his mother-in-law's approval. Emma belonged with her father. He was a good man. The baby would come to no harm in his care. Abby refused to believe otherwise and hoped her mother would come to see the truth of it, too.

Abby tried once more to sway her. "We must seek the Lord's guidance and wisdom and pray for a happy outcome."

"The Good Lord would surely have His work cut out for Him to raise *that* man up from the low place he's sunk."

Although negativity was something Abby had come to expect from the older woman, she wished that just once her mother might surprise her. There were far worse depths a man could fall than the place Elias was in.

He had not turned to drink or vice. He wasn't cruel or violent. He'd simply become locked in his own misery—and that was hardly blameworthy. The worst that could be said against him was that he led a solitary life, avoiding interactions with others whenever possible.

Emma's arrival in his home could only help with that, forcing him to reach outside himself to the child who needed him. It would be good for them both.

Unfortunately, Emmaline Warner's heightened emotions blinded her to that fact.

Rebecca's passing had been a loss to all of them. Not only her mother but also her father. As well as Elias. Poor, motherless baby Emma. And Abby. No one remained unaffected.

Lord, please heal our family.

Chapter Four

The next morning, Elias was at his wit's end after a sleepless night spent tending his fractious child. Now he sat at the kitchen table with Emma balanced on his lap, attempting to feed her breakfast and feeling decidedly inept. More oatmeal ended up decorating the baby, as well as Elias's clothing, than in her mouth.

A knock sounded on the front door, and he breathed a sigh of relief that Abby had finally returned. The past fifteen hours had been difficult for both him and his daughter, the tense atmosphere making the time since yesterday evening seem as though it had dragged on forever.

Rising from his chair, he tucked Emma against his chest and hastened to the front door to open it.

"Good morning," Abby greeted in a cheery tone.

He barely stopped himself from grimacing in response. It was morning all right, but he wouldn't call it *good*. Especially not when he spotted his former mother-in-law standing behind Abby.

Mrs. Warner was a short, buxom woman whose

frame had acquired a good deal of padding as she grew older. In her midforties now, her blond hair was threaded with gray.

Rebecca had taken after her mother in appearance. Was this what she might have looked like in two decades, had she lived?

There was no sense in Elias speculating on pointless what-might-have-beens. He'd never know, and thinking about it only acted as a knife jab to unhealed wounds that were best left alone.

Abby folded her hands at her waist. "I'm sorry for showing up here unannounced."

Since he'd expected her, the apology had to be for Mrs. Warner's uninvited presence.

The older woman pushed past her daughter. "It seems I've arrived not a moment too soon. What have you done to my grandchild?"

Plainly, his former mother-in-law wasn't inclined to give him the benefit of the doubt. Unlike Abby.

Whether he agreed with the assessment or not, he found that Mrs. Warner's lack of faith still stung. "I haven't caused irreparable damage to Emma," he assured the older woman, though that much should've been obvious. "Things got a bit messy while I was feeding her breakfast." Shifting the baby in his arms, he glanced down at her.

She looked a sight, but at least she wasn't crying or screaming. In fact, a sunny smile split her oatmeal-dotted face as she reached out her arms toward the two women.

Mrs. Warner was closest, but she took a hasty step back out of range of Emma's sticky fingers. "No, no, darling, we mustn't soil Grandmother's brand-new dress."

Elias didn't suppose the older woman would stand for being kept waiting outside on the doorstep for the whole of her visit. Moving aside reluctantly, he allowed her to enter the house.

"Mother won't stay long," Abby remarked as she stepped into the front hall behind the older woman, apparently recognizing his half-hearted welcome to his unwanted guest. "She has errands to attend to, but she wanted to come and check on Emma first."

Wanted to check up on Elias was more like it, but he refrained from voicing that thought out loud.

Mrs. Warner sailed down the hallway and toward the kitchen as if she owned the place. Perhaps she imagined she had more of a claim on it than him, since she and her ladies' society had been instrumental in its construction and furnishing.

Following behind her, he reached the kitchen in time to see her subject the room to a cursory look, her mouth pinched up as if she'd taken a sip of lemonade with insufficient sugar.

"The state of this kitchen is simply disgraceful," she pronounced.

Sensing Abby at his back, he turned to glance at her.

She didn't seem to share her mother's aversion to the mess. "We clearly came at an inopportune time, Mother. But how can you have any complaint about Elias feeding Emma before he cleans up the kitchen?"

The other woman's sour expression didn't change, but at least she kept any further criticisms to herself about his apparently deplorable housekeeping.

Elias cleared his throat and shifted from one foot to the other. "I'm sorry I can't offer you a cup of coffee."

He'd had his hands full with Emma, focused on seeing to her needs, and hadn't gotten a spare minute yet this morning to brew a pot. And actually, he wasn't truly that sorry he couldn't provide refreshments. He preferred not to give Mrs. Warner any additional excuse to linger once she satisfied herself that Emma wasn't in imminent danger of coming to harm in Elias's care.

The older woman stuck her haughty nose in the air and moved to inspect the half-full bowl of porridge he'd left sitting on the table. "I'd like to say I'm surprised by your lack of proper manners, Mr. Dawson, but I know better than that. Fortunately, I didn't come here anticipating social niceties from you."

No, she'd come, it seemed, to find fault with him and judge his worthiness—or lack thereof—as a fitting father to his own child. Though he still harbored doubts of his own in that regard, he resented her presumption in rushing to convict him. She wasn't offering any help, only censure.

Uncaring whether she thought him rude for not continuing to stand while ladies were present, Elias took a seat at the table and propped Emma on his lap once again. Abby pulled out one of the other chairs and sat down, as well.

He reached for the half-finished bowl of porridge, but Abby got there ahead of him. She spooned some into Emma's open mouth, expertly catching the dribble that tried to escape down the baby's chin.

Emma patted the table directly on the spot where a glob of oatmeal had landed while Elias struggled to accomplish this task on his own a short time ago. She appeared fascinated by this new tactile sensation, and she curled her fingers around the squishy substance before bringing her fist to her mouth for a taste.

"No, no, Emma," her grandmother scolded. "We must use utensils when eating. We mustn't use our hands."

Abby shot a look at the older woman. "Don't you think she's a bit young to be worrying about proper table manners?"

"One is never too young to start learning the rules of etiquette. I can't be expected to leave it up to certain other persons to instruct her."

Elias chose to ignore the blatant dig aimed at him, but he felt the weight of Mrs. Warner's implacable stare on him as Abby continued to feed Emma.

After several uncomfortable minutes, his former mother-in-law apparently deemed her duty to her granddaughter done, at least for the moment. "Well, I must be off. Lydia Freedmont, our club president, asked me to meet with Mr. Greene, the carpenter, to discuss plans for a schoolhouse the Silver Springs Ladies' Benevolence Society intends to have built. The town council has already donated a plot of land on the west side of town, near Preacher Linton's church."

With a wave of her fingers and air kisses in Emma's direction, the older woman moved toward the doorway. "Come along, Abigail. Your father's expecting you at the mercantile to assist him with customers."

Elias wanted to protest that Abby couldn't leave him yet, but he clamped down on the words before they could escape. He didn't want to give Mrs. Warner further justification for her low opinion of him. Not that she needed any additional proof against him.

Abby's mother sent her an impatient look when she didn't immediately jump to her feet. "Don't dawdle, Abigail. You know your father doesn't like to be kept waiting."

Actually, it was her mother who made a fuss about such things. Very little bothered Abby's father, which was a good thing. Otherwise, he likely wouldn't have weathered the past twenty-five years married to a persnickety woman. For the most part, he simply let his wife have her own way to avoid friction in their household.

This also meant he preferred not to get in the middle of any disagreements between his wife and daughter and rarely interceded on Abby's behalf during her mother's many rebukes. Which left Abby feeling as though she wasn't important enough to him that he would stand in defense of her.

One of the few times he'd put his foot down hadn't been for Abby but rather when he'd made the decision to move his family to Oregon Country several years ago. His wife hadn't wanted to be separated from their eldest daughter and had protested rather vehemently against leaving their home in Tennessee. Rebecca had been newly married to Elias, who had worked hard to establish himself as a doctor and owned a prosperous clinic in Nashville.

When Thomas had been unswayed by her protests, his wife had accepted the inevitability of the move—but even then, she had sought to manipulate circumstances to her liking. She'd arranged a doctoring practice for Elias in Silver Springs, hoping to compel him to pull up stakes in Tennessee and bring Rebecca to Oregon Country.

The only thing Emmaline Warner hadn't accounted for was what had happened to Rebecca during the perilous journey.

Abby's mother liked to put all the blame for that tragedy on Elias. She never acknowledged that her self-serving actions had started the entire chain of events. Nor would she concede that Elias had been affected as greatly as her, his pain as profound.

Abby couldn't treat Elias in the same dismissive manner. *She* wouldn't abandon him without a backward glance.

"Papa won't mind if I get there a bit later than expected. Not once I explain that the cause of my tardiness was to spend a few extra minutes with Emma."

Irritation flashed across the older woman's face. "I haven't time to debate the point with you now. I want your word that you'll head to the mercantile within the next quarter hour."

Abby tucked her hand into the folds of her full skirt and crossed her index and middle fingers. "Of course, Mother."

Only slightly mollified, the older woman gave a curt nod, then pivoted on her heels and exited the kitchen. Her footfalls retreated down the hallway, and a moment later, Abby heard the sound of the front door opening and closing.

Relaxing her rigid posture, she returned her attention to Emma and Elias. He'd seemed on edge since their arrival, but a good bit of his tension appeared to dissipate with the older woman's departure. She had that effect on a number of people.

"I apologize for my mother. She shouldn't have said those uncharitable things."

Elias shifted Emma on his lap and leaned back in the chair. "You don't have any cause for apology. It's your mother who ought to make amends for her own behavior. No one holds you responsible for her actions. Least of all, me."

After finishing the last of the oatmeal, Emma reached out her arms toward Abby.

She deposited the spoon inside the empty bowl and leaned forward to take the baby without a second thought.

Elias stopped her with a shake of his head. "Trust me when I say that you don't want to hold her right now or you'll look no better than me in a moment."

She scanned the part of his shirt that was visible above the table. Smeared oatmeal stood out in stark contrast against the dark brown cotton. She'd venture a guess that his trousers had been subjected to the same maltreatment.

Her gaze settled on his face, and her lips curved up the tiniest bit. "Did you know you have some oatmeal in your beard?"

"No, but I'm not surprised to hear it." He glanced down, his eyes crossing comically in an effort to see for himself.

She couldn't contain her laughter.

Elias's gaze came back up to clash with hers, his eyebrows lowered in mock outrage. "You think this is funny, do you? Perhaps I should've let Emma make a mess of your clothing. I can just imagine how your mother would react if you assisted customers at the mercantile while wearing a stained dress."

Abby's good humor fled abruptly at his words. "I don't have to imagine that because I've suffered through it a fair number of times already."

"I didn't realize your relationship with your mother was quite so contentious."

"Has there ever been a time that she's failed to let you know about her disapproval of you?"

"Only when I'm doing what she wants."

"Exactly."

His eyes widened in understanding, and then something that looked uncomfortably like pity entered his gaze. "She has no call to be criticizing you," he said. "I'm sorry she's so hard on you. Having no mother seems almost preferable."

"I wasn't trying to garner sympathy. I merely sought to point out that you're not alone in drawing her censure."

He appeared immediately contrite. "I apologize for teasing you about it." Keeping Emma upright with one palm braced against her tummy, he rubbed his other hand in circles across her back. "I'm all too familiar with the way your mother behaves toward me, but I didn't consider that—"

"I'm on the receiving end of her frequent displeasure, as well?" She ducked her head, not wanting him to read in her expression how much it hurt her to admit to the true state of her relationship with her mother.

She pushed her chair back from the table. "Thank

you for sparing me an angry harangue on this occasion." Carrying the dirty dishes to the washbasin, she dampened a cloth and moved back toward Elias. "Let's get Emma cleaned up."

After wiping the baby's face and hands while Elias held her still, Abby removed the towel that he'd had the forethought to tuck around Emma's neck prior to their breakfast mishap, protecting her clothing from the worst of the spilled oatmeal.

Abby set aside the soiled linens and turned her attention to the rest of the room, also in desperate need of a good scrubbing. "Now for the kitchen."

"Why don't you take Emma while I handle this lot?" Elias asked. "There's an apron over there, hanging on a hook by the back door. You can put that on to protect your dress from getting dirtied."

She did as he'd suggested. "I didn't take you for the apron-wearing type," she mused, as she tied the apron strings into a bow at the back of her waist and accepted Emma from him.

"If I was, do you think I'd look like this?" He spread his arms wide and then let them fall back to his sides. "It belongs to Mattie, but I'm sure she won't mind you borrowing it."

"I'm certain she wouldn't have objected if you'd borrowed it, either." She cocked her head to the side as she inspected him. "Perhaps, you should rethink your anti-apron stance."

He eyed askance the white-and-navy-checked gingham, edged with a gathered strip of dark blue fabric. "I'd look ridiculous in ruffles."

"I hate to tell you this, but it would be rather difficult

for you to look any more ridiculous than you do right now, sporting a suit of splotched oatmeal."

Glancing down at himself, his expression turned wry. "You've got a point there. As soon as I'm finished cleaning the kitchen, I'll be sure to remedy this situation, as well."

She noticed that he hadn't made any mention of donning the apron next time, but she didn't call him on the omission.

With Emma cradled in her arms, Abby watched Elias wet a rag and start wiping up the mess, which was spread over most every surface in sight, from the counter and stove to the table, and even the wooden floor. It seemed Emma had quite an impressive talent for hurling oatmeal.

Abby was frankly surprised not to see traces of it stuck to the ceiling. "It appears you and Emma had an eventful morning before my mother and I showed up."

He rubbed the underside of his jaw through his thick red-hued beard. "It's been an eventful day and a half."

Strictly speaking, he hadn't spent a full day with Emma yesterday, and it was barely gone eight o'clock now—but she figured he wouldn't appreciate her correcting him on those facts.

"Did Emma start screaming again last evening once I'd left here?" she queried instead.

"No, but when I put her to bed, it took a long while for her to settle." He didn't pause in his cleaning as he spoke. "Then after she finally drifted into an exhausted slumber, she whimpered in her sleep throughout the remainder of the night. *That* was even harder to endure than her earlier temper tantrum."

Abby's heart twisted at the mere thought of it. How much worse must it have been for Elias to witness? From the sound of it, he hadn't slept at all.

"Were you awake the whole night?"

He gave a weary nod in response. "I tried to lie down and get some rest, but it proved impossible. I doubt I dozed for more than five minutes at a stretch."

She felt a tug on her heart for him, as well. "I'm sorry it was so difficult for you and Emma last night." Hugging her niece close, she kissed the baby's rosy cheek. "But things will improve, given time."

"They have to, I guess. Let's just hope it happens soon." He stifled a yawn behind his hand. "Some sleep would sure come in handy before too long."

Several minutes later, the kitchen looked almost like new again.

"Fine work," she commended.

His mouth quirked up in a lopsided grin. "I reckon I should go and get cleaned up now. That is, if you don't mind keeping an eye on Emma for a bit longer while I'm upstairs."

"Go ahead. I'm happy to watch her."

"Thank you." He yawned a second time as he shuffled out of the room.

His yawns reminded Abby that he hadn't yet gotten any coffee this morning. She balanced Emma on her hip and walked to the stove to start a pot brewing.

It took a bit of juggling to complete the task one-handed, but Emma seemed to delight in her fumbling. Especially when Abby exaggerated her struggles. She playacted letting Emma slip in her grasp with a mock gasp, then hitched her up again, sending the baby into peals of laughter.

"It's a nice change to hear her laughing after last night," Elias remarked from behind them.

Abby twisted around to face him. "You're back," she said needlessly.

And looking handsome in a fresh shirt and trousers, with his hair and beard damp from a recent washing.

She shook her head to erase such thoughts from her mind. "The coffee will be ready in a minute."

"Thank you for fixing it. I could sure use a cup about now." He moved to the open shelves next to the stove and reached for an enamel mug. "Will you join me?" he asked, his hand hovering over a second mug.

She hesitated a moment before answering. "I should be going."

Elias wasn't ready for Abby to leave yet, but he didn't try to talk her into staying. Not because his pride wouldn't allow it—he'd have gotten down on his knees and begged if he'd thought it would've done any good. Only the certain knowledge that no amount of pleading could alter the inevitable outcome served to keep him silent. She'd already earned her mother's displeasure by staying this long. She couldn't linger all day—not when her father was expecting her at the mercantile.

Besides, it was downright pitiful for a grown man to be quaking in his boots when faced with the prospect of being left alone with his infant daughter. But Elias hadn't spent any significant amount of time on his own with Emma prior to the previous day.

Before that, there had always been a female relative

or two hovering about, ready to step in at a moment's notice and take charge of the baby at the first hint of trouble. Having that safeguard ripped away had left Elias fighting to find his footing.

His heart pounded in his chest as memories of the previous night overtook him. He recalled in stark detail the tears running down Emma's cheeks, even in her sleep, and how the sight had very nearly broken him.

He'd spent the long hours of darkness plagued by doubts and fears that he wasn't up to the monumental responsibility of caring for and protecting his child's life—that, ultimately, he would fail his daughter, as he had failed her mother.

Perhaps Abby sensed his unease with the situation. Indecision shadowed her expression for a moment, then cleared. "I suppose I could spare the time for one cup of coffee. A few more minutes won't make much difference."

He grabbed the second mug from the shelf and filled both cups with rich, dark coffee, then handed one to her. She smiled in gratitude.

By unspoken agreement, they headed to the table and sat down again. He noted Abby's deftness in keeping the mug out of the baby's reach as she blew on the hot liquid and took a cautious sip. Her cheeks were flushed a light pink by the steam drifting up from the coffee.

He remembered how she had looked moving about the kitchen carrying Emma in those seconds he'd paused in the doorway unobserved, before making his presence known.

She was tall for a woman and slender—unlike Rebecca, who'd been petite and curvy. His late wife had barely come up to the center of his chest, while the top of Abby's head was on a level with his nose when they stood facing each other.

She finished her coffee and rose gracefully from her chair, with Emma clasped securely in her embrace. After setting the cup in the basin, she approached Elias.

Her eyes were focused on her niece, not meeting his gaze. "Time to go to your papa, so I can head on over to the mercantile," she addressed the baby.

Elias held out his arms to his daughter, and she came to him willingly enough. He tucked her against his shirtfront.

Her tiny hand patted his chest. "Papa."

His heart melted at hearing her utter that single word.

The realization of his vulnerability terrified him. Still, he made a vow to do his level best for his baby girl—no matter what that might entail nor what it meant for his own unsettled and chaotic emotions.

Unfortunately, he didn't have much more than a vague notion about what was required of him in any real and practical sense. Yesterday, he'd fed Emma supper, and then it had been time to change her and put her to bed. But now, the hours until nightfall stretched out in front of him. A gaping void, which needed to be filled somehow.

He glanced up at Abby. "What am I supposed to do with her?" As soon as the question left his mouth, he shook his head and held up a hand to stop her before she could respond with a sharp remark. "Wait. That came out wrong. I didn't intend to make it sound as though I have something better to do with my time or that Emma will be in my way. That's not the case." Obviously.

Since he hadn't any more pressing matters—or matters of any sort—in need of his attention. Only Emma.

"I should have said, how do I ensure she stays happy and content after you leave? I'm in need of some guidance here, is all. What exactly does a nearly one-year-old child do all day long?"

"Play, eat and sleep, mostly. Give her toys to keep her occupied for a while, or you could try reading to her. Feed her around noon. Clean her—and yourself—up again afterward." Her eyes sparkled with mirth at that last one as she reached around to untie the apron from her slender waist. "Put her down for a nap midafternoon. That sort of thing. All fairly simple."

"Easy for you to say," he grumbled.

After hanging the apron back on its hook, she returned to his side. She placed her hand on his arm and squeezed briefly in tacit support, then smoothed a wispy red curl from Emma's forehead. "I'm sure you'll manage just fine together. I'll see you both later. Have a good day."

Then she was gone.

He turned to look down at Emma. She babbled what sounded like complete gibberish to him, though it probably made perfect sense to her, and blew bubbles with her mouth, causing the dimples in her cheeks to appear.

"I guess it's just you and me again now, baby girl."

Lord help them both.

Chapter Five

On Sunday morning, Abby walked with her parents toward the church on the far side of town. They passed Mrs. Wheeler's boardinghouse, the bank owned by Mr. Freedmont, a restaurant, the sheriff's office, her father's mercantile, Rothmeier's Livery Stable and a few dozen homes. Silver Springs was small but growing rapidly, albeit by fits and starts, as more people arrived from the East each autumn.

Reverend David Linton and his family had been among the group that had journeyed on the wagon trail from Missouri the previous year along with Elias and Rebecca. The young preacher had chosen to settle in Silver Springs with his wife, Tessa, and their two small children. The construction of his church had only just been completed a few weeks ago.

It was a simple wooden structure with a steeple, situated on a slight rise a short distance apart from the town proper. Painted a bright white, the church stood out against the dark green trees directly behind it and the indigo mountains farther off on the horizon. The sight never failed to bring Abby a feeling of hope.

Surely, no one could remain unaffected by the tranquil beauty of this house of worship surrounded by some of the Lord's most awe-inspiring landscape this side of Heaven.

Abby could never regret the move to Oregon Country, though it had been a wrench at the time to leave her older sister behind in Tennessee. She only wished their separation hadn't been made permanent by Rebecca's death.

It remained a scar on Abby's heart, which she feared would always be there, but attending the preacher's weekly sermons gave her a measure of comfort and peace.

She prayed it might be the same for Elias, as well. That today he would finally come here seeking the Lord and would lay his burdens before Him.

Elias had been conspicuous in his absence from Sunday services, while Mattie and Josiah had brought Emma to church each week. Abby hoped this would change, now that Elias was caring for his daughter. That he would join the rest of his family in attending at last. Open himself up enough to listen to the preacher's words—and hear the Lord speak to him through the Scriptures.

As she entered the church, she scanned the rows of wooden pews in search of Elias and noted that the Dawson family hadn't arrived yet. Following her parents up the center aisle, she skirted around the cold woodstove and greeted people as she passed.

"Good morning, Mr. Rothmeier," she addressed the white-haired widower who owned the livery stable.

He didn't smile as he nodded in acknowledgment, but she was certain she saw a hint of warmth in his eyes, despite the dour expression on his lined face.

The church was half-filled with fellow parishioners, and Abby and her parents found empty spaces near the front.

The faint smell of fresh-sawed timber still lingered in the air, overlaid with the scent of the beeswax polish used to clean the pews. The rough wooden walls of the interior were unadorned, except for a solitary carved cross that hung above a window behind the pulpit.

According to her mother, the ladies of the Benevolence Society had discussed ordering stained glass from back East to fill the window frame. They'd decided against it after concluding the cost was prohibitively high. Much to Emmaline Warner's dismay.

It was an inescapable truth that there were things readily available in Saint Louis or New York that the inhabitants of this rough country often had to wait long months to obtain if not do without entirely.

Fortunately, material ornamentation wasn't necessary to show the community's devotion to the Lord. He didn't require fancy windows in His house, only faithful, loving hearts willing to offer kindness and compassion to others.

Abby twisted around in her seat to face the back of the church and watched the door for the Dawsons' arrival.

A minute or two later, Mattie entered, carrying Emma nestled in her arms. Josiah came in behind his wife. Several seconds ticked by with no sign that Elias had accompanied them, and Abby's hopeful anticipation trickled away.

As the Dawsons sat down in the last row, Mattie glanced in Abby's direction and caught her gaze. She smiled a greeting, and Abby's lips automatically curved up in response. But after she had turned back around toward the front once more, her face fell and her shoulders slumped.

"It's extremely unbecoming to slouch, Abigail," her mother chided. "Please, do sit up straight."

Abby wordlessly obeyed the dictate as the preacher took his place at the pulpit and began the service.

He addressed the gathered congregation in a strong, resonant voice as he directed their attention to a number of selected passages from the Bible. "Let us now turn to Galatians chapter six, verse nine, which says, 'And let us not grow weary while doing good, for in due season we shall reap if we do not lose heart.'"

The preacher's words seemed especially relevant to Abby's current situation. Hearing them spoken aloud, she felt as though she wasn't alone in this struggle, that God was with her, encouraging her to hold on to hope.

She would continue to pray for Elias and Emma for as long as necessary.

Please, Lord, turn him away from despair and toward hope, that through his daughter he may find joy and contentment in his life once again.

Abby didn't want anything to hurt Emma, prayed no pain would ever touch her again. That she would know only happiness, acceptance and love, along with daily blessings from the Lord. At barely a year old, she had already suffered greater loss in her young life than some adults ever experienced. She shouldn't be made to face any more.

A short time later, the preacher closed his Bible and led the group in a final prayer. Then he moved to the back of the church and took up a position by the open door.

Abby got to her feet and joined the others filing outside. Pausing to shake the preacher's hand, she expressed her appreciation for the message he'd delivered. "It was a lovely service, Preacher Linton. I found today's sermon to be not only inspiring but timely, as well."

He squeezed her fingers briefly before letting go. "Sharing the Lord's Word with others is a privilege that I don't take lightly. I'm pleased to know this week's selection touched a number of people here today. I look forward to doing the same again next Sunday."

He exchanged a few words with her parents, then Abby's father shepherded his wife and daughter down the steps.

"Mrs. Freedmont," Abby's mother hailed, as she hurried after the dark-haired society matron.

Abby turned to her father. "I'd like to visit with Emma and the Dawsons for a bit, if you don't mind."

"Not at all." He tucked his hands in his pockets and rocked back on his heels. "I'll just be joining that circle of menfolk across the way. I'm sure our talk wouldn't be of interest to a young girl like you. I'll be along shortly to see Emma."

"Thanks, Papa." She kissed his whiskered cheek and

made her escape while her mother's attention was occupied elsewhere.

After greeting Mattie and Josiah, Abby eagerly accepted Emma and cuddled her close, inhaling her sweet, powder scent. The baby was dressed in a cotton bonnet and a white gown with light blue embroidery along the hem and collar.

Abby fingered the stitches, marveling over the intricate floral detail. "I didn't realize you were so skilled with a needle, Mattie."

The other woman made a face in response. "Oh, I'm not. That's my sister, Adela's handiwork."

Abby didn't know Mattie's sixteen-year-old sister well. She'd only had occasion to meet the younger girl a handful of times. Adela Prescott lived in Oregon City with her aunt and uncle, and it was quite a long trip to Silver Springs from their home, taking a day or more.

Abby traced the tiny periwinkle flower design just below Emma's chin. "I admire your sister's talent. I've never been much good at needlework." But put a piece of charcoal in her hand, and it was an entirely different matter.

"Adela stitched several gowns for Emma while we were on the trail heading toward Oregon Country." Mattie's expression dimmed suddenly, as if dark memories had intruded without warning.

Abby could imagine the other woman was thinking about what had happened to Rebecca. She hugged Emma tight to keep her own dark thoughts at bay.

Josiah cleared his throat awkwardly and moved nearer to his wife.

Mattie shook her head, as though dispelling the unhappy images from her mind. "You and your parents are welcome to join us at Elias's house for Sunday dinner," she invited, effectively changing the subject. "We're having pot roast with carrots and potatoes, and I baked a peach pie for dessert."

"It sounds delicious. I'll have to check with my parents first, of course, but I'm certain they'll be agreeable."

The slight breeze caught a lock of Mattie's hair, which had escaped from the bun at her nape, and she tucked the strands behind her ear, then reached over and adjusted Emma's bonnet to protect the baby's delicate skin from the bright sunshine. "Dinner should be ready by around one o'clock. We'll look for you then."

Abby passed Emma back to Mattie. After mentioning that her father wanted to see his granddaughter before they departed, Abby excused herself and headed toward her mother. A quick glance across the churchyard revealed that Mrs. Freedmont had already moved on, leaving Emmaline Warner standing alone for the moment. When Abby reached her side, she relayed Mattie's invitation, and was taken aback by her mother's refusal.

"Unfortunately, we won't be able to accept her kind offer."

Abby swatted at a gnat buzzing around her face. "Why not?"

Did the older woman have some silly aversion to sitting down with Elias and sharing a meal? It wouldn't surprise Abby in the slightest to discover such a thing.

Her mother's mouth curved into a self-satisfied smile. "Lydia Freedmont has promised that she and her husband shall dine at our house." She preened with triumph at her accomplishment. "Which will afford you an opportunity to make a good impression on Augustus's parents."

Abby barely resisted rolling her eyes at her mother's persistent bids to pair her with the banker's twenty-one-year-old son. "Augustus isn't interested in me, Mother." And more to the point—at least to Abby's mind—*she* had no interest in *him*.

He was puffed up with his own importance and entirely too concerned with appearances for her liking.

A trait that her mother viewed with great favor. "Perhaps you might catch his attention, if you'd bother to put a bit of effort into your appearance." She eyed Abby critically.

Abby wondered what precisely her mother took exception to. Since she hadn't been outdoors sketching in the meadow before the church service, her dress wasn't stained, her hair remained tidily restrained, and her fingers were free of charcoal smudges.

What more did her mother want from her? Other than for Abby to make herself over completely into Rebecca's image—which was impossible. She was too tall and too thin, her hair a dull brown rather than golden blond. She wasn't nearly as pretty as her sister had been, and all the effort in the world wouldn't alter that simple truth.

"You'll never possess Rebecca's beauty," her mother continued, as if reading Abby's thoughts. "But that's not to say you should lower your expectations when it comes to selecting a husband. I shouldn't need to remind you that Augustus will inherit his father's bank one day."

Another thing the older woman prized highly, which was of no consequence to Abby. She had a wholly differing set of criteria when it came to a prospective spouse.

Certainly, Abby prayed for a man capable of supporting his family financially, but she valued inner qualities over external trappings. She didn't covet a life of social prominence and extravagance; instead, she desired a marriage based on love and respect.

There was no sense arguing with her mother about Augustus Freedmont's merits as a suitor, however, so Abby decided to try another tack. "I'm surprised you trust me not to do anything unfortunate in Mrs. Freedmont's presence."

Abby felt a sharp pang when it seemed as though her mother was giving the possibility serious thought.

But if the older woman's proclivity to expect the worst from her daughter could be used to Abby's benefit, she'd willingly endure a few bruised feelings. "You won't have to worry about that if I'm eating dinner elsewhere."

"Perhaps we *would* be better served if you don't join us this time, given that Augustus won't be in attendance. Very well. You have my permission to dine with the Dawsons instead." She held up a hand, halting Abby's attempt at an immediate departure. "However, I'll need your help preparing the meal for the Freedmonts before you run off."

Abby resigned herself to the delay with ill grace, but excitement over her afternoon's plans soon took over.

Not only was she looking forward to spending more time with her niece but she also felt a strong urge to see Elias. It had been a few days since her last visit, and she was eager to find out how he was faring and whether things had gotten any better for him and Emma yet.

Abby didn't want to read too much into his continued absence from church…but there was no denying it had raised concerns that perhaps he wasn't adjusting as well as one might hope.

And if that was the case, what could she do to help?

Elias sat in his upstairs parlor with Josiah, watching over Emma as she played on the floor amid a scattering of toys. She'd been left with the two men following her noon feeding, while Mattie prepared dinner for the rest of the family—and certain former family members, as well.

After nearly three-quarters of an hour, during which the baby had entertained herself well enough, Mattie called up to them that the food was ready.

"That means it's time to put Emma down in her cradle for a nap," Josiah remarked, without shifting from his relaxed pose.

It was a continuation of the younger man's hands-off—in the literal sense—child-minding policy, which had gone into effect upon their return from church.

Well then, so be it.

Elias pushed himself out of the chair and scooped up his daughter from the rug. Her rag doll came with them, but the other toys were abandoned where they lay. He carried Emma into her bedroom and settled her

in the cradle. A few minutes of rocking, and her eyelashes began to droop as she fought sleep.

He'd noticed that she seemed less prone to sudden
fits and outbursts with Josiah and Mattie here. But what
would happen when they returned home again? He had
an insidious suspicion that things would take a rapid
downturn once again.

It pained him to think of Emma's emotions see-
sawing wildly each time Mattie and Josiah put in an
appearance. And there was nothing Elias could do to
fix it.

He brushed back a wayward curl from his baby girl's
forehead.

Once she'd drifted off into slumber, he drew the curtains closed at the window to block out the sunlight and
quietly exited the bedroom, heading across the sitting
room toward the staircase.

"Abby's here," Mattie announced from the foyer
below.

Elias started down the stairs, with his brother bringing up the rear.

Josiah's wife stepped back from the open front door
to allow their guest to enter.

Abby wore a gown of cream-and-burgundy-striped
fabric, with burgundy piping along the bodice. The red-
dish hue enhanced the color of her blue eyes. Her light
brown hair was pulled back into an elegant knot at her
nape, revealing the graceful lines of her neck, while a
few curling wisps had been left loose to frame her face.

"Doesn't Abby look lovely today, Elias?" Mattie
prompted.

"Very nice," he agreed.

Abby's cheeks flushed at his words. Though he'd meant them more as a statement of fact rather than as any sort of compliment, he had no objection if she chose to be flattered by his words. She wouldn't have attributed some great significance to a polite utterance from him, in any case.

Elias was thankful to learn that Abby's parents— or more specifically, her mother—had decided against joining them. This way, his prospects for a pleasant meal were much improved, though not guaranteed.

Somehow, Elias doubted Josiah and Mattie would suddenly refrain from voicing any further opinions in regards to his handling of Emma. He didn't need them to enumerate his inadequacies as though he wasn't well aware of them already.

Abby alone had exhibited a seemingly undauntable faith in him.

After the group had moved into the kitchen and sat down at the table, Josiah asked a blessing over their meal.

Though Elias bowed his head in seeming prayer, his mind shied away from focusing on his brother's discourse. Instead, he allowed his thoughts to simply wander here and there, alighting on nothing of import, until Josiah had finished saying grace.

"Your pot roast is one of the best I've ever tasted, Mattie," Abby commended after savoring a bite of meat covered in thick brown gravy. "What spices did you use on it?"

Elias didn't pay much notice to Mattie's answer as he tucked into his plate of food. But he was drawn from his aimless thoughts when she directed a comment toward him.

"I meant to tell you earlier, Elias, but with Josiah and I taking Emma to church in your stead, it slipped my mind."

When she and his brother had first reached town this morning and dropped in on him and Emma, he'd declined to accompany them to the Sunday services. They had made their discontent plain at the time, as they did every week, but hadn't pressed him to reconsider.

Was Mattie now trying to needle his conscience deliberately? Or were his own conflicted feelings causing unwarranted suspicions?

He deemed it wisest to let the last part of her remark pass by without acknowledgment. "What did you forget to mention?" he asked instead.

"I received a letter from Adela."

He raised an eyebrow in silent inquiry and waited for her to go on.

Abby's face brightened with interest. "Did she write of some exciting news?"

Delight and anticipation suffused Mattie's expression as she nodded. "Adela, Aunt Lavinia and Uncle Ephraim are coming to Silver Springs for a visit in a few weeks' time."

Abby smiled wide in response to the announcement. "You must be thrilled to see your family again. It's been two or three months since their last trip here, hasn't it?"

"That's correct." Mattie shifted her gaze from Abby to Elias. "Even though the situation here has changed for you, and Josiah and me, my family will still wish to spend some time with Emma. I hope it's all right with you if they come by here to see her once or twice while they're in town."

"Of course. You can tell them that they're welcome anytime."

In fact, should they wish to stay the night with him instead of taking rooms at Mrs. Wheeler's boarding-house, he'd have no objection. It would save him from lying awake, worrying whether he would hear Emma's cry if he fell asleep for longer than a quarter of an hour.

However, he couldn't quite envision Mattie's well-to-do relations agreeing to the arrangement. Three adults, one young girl and a baby stuffed into a couple of small bedrooms—with at least two people obliged to make a pallet on the hardwood floor—wouldn't be anybody's first choice of lodgings. And most especially not the Prescotts. As it was, the boardinghouse lacked many of the amenities to which they were accustomed.

Mattie paused between bites of food. "Are you ab-solutely certain you want me to tell my sister that she has an open invitation to come and visit? It's a very short walk from the boardinghouse, and Auntie Adela may well be over here at all hours of the day, wanting to cuddle her niece," she warned.

Although "Auntie Adela" wasn't Emma's aunt in ac-tual fact, she'd taken on that role from the time of the baby's birth since her sister had acted as Emma's sur-rogate mother. Adela Prescott had adopted his daugh-ter as a part of her own family, and he didn't intend to stand in the way of that bond. Not when Emma loved spending time with her Auntie Adela.

Besides, with Adela hanging about the place, it should take a bit of pressure off him. A relieving of the tension that seemed to have his insides tied up in knots whenever it was just him and Emma. Which was something he sought to avoid as much as possible.

He nodded his assent as he chewed a chunk of roasted potato.

Josiah looked at him sideways out of narrowed eyes. "You're in an awfully accommodating mood all of a sudden."

Elias opened his mouth and then couldn't think what to say. Speaking the truth would only confirm his brother's worst doubts about him, and he found he didn't want to do that.

He was spared from having to make any response to Josiah, however, when Abby addressed him.

"Elias, perhaps now's a good moment to ask you and Emma to join me on an outdoor excursion. The weather has been so nice lately, warm but not too hot." Her expression was so adorably earnest.

He couldn't resist teasing her a little. "Can't this outing wait until after we finish eating?"

"I didn't mean right this second." She patted her lips with a napkin, the gesture failing to mask the slight blush that had appeared high on her cheeks.

His mouth twitched as he fought to restrain a grin. "I'm glad to hear it, since I don't care to miss out on Mattie's peach pie." He picked up his glass and took a drink. "If you don't mean to deprive me of dessert, then when did you have in mind for your excursion?"

"I was thinking of sometime early next week. Would Tuesday or Wednesday afternoon suit you?"

He didn't have any plans for either day. All in all,

a typical state of events for him. "Whichever one you prefer is fine by me."

"Tuesday, then."

"I'll look forward to it." And, surprisingly, he realized he'd spoken the absolute truth.

Chapter Six

Abby walked toward Elias's home on Tuesday, just slightly past noon, mulling over certain troubling remarks that her mother had expressed over breakfast that morning.

Had the older woman been in earnest? Even if she did intend to do as she'd said, surely it would come to naught. Still, wasn't it better that Abby mentioned it to Elias, either way? Or was she making too much out of nothing?

She hadn't arrived at any firm conclusions by the time she reached her destination.

Elias must've been watching for her, because the front door opened at her approach.

He stood in the doorway with a fussy, squirming baby in his arms.

Abby hitched her canvas bag higher on her shoulder. "I didn't realize you two were so eager to take this trip."

"I've been having some difficulties with Emma today," he admitted. Mussed chestnut hair stuck up from his head in uneven tufts, and his eyes were hazed with exhaustion. "After another bad night, we're both tired and suffering from lack of sleep. She's in a fractious mood, and nothing I do seems to please her."

Abby felt for them both. "Has she had her midday meal yet?"

"In a manner of speaking. I tried to feed her, but she wasn't much interested in the food." He adjusted his hold on Emma as she started to slip. "I think we both could do with a change of scenery now that you're here."

"Why don't I pack a basket of goodies to take with us in case she gets hungry while we're away?"

He moved back in silent assent.

Abby headed toward the rear of the house. "Let's see what you have in the kitchen in the way of foodstuffs to tempt Emma's appetite."

"Mattie made arrangements for a delivery that arrived just yesterday from the mercantile," Elias spoke from behind her. "So there should be a number of things to choose from. And there are some biscuits left over from Sunday dinner."

After setting aside her canvas bag and locating a wicker hamper, Abby began opening cupboards in search of items to fill it. She selected a jar of sliced peaches and a few apples, then added some of the two-day-old biscuits.

Twisting around, she glanced over her shoulder at Elias. "Do you have a quilt we can use to sit on to protect Emma from the dirt and grass?" Although it wasn't something Abby normally bothered with just for herself, she'd prefer that Emma not lie directly on the ground. Among other concerns, she was likely to find a variety of things that she'd try to put in her mouth. Better to forestall that, if possible.

"I'm sure I can find something."

Once Elias had gone from the room, taking the baby with him, Abby shifted her focus back to her task. She filled a container with cool, clear water from the pump and placed it in the basket, along with tin plates, utensils and napkins.

Upon Elias's return, she accepted the colorful patchwork quilt he held out and laid it atop the other items inside the hamper. "Shall we go?"

He indicated for her to proceed. "Lead the way."

She hefted the large hamper, waving him off when he moved to take it from her. "I can carry it." Collecting her canvas bag, she set off in front of him and Emma.

Once out on the street, Elias fell into step beside her. "Where are we heading?"

"Just outside of town. There's a large grassy area with only a few trees."

They walked on in companionable silence for a few minutes, the quiet leaving Abby's mind free to meander. Unfortunately, the path it followed took her straight back to her earlier concerns.

Would Elias want to hear about her mother's threats, said over the Warners' breakfast table? Or would telling him merely add one more worry to those he already carried?

She looked to the Lord for guidance. *What should I do, Lord?* Though there was no immediate answer, she felt a measure of peace for having laid her troubles at His feet.

After passing through residential lanes lined with

houses, they continued on for a bit farther, traveling across open, uncultivated land.

The day was pleasantly warm, with a light breeze sighing through the tall grasses and rustling the leaves in the trees.

Abby came to a halt beneath the sprawling branches of a shady oak tree. "This is it." Setting the basket on the ground, she removed the quilt and spread it over the grass.

Elias glanced around, taking in their surroundings. "It's a nice spot. Quiet and peaceful, but still within sight of town." He deposited Emma on the quilt, then lowered himself to the ground and settled beside her.

Watching him with his daughter decided the matter for Abby. Still, she hesitated to broach the subject, which was sure to darken the mood of their outing.

She sat down next to Elias on a corner of the quilt and curled her legs beneath her. As she arranged her skirts, she used the time to mull over the best way to go about this.

In the end, she simply blurted it out. "Mother has taken issue with the fact that you don't attend church."

His eyebrows shot upward at her stark statement, but on the whole, he seemed quite unconcerned. "I don't see how that's any business of hers."

"She believes it is—she's opposed to a non-church-going man raising *her* grandchild."

"Well, I don't require her approval. It's a good thing, too, since she's made it plain she hasn't cared for any of my actions lately."

It was apparent he didn't yet comprehend what was truly at stake here. For him. And for Emma.

Because of Emmaline Warner's renewed machinations.

After voicing her complaints for several days, the older woman had worked up a good head of steam and planned to take steps beyond mere idle talk.

"She aims to do something about this situation," Abby forewarned him, determined to reveal every horrid detail of her mother's schemes. "My mother intends to remove Emma from your care. Permanently. Her goal is to wrest your daughter away from you by any means so that she can bring up Emma herself."

He was silent for a long moment before he replied. "Perhaps that would be for the best."

"What?!" She gasped at his words, feeling as though the wind had been knocked out of her, and then shook her head in instant denial. "No."

It was the last thing she'd expected from him. But surely, he hadn't meant it. He couldn't.

Please, Lord, don't let him mean it.

Looking into Elias's eyes, she silently begged him to retract the words.

He lowered his gaze, severing the tenuous connection and concealing his thoughts from her. It seemed to be an admission of sorts. A confirming of her worst fears.

That first evening after Mattie and Josiah left the baby with Elias, he'd tried to pass his daughter off to Abby. She'd put his actions down to panic at finding himself confronted with a wagonload of responsibilities he hadn't seen coming.

Now she worried that there was more to his reluctance than she'd realized. Perhaps her assumptions about his feelings toward his daughter had been wrong, too. Would he truly give Emma up? Had he been searching for a way out even then, right from the very beginning?

Abby was troubled by the implications, that his child might mean so little to him. If that was true, then how could she continue to argue that Emma should stay with Elias? She envisioned Emma growing up with the knowledge that her father didn't want her. Perhaps believing he blamed her for her mother's death.

The thought brought equal parts shock and dismay. Abby knew exactly how it felt to try so hard to gain a parent's unconditional affection while never quite succeeding. She didn't want that for her niece. Didn't ever want Emma to feel as though she had to earn her father's love. She definitely didn't want Emma to feel the pain of failing at that task.

Elias's hand curled into a fist on his thigh. "I don't know whether or not Emma should continue to stay with me."

Abby couldn't help but question if his concern was for his daughter's sake—or for himself.

Had he considered Emma's happiness at all in this? Was he thinking of *her* well-being? Had he given any thought to what it would be like for Emma to be raised by Abby's mother? Did he truly believe that would lead to a better, happier life for his daughter? Or was he motivated only by his own interests? What were his reasons? Why was he seemingly conflicted about taking on the rearing of his child?

Abby needed to find out the truth, no matter how

painful. She wasn't letting him get away with avoiding an answer. Not this time.

She had to discover exactly how he felt about his daughter, what emotion filled his heart for Emma. Love or something else. Abby had to hear him say the words one way or the other. Reaffirming her faith in him. Or crushing it completely into ruins.

"Why wouldn't you want her with you?" Abby glanced toward the baby, lying asleep on the quilt. "Don't you love her?" Her gaze shifted back to Elias, her heart sputtering to a halt as she waited for his response.

"Of course I love her." The reply burst out of Elias, instant and emphatic.

It was because he *did* love his daughter that he wanted what was best for her. If he wasn't capable of providing that, then didn't it mean he should—no, that he *must*—give her up, regardless of his personal inclinations on the matter?

Emma had been in his care for almost a week now. Yet he was doing no better than he had done on the very first day. Each new dawn brought with it more struggles, which he felt ill equipped to handle.

Only yesterday, he'd set Emma down on the kitchen rug in order to see to other things. But she hadn't stayed put in one place for long. His daughter had very nearly burned herself on the cast-iron stove because he'd been splitting his attention between her and fixing a meal. And on another occasion, she'd gotten ahold of some lye soap while he was tending to the washing, and he had only just snatched it away from her in the nick of time before it had gone into her mouth.

At other times, she'd screamed when he tried to put her down at all. It seemed she didn't like to be ignored. And if his focus strayed from her for even a moment, she endeavored to reclaim it.

He'd tried to complete household chores while holding or watching Emma, but he'd found that he lacked the knack for doing two tasks at once—and ended up failing miserably at both whenever he attempted it.

If Mrs. Warner was prepared to take Emma into her own home, wouldn't it be in his daughter's best interest for Elias to let her go?

"It's not that I don't want her with me," he attempted to clarify. The thought of handing his daughter over to somebody else to raise sent a shaft of pain arrowing through him. "But what *I* want doesn't matter. If Emma would be better off elsewhere, with someone other than me—"

"How can you think that she would be better off away from you?" Abby laid her hand over his clenched fist. "It's *not* true."

How could he explain all the doubts that hounded him so that Abby might understand? By admitting his failings aloud…she would realize she'd been wrong about him. And he didn't know what he'd do if she lost her belief in him.

But Emma's welfare was more important than his selfish reasons for wanting to hold on to something that had never truly been his in the first place. He wasn't deserving of Abby's support, had done nothing to earn it.

Elias flexed his fingers beneath her palm, and her

hand fell away from his. He missed the warmth of her touch, but he'd have to get by without it.

Drawing his knee up toward his chest, he looped his arm around his bent leg. "I feel as though I'm floundering, completely out of my depth. Half the time— no, most of the time, I have no idea what Emma needs when she cries. And that's not fair to her."

It was a given that he would make more mistakes— and what if they led to serious consequences for Emma? Possibly far-reaching and life-altering ones. What if he did something wrong, allowing her to come to harm in some way through his own ignorance?

He felt physically ill at the thought. His heart pounded, the rapid acceleration of blood through his veins throbbing at his temples. Sweat dampened his forehead as he imagined everything that could go awry. The myriad dangers he might yet face, that waited to ambush him and Emma at some unknown point in the future.

All the while, he'd be worrying that he wouldn't have it in him to right things, come what may. It scared him witless how many potentially disastrous choices he could make. There were an infinite number, in fact. Any choice—or all of them—might turn out to be the wrong one.

Having the responsibility for an innocent child's very life… It most definitely was not an undertaking for the faint of heart.

And what did Elias know about being a proper parent to Emma anyway? He who had grown up feeling the lack of a loving father, and without a mother's comfort for most of his childhood. He wouldn't wish that on anyone—especially not his own daughter.

The last thing he wanted to do was to follow in his father's footsteps. Samuel Dawson had been grim and remote, closing himself off completely from his only child. His household had been devoid of the softness of a woman's influence after he renounced his wife and their marriage vows.

Elias had few memories of his mother, Louisa, the images turning faded and indistinct in the intervening twenty-five years.

If Rebecca were still here, things would be different. Then he wouldn't be on his own, left to muddle through as best he could alone.

To put it bluntly, he didn't know if he was up to this task. Could he be the kind of father Emma needed? He had kept himself detached and distant from her for almost a year. What if he couldn't change that? Couldn't give her the closeness and open affection, the feeling of acceptance and security, that every child craved and deserved? It was the not knowing with any certainty that truly troubled his mind the most.

He wished he'd paid more attention during the numerous visits Mattie had insisted upon instead of stonewalling her each time she'd started to tell him about anything to do with Emma. He regretted that he hadn't been more receptive when Mattie had urged him to hold his daughter or take a hand in her care during those visits—be it feeding her, changing her or soothing her tears when she cried.

It shamed him to admit, but at the time, his sole aim had been to hand Emma back to Mattie as quickly as possible so that he could return to the emotionless existence where he didn't have to feel the pain from his loss and wasn't reminded of the mistakes in his past.

Only now did he realize that his actions over the past eleven months were to his detriment. And Emma's. If he hadn't resisted Mattie's offers of advice and countless attempts to help him, he wouldn't be in such dire straits at the moment. And staring at more of the same ahead.

Accepting that the fault lay with him did nothing to resolve his present predicament, however.

His gaze was drawn inexorably to his daughter. She shouldn't be made to pay for his shortcomings.

He would do whatever it took, go to any lengths necessary, to ensure that never again was she made to suffer because of him. He refused to be the cause of further pain and misery in her life.

She'd been through enough already in the short span of time she'd spent on this earth. Too much for one so young.

No more, he vowed. Particularly not at his hands.

Abby shifted beside him. "You merely need to give yourself time to adjust. You'll see. In a few weeks, things will be different for you and Emma."

How could she hold on to such a strong conviction in his worthiness to parent his child, even after everything he'd told her? "Don't you see, Abby? My daughter deserves so much more than I've been able to provide, more than I can ever possibly hope to offer her."

Abby twisted her fingers around a clump of grass. "Letting my mother take charge of Emma is *not* the solution. Trust me on that."

"It's preferable to the current situation," he contended. To his mind, most anything would be.

"No, it isn't." She yanked the grasses out by their roots and then tossed them aside. "Mother isn't without flaws of her own. She expects everything her own way and has very definite notions about the proper ordering of matters. She's overcritical of anyone who has the audacity to try to go against her plans or who dares to disagree with her opinions."

Abby didn't need to tell *him* that. During the last several months, it had been Elias's misfortune to make close acquaintance with those particular aspects of his former mother-in-law's nature. He often felt that she viewed him much the same as she would a pile of horse droppings left in the middle of the road.

"I do know what your mother is like," he acknowledged.

Abby's eyebrows lowered over her wintry blue gaze. "Then, how can you think to entrust your daughter to her without a single qualm? Do you imagine Emma will be a perfect little darling, never giving Mother a moment of frustration and never incurring her ire?"

To him, Emma *was* a perfect little darling, his precious baby girl—but that wasn't to say she wouldn't ever misbehave.

He recalled Mrs. Warner's reaction to Emma wearing a significant portion of her breakfast a few days ago. If his daughter had acted in that manner while in her grandmother's care, the older woman likely would have punished Emma for behaving as a normal child. And it was this that Abby meant for him to realize.

"Well, I…" He shook his head as he trailed off, his

mind a mass of confusion and doubts. Even more so than it had been just a few minutes ago.

He had to concede that Abby made a valid point.

Until that moment, thoughts of Mrs. Warner's fittingness hadn't occurred to him at all, though he wondered how he could've overlooked such a concern. Now that it had been brought to the forefront of his mind… he was no longer sure of much of anything.

Abby took advantage of his muddled state to press her case. "Can you see my mother tolerating a young child making a mess in her immaculate house?" She didn't wait for a reply before continuing. "And besides that, Mother's involved in community organizations and social activities, which claim a good deal of her time. She won't care to give up those interests in order to stay home with Emma.

"You know as well as anybody how much attention a baby requires. I don't believe Mother's truly prepared to take on the day-to-day care of her grandchild, whatever she might say to the contrary."

His mouth dropped open in disbelief. "Then, why are we even having this conversation?" He ran his hands through his hair, pushing the strands back from his forehead. "What did you hope to achieve by telling me about your mother's intentions if you believe nothing will come of them anyway?"

"Would you rather I hadn't told you?"

"Maybe."

"Well, as it concerned you, I figured you had a right to know. Besides, I can't be entirely certain of anything when it comes to Mother. *I* can see that she wouldn't enjoy spending all her time caring for a baby, but she may not realize as much herself until she's already taken Emma away from you. When she sets her mind on a certain course, she rarely allows anything to divert her. Who's to say what she may or may not decide to do? What if she actually does try to follow through on her threats? She could make things very difficult for you as long as she's got this bee in her bonnet."

He released a weary sigh. "You're correct." On all counts.

It was far preferable that he was forewarned as to what he might be up against rather than being kept in the dark, unaware of any lurking hazards.

There was no doubt in Elias's mind that Emma would be better off with a loving couple, such as his brother and sister-in-law, rather than a shell of a man, empty inside. Josiah and Mattie weren't an option, however. Given the choices he currently faced—would his daughter truly be better off with *anyone* other than him? Or had his lack of faith in his own capabilities almost led him to react unwisely, potentially putting Emma in an even worse situation?

How could he have suggested placing his child entirely under Mrs. Warner's influence without a thought for the likely outcome? It wasn't as though he had no evidence to judge by. He knew all too well what she was like. Yet he hadn't taken that into account.

The last thing he wanted was his former mother-in-law endeavoring to turn his baby girl into a miniature copy of herself. If her daughters could be taken as examples, it would end in either Emma turning willful and determined to have her own way because the older woman had her thinking she could do no wrong, as had been the case with Rebecca. Or Emma would constantly struggle against her grandmother trying to stifle her spirit, as Emmaline Warner seemed bent on doing with her younger daughter whenever Abby didn't act according to her mother's wishes.

But could Elias hope to do any better by his daughter? Or would his mistakes be just as damaging to an impressionable child?

"I don't know what to do, don't know which course is the right one." Only that whatever he decided, it would have to be solely for Emma's sake, not for his own reasons or selfish considerations.

Abby reached out and gave his hand a quick squeeze. "The fact that you care this much about her best interests proves you're the right person to raise your daughter."

He nodded, though in his heart he didn't share her certainty. At least not yet. But perhaps with time?

It remained to be seen, but he felt a tiny spark of hope, like a candle in the night, fighting back the absolute darkness.

Chapter Seven

Abby's gaze rested on Elias, seizing full advantage of an opportunity to study him at leisure without his awareness. He'd leaned back against the tree trunk and closed his eyes several minutes ago, and now he appeared to be sleeping, his measured breathing deep and steady.

The past few days' trials were stamped on his features. Lines grooved his forehead and his eyebrows knitted together above the bridge of his nose, as though his worries had followed him into slumber. Dark circles under his eyes attested to recent nights spent awake with Emma. Fatherhood was wearing him out. She could only hope that he'd be willing to see it through, all the same.

If Abby hadn't entirely convinced him to see things from her point of view, at least she'd gotten him to concede that he should give the situation more thought before he made a decision. She would have to be satisfied with that for now.

In that moment, it was almost as though she could

hear God's voice whispering on the breeze. A fanciful thought, perhaps, but one that brought her peace. It was part of the reason why she sought quiet moments surrounded by nature after a discouraging encounter with her mother. Feeling closer to the Lord never failed to renew her spirits and lift her up.

Her eyes were drawn to Emma, sleeping peacefully in the dappled shade, without a care. As it should be. Reaching out, Abby smoothed down an errant mahogany curl. Emma's stubby dark red eyelashes formed crescents against her rosy cheeks, and her tiny mouth worked.

A tender smile curved Abby's lips at the sight. Then she returned her attention to Elias. Her fingers itched to smooth his hair, as well. To caress the soft chestnut lock that had flopped forward to lie against his forehead and brush the strands away from his face.

When she realized she'd unwittingly began to act on that desire, her arm stretching out toward him, she jerked back as if he'd burned her, though she hadn't been within a foot of making contact. She fisted her hand in her lap, tucking the offending appendage amongst the folds of her navy blue skirt.

Clearly, she needed to find something to keep her hands occupied. Good thing she'd brought along her sketching supplies. Digging in the canvas bag, she extracted her sketchbook and charcoal. She flipped to a fresh page, and within moments, she was lost in her drawing. The smooth strokes of the charcoal pencil served to soothe her while the minutes passed by unnoticed.

Some time later, she was pulled from her focused

absorption when Emma started shifting and making fussy noises. Merely snuffles at first, they quickly escalated from there.

Setting aside her work, Abby reached for her niece. Elias came awake as she picked up the baby and tucked her into a secure embrace.

"What's going on?" he asked, plainly still bleary from the nap.

"Emma might be hungry now," Abby speculated.

Elias moved toward the hamper and opened the lid to peer inside. "What do you think she'll want?"

"Let's see if she'll eat some peaches. They're one of her favorites."

His eyebrows arched in inquiry. "Is that so?" At Abby's nod, he smiled. "I guess she gets that from her papa. Mattie makes peach pies especially for me since she knows how much I like them."

After retrieving the jar of fruit and unscrewing the cap, he held it out toward Abby. Emma cawed in delight at the sight and extended her arms out in front of her, little fingers clenching in hopes of grasping the tantalizing prize that hovered just out of range.

Elias's grin grew wider. "I suppose I should've tried peaches earlier today." His mouth turned down slightly at the corners. "But aren't these slices too big for her to manage?"

"They need to be cut into small chunks before you give them to her," Abby explained.

"Oh." His expression turned sheepish. "I should have realized that on my own, shouldn't I?"

Abby figured he wasn't truly looking for an answer,

so she didn't respond to his question directly. "There's a plate and knife in the basket."

Once he'd completed the task of dicing the fruit into little mouse-sized bites, he handed the tin plate to Abby. She balanced it on her knee, within easy reach for Emma. The baby wasted no time grabbing a tiny piece of peach and stuffing it in her mouth. As she scooped up another bit, twin dimples appeared in her round cheeks and she bounced in Abby's lap.

Elias laughed at her antics. Warmth spread through Abby's heart to hear the sound, which she knew had been all but absent from his life for far too long.

Securing the lid on the glass jar, he put it back in the basket. "I wish I'd known sooner that a few peaches were all it took to make her happy."

"Well, there's no denying she is her father's daughter in that respect."

Though Emma's physical resemblance to Rebecca was marked, Abby could see Elias just as strongly in their child, through her temperament and mannerisms.

Abby's gaze returned to Elias, and she was gratified to see that he seemed pleased by her comment.

He fixed his attention on his daughter, the look in his eyes now containing a kernel of optimism mixed in with the prevailing trepidation. "I intend to do my best by Emma. I want her life to be filled with joy and contentment, above all other things."

The small embers of hope inside Abby flared bright once more. "You and I will make sure of it."

For the first time, Elias appeared as though he might actually believe her. Still, he cleared his throat and shifted under her steady regard, seemingly discomfited to be the object of such pointed focus.

Glancing away from her, he squinted at the sun marking the hours of the afternoon as it tracked across the sky. "How long was I asleep?"

"Almost an hour." At least, as near as she could figure without a watch.

Surprise suffused his face, and he turned back to her. "You should have woken me."

"I didn't mind sitting here while you and Emma rested." Abby used a napkin to wipe a dribble of juice from her niece's chin, then tucked the cotton square around the baby's neck to protect her clothing. "I enjoy spending time out of doors."

And the truth was that when she sketched, she often lost all awareness of the passage of minutes and even hours.

The midday shadows had lengthened without her noticing. She hadn't realized the day was becoming so advanced until he'd drawn her attention to it. Had she been on her own, she might not have surfaced from her sketchbook until sundown, putting her at the risk of her mother's umbrage.

But as it stood now, Abby had a bit of freedom left yet before she needed to head home.

Since there was no place else she had to be and no call to rush, she welcomed the opportunity to simply enjoy the occasion, letting Emma do as she pleased, instead of hurrying things along and worrying over the length of time they remained here.

It was a sticky business allowing the baby to feed

herself, however. Emma ended up covered in peach juice in short order.

Fortunately, Elias didn't seem to mind. "She certainly appears to be enjoying herself," he remarked, a slight smile playing around the edges of his mouth.

"Mattie told me that she and Josiah started taking Emma on outdoor excursions such as this just as soon as spring arrived and the weather warmed up. Apparently, Emma likes going on picnics."

"I find that I do, as well." Sincerity shone in his eyes, making it evident he hadn't merely said the words to be polite. "Thank you for inviting me along on this outing."

"Thank you for agreeing to accompany us," she replied in turn.

Emma bumped the plate, and it slid off Abby's lap before she could catch it. Peach bits tumbled onto the quilt, narrowly missing Abby's sketchbook, which she'd left open to a half-finished rendering of the summer landscape that surrounded them.

Elias moved to clean up the spill. "At least the quilt can be laundered. However, we had best put this somewhere out of harm's way." He indicated her sketchbook. "I would hate to see your efforts spoiled by an accident."

As he took the sketchbook in hand, his gaze settled on the top page, taking in the partially completed scene. His lashes lifted, and his eyes met hers. "May I?"

Abby nodded with some reluctance. She never showed her drawings to anyone. Not since she'd been much younger and her mother had made her opinions about them clear. Afterward, the activity had become a private pleasure, something Abby did for herself that wasn't intended to be seen—or judged—by anyone else.

She reached for the container of water and used it to dampen a corner of the napkin, then cleaned up Emma's sticky fingers and face. Wrapping one arm around the baby, Abby tucked her close and tried to gain comfort from the solid little body snuggled against her.

What would Elias think of her sketches? Would he believe she had a measure of talent? Or would he, like her mother, see nothing more than a useless and frivolous waste of time?

He didn't say anything while he studied the first picture, then flipped back through several of her previous sketches featuring various landscapes in and around the town of Silver Springs.

Her nerves pulled tight as the silence stretched on and on. She wanted to yank the book away from him and slap the cover closed, protecting her shaky self-confidence from the possibility of harsh critiques. The fingers of her free hand gripped her cotton skirt in a bid to keep herself from acting on the craven impulse.

Finally, Elias raised his head. "These are incredible." His eyes were filled with awe and admiration. "I had no idea you possessed such talent."

Her cheeks heated slightly at the unaccustomed praise. A warm glow spread through her that he could find value in something that meant so much to her.

"I've been drawing since I was little," she revealed.

He raked back a lock of hair from his forehead, his expression perplexed. "I can't believe I didn't know this about you. Why is that?" The corner of his mouth tipped up, and teasing lights danced in his eyes. "Is it a family secret?"

"In a way." And there was nothing amusing about it. Not to Abby. "Mother doesn't think it's a worthwhile endeavor. She would rather I didn't dirty my hands by drawing at all, but barring that, the next best thing is to never make mention of it to others."

"Well, your mother is wrong. And not for the first time, I might add."

She couldn't contain a tiny smile at that.

Elias reached for her hand and turned it palm up. She instinctively tried to curl her fingers into a fist to conceal the charcoal smudges from sight, but he stopped her.

"There's no need to hide the marks on your hands from me. If drawing brings you joy, that's reason enough to afford it merit." His thumb rubbed across her palm, then he released her.

She closed her hand over the spot, as though she could physically hold on to the effervescent feelings his touch had elicited.

Hugging Emma against her with her other arm, Abby kissed the baby's downy head, warmed by the belief that Elias would be just as accepting of his daughter's preferred pastimes in the years to come.

It seemed she needn't worry that her niece would grow up as Abby had, the focus of ceaseless parental censure. She prayed Emma would forever be spared that, never even once feeling as though she'd disappointed her family simply by being herself.

Elias had renewed Abby's optimism on that score.

And she thanked the Lord for it.

* * *

The following Sunday found Elias mere paces from the church steps, in the company of his brother and sister-in-law, and with Emma in his arms.

Ever since he'd spent the afternoon with Abby on Tuesday, he had acknowledged that he wasn't prepared to hand his daughter over to someone else to raise unless he'd first determined that it would be the best arrangement for her—and not merely what was easiest for him. Whatever he decided, it had to be for Emma's sake. His daughter's needs came first.

Perhaps that meant staying with him. Perhaps not. But he wasn't going to let someone else make that decision for him.

In the meantime, he'd set about searching for a way to circumvent his former mother-in-law's schemes until he reached a firm conclusion in his own mind.

If Mrs. Warner had an issue with Elias's prolonged absence from church? Well, that was a problem that could be fixed readily enough. After all, there was no sense in making things more difficult for himself than need be.

However, he no longer felt quite so nonchalant about appearing for Preacher Linton's sermon, now that the moment had arrived.

A knot of tension had formed across his shoulders as he approached the small church. Several clusters of people were scattered around outside, chatting with friends and acquaintances. Elias counted as neither.

When he scanned the churchyard looking for a welcoming face, he found none. Most everybody in town was a stranger to him. But they knew plenty about him, he was sure. He could well imagine the kinds of tales Mrs. Warner had spread after his actions supposedly threatened her social standing in the community.

To hear her tell it, his behavior reflected poorly on her due to their former familial connection. However, he suspected she'd made much of her son-in-law "the doctor" prior to his arrival in Oregon Country and was subsequently embarrassed when Elias had fallen far short of the paragon she'd described.

He found he couldn't drudge up even a smidgen of sympathy for her. Not when her wagging tongue had likely contributed to his current predicament, as well.

He felt as though everybody present was staring at him. It didn't help that he no longer had a thick, overgrown beard to hide behind. When he'd made the decision to attend services today, it had seemed like a good idea to try to make himself appear more respectable—which was how he'd come to be standing here, dressed in his nicest coat and trousers with his face clean-shaven. A choice he now regretted.

Shifting Emma to a more comfortable position against his chest, he did his best to school his expression and give away nothing of his thoughts. Still, he wondered if the others could see that his heart wasn't in this. Though he'd been compelled to come, his mind remained closed to the Lord.

Josiah clapped him on the back, breaking into his dark musings. "It's good to have you back."

If his brother believed this event signified more than Elias's physical return to church, then he was sadly mistaken. Despite outward appearances to the contrary, Elias was no different today than he'd been the day before. Not deep down inside where it mattered. He remained a hollow shell of the man he used to be. There was no going back for him. Never again could he be the person he'd been prior to Rebecca's death. That man was gone forever.

But he left Josiah with his illusions, staying silent on the fact that even though he was here in body, he remained absent in spirit.

"Elias!" Abby's voice called out behind him, her tone bright and cheerful.

He pivoted on his heels and spotted her walking up the path from town. Leaving her parents in her dust, she hurried toward Elias, her face lit with happiness.

It took him by surprise when she enfolded him and Emma both in a hug, her arms curving around his back. He stood frozen, at a loss as to how he should respond. He need not have worried, however, since Abby apparently didn't expect anything from him in return. Her spontaneous gesture was over almost as soon as it had begun.

Oddly, Elias felt a pang of something almost like disappointment that the embrace hadn't lasted a tad longer.

He brushed off the peculiar sensation. It had likely been nothing more than a subconscious reaction to the first hint of welcome he'd encountered after facing down a sea of aloofness from the rest of the congregation.

Abby linked her hands together in front of her, a wide smile and the hint of pink in her cheeks transforming her features from rather ordinary to radiantly lovely. "I'm so glad you decided to join us." She turned and greeted Mattie and Josiah, then asked, "Why don't we share a pew today?"

Her mother reached them, huffing a bit from her exertion after rushing to catch up with Abby.

The older woman didn't hesitate to insert herself into the discussion. "We must try to find a seat beside the Freedmonts, Abigail, so that you might share a hymnal with Augustus."

Good ol' Gus, the banker's son, Elias silently mused. Though he'd not yet had the dubious pleasure of meeting the young man, Elias had already heard somewhat more than he cared to about the junior Mr. Freedmont from Abby's mother.

It hadn't escaped his notice that Mrs. Warner never missed an opportunity to drop the esteemed family's name into any conversation. And her endless maneuvering to arrange a match between her daughter and the heir apparent was by no means subtle.

It was just as plain that Abby didn't appreciate her mother's constant meddling. She chewed the corner of her lip in consternation but didn't openly contradict Emmaline Warner. Doubtlessly, she had learned long ago the futility of voicing protests.

Elias caught the commiserating look Mattie sent Abby behind the older woman's back.

"The others have started to head inside," Josiah commented. "We should do the same."

"Come along now, Abigail," Mrs. Warner urged, drawing her daughter away from the Dawsons.

Thomas Warner trailed behind his womenfolk, in silence as usual. He was a slender man of medium height, with shoulders slightly stooped from more than three decades spent hunched over a counter while figuring customers' accounts. Somewhere near his fiftieth year, he had thinning hair the same light brown shade as Abby's.

Elias had no issue with his former father-in-law, apart from the fact that most of the time the older man seemed to lack the slightest inclination to rein in his managing wife.

After making their way into the church, Elias's family ended up seated in the row behind Abby and her parents. Mrs. Warner had been foiled in her aim to sit beside the Freedmonts, who'd taken a place on the opposite side of the center aisle.

A state of events that pleased Elias rather more than it should have.

He found that the thought of Abby and Augustus together was not to his liking but assured himself such sentiment didn't stem from any feelings of a romantic nature toward her on his part. He looked on Abby as he would a sibling and as a friend. Like Josiah, only prettier.

And it was for this reason that he wanted to see her happy. He didn't believe she would be with Augustus Freedmont. Ol' Gus wasn't the right man for her.

Although he came from a prominent family and stood to inherit a profitable bank one day, it didn't automatically follow that Augustus was good enough for Abby.

She deserved a husband who would appreciate her and support her. One who would never think to stand in the way of anything that gave her joy. Could she expect that from the banker's son? It seemed unlikely.

It had been Elias's experience that money and power that was conferred by an accident of birth, rather than earned through one's own endeavors, more often than not seemed to have a corrupting influence on a man's character. He'd met many an arrogant cad who considered their wants of greater import than all others and who often acted without a single thought for those crushed beneath their ruthless will.

Elias would hate for Abby to be tied for life to such a man. It would surely break her spirit, as the many years battling Emmaline Warner had failed to do.

Hopefully, her marriage would not be the trial that living with her forceful mother was for Abby.

And while it was true he didn't know Augustus Freedmont well enough—or at all—to judge him, from what Elias *had* learned of the other man, he couldn't envision Augustus approving of the things that brought Abby joy, such as picnicking outdoors with her niece and sketching.

Elias doubted the banker's son would view independence and determination as desirable qualities in a spouse. Instead, he'd want a meek woman who enhanced his image within the community and never opposed him.

It was Augustus, in particular, who Elias took issue with Abby being paired with. Never mind that he didn't care for the thought of her married to any of the other local men, either.

He shifted restlessly on the hard wooden pew. The church felt hot and stifling with several dozen bodies packed into the small space and the late July temperature rising outside. No drifts of air moved through the building, even though the door and windows were thrown open wide to catch any hint of a breeze.

Elias stuck a finger beneath the stiff, starched collar of his shirt, feeling overly warm, as well as ill at ease.

A few minutes later, David Linton took his place at the pulpit. "Let us begin with a prayer."

Heads bowed all around Elias, but he didn't follow suit.

Seeing the preacher for the first time since their arrival in the Willamette Valley dragged Elias back to that terrible day on the trail during their overland journey when all his supposed knowledge and doctoring skills hadn't been enough to thwart death and save his wife. When his appeals to the Lord had fallen on deaf ears.

Elias remembered little about the funeral service held on the side of the trail, but he would never forget the sight of a lone wooden cross on a hill in the middle of nowhere, left behind on the vast empty prairie as their wagon train had moved on. Nor could he forget the feelings of guilt that had consumed him afterward. And continued to torment him even now.

What purpose had Rebecca's death served? What purpose *could* it serve to take a young woman from her husband and newborn child? Elias didn't have the answers, which set him adrift in angry confusion and helplessness. It was a state he despised, but he couldn't seem to escape it.

Finally, he admitted to himself that he wasn't only angry with himself for his failure and angry with God for ignoring his desperate pleas to spare Rebecca. Though it shamed Elias to acknowledge it, some of his anger was directed toward his dead wife.

He was angry with Rebecca for leaving him alone with their child, and so much more, besides.

She'd kept her pregnancy a secret from him before they left Tennessee, knowing that if he'd been aware of her condition he would've insisted on postponing their journey until the next year, at least. She hadn't let anything—including her husband's desire to keep her safe—stand in the way of her own wishes.

He had understood that she'd missed her family dreadfully and wanted to be near them again. However, he couldn't forgive her disregard of him. Not when her lack of honesty had cost her life. He had no doubt that the rigors of the trail had led to their daughter's early arrival and the tragic events that followed.

If they had not made the journey, perhaps Rebecca would still be alive. He blamed himself and his failure for what had happened. But he blamed her, as well.

Sweat dampened the back of his shirt as he let the preacher's voice wash over him. His mind had roamed in a deliberate effort not to focus on the words or pay attention to their meaning, but he didn't like the direction his thoughts had taken as a result. The time until the sermon ended couldn't pass soon enough for him.

After Preacher Linton concluded the service, Abby rose with the rest of the congregation to make her way outside. Though separated from the Dawsons by several other parishioners, she was nonetheless close enough to overhear the words Elias and his family exchanged with the preacher as they exited the church.

"It was a lovely sermon as always, Preacher Linton," Mattie complimented.

"Thank you, Mrs. Dawson," he said, and then addressed Elias. "It's good to see you again. We've missed you at Sunday services these past months. Can we look forward to you joining us again next week?"

"I'll be here," Elias replied.

Abby was gratified to hear that, since after their conversation during the outing on Tuesday Elias hadn't committed himself to any specific course of action. She'd hoped that he would come to church today but hadn't wanted to expect too much and end up disappointed. Learning that he planned to attend weekly Sunday worships once more seemed an answer to her most fervent prayers. Proof of the Lord working in Elias's life.

But did Elias's actions signify a true healing had begun in his heart at long last? It could be that, since learning of Emmaline Warner's plans, he merely felt a sense of duty and responsibility toward his daughter but was still weighing all his options before deciding on a course to take.

Please, Lord, let it be his love for Emma guiding him, and not something else.

Though there was no immediate response, Abby gained courage and solace from putting her hopes into words and knowing the rest was in God's hands. She refused to allow grim doubts so much as a toehold from which to blot out the bright rays of optimism she'd felt a short time earlier, upon her arrival at church.

Elias was here now. That showed significant progress from a week ago. A fact not to be taken lightly, no matter his motivation.

When she had first spotted the handsome chestnut-haired man standing with Josiah and Mattie in the churchyard before the service started, she'd barely recognized Elias without the thick growth of red-hued whiskers. It had been over three years since Abby had seen him clean-shaven. She was surprised to discover that her memories of his square jaw and strong cheekbones had fallen far short of his true appearance. Though it didn't seem possible, he was even more good-looking than she'd remembered from her countless girlish fantasies.

In those long-ago days, she hadn't known the kind of man he was deep down in his heart. Her supposed tender, romantic feelings toward him had owed more to an idealized image in her own mind than Elias's true character. Now that she'd gotten glimpses inside him— to the imperfect man who was hurting yet still sought to provide what his daughter needed—her esteem for him had become anchored in a foundation much more substantial than mere illusion.

She admired his core of strength and courage in facing up to the things that were difficult. Her heart contracted at seeing him step out of his self-imposed isolation in consideration for his child.

But no matter how he affected her emotions, she couldn't allow herself to return to her old, foolish habit of weaving ridiculous fairy tales about her and Elias living happily-ever-after together.

Even though Rebecca was gone, she still stood between Abby and Elias, her shadow continuing to hover over their lives. Abby had no more chance of gaining a significant place in his heart than she ever had all those years ago when she'd been fifteen.

Chapter Eight

❧

Two days later, Abby raised her fist to knock on Elias's front door, balancing a peach cobbler in her other hand.

When he opened the door a few moments afterward and greeted her, she was once again struck by how handsome he looked with his strong jaw visible. Although he'd shaved his beard, he hadn't trimmed his hair, and she noted the chestnut strands brushed the collar of his cotton shirt. The overlong locks did nothing to detract from his appeal.

Abby imagined she wasn't the only one who had been caught off guard by his attractive countenance. In particular, he'd seemed to draw the notice of the females in attendance at church the day before yesterday. Abby feared that every unmarried lady in and around Silver Springs would view Elias's altered appearance as a sign that his mourning had come to an end. They'd likely believe he might be on the lookout for another wife to act as a mother to Emma. How many women would set their sights on filling the role?

She very much doubted that he'd begun to contemplate sharing his life with any woman who wasn't Rebecca. But that wouldn't always hold true. Some day in the future, surely, he *would* be ready to open his heart again.

It pained Abby to picture him married to somebody else. She was ashamed to admit that the feeling had nothing to do with thoughts of her sister. Rather, it was for selfish reasons that Abby didn't want to see Elias with anyone other than herself. Even though it would be foolish of her to wish for a life with him beyond the companionable bond they shared through Emma. Abby recognized that hoping for anything more would only lead to heartache for her.

All her life she'd felt second best to Rebecca in her mother's eyes. She refused to feel that same emotion in her marriage. And how could she hope for anything else in a situation where comparisons with her sister, Elias's first wife, would be inevitable? In any contest between her and Rebecca, Abby would forever come up short. Past experience had taught her that.

Preferring not to go down that path again, she halted her dark musings before they could gain any more ground inside her head and focused back on Elias instead.

He stood in the doorway, his gaze riveted to the dessert she carried in her hands. "What do you have there?" Leaning forward, he inhaled the fragrant steam wafting up from the tin, which was just minutes out of the oven. "Do I detect the scent of peaches coming from this mouthwatering cobbler?" A hopeful look lit his dark brown eyes.

"Indeed you do. I figured you deserved this after braving the masses on Sunday morning."

He grimaced in response. "I felt as though I was a hapless ant caught beneath a magnifying glass as the sun's merciless rays scorched through the lens." Then his mouth stretched wide in a grin. "Peach cobbler sure goes a long way toward making up for that, though. Thank you, Abby." He bent down and placed a quick kiss on her cheek, then took the tin from her suddenly nerveless fingers.

Her heart fluttered like a silly moth in danger of flying too close to a flame, and she tamped down the reaction.

Logically, she knew better than to read anything into a simple gesture of appreciation. It was the kind of peck a man might give his maiden aunt—or his wife's sister. She hammered home that point ruthlessly lest she forget.

The kiss had been utterly lacking in romantic sentiment. It meant nothing more.

And it was best that she never think otherwise.

Elias caught another whiff of air scented with peaches and brown sugar. In that brief moment when he'd pressed his lips to Abby's soft cheek, he had noticed that the delicious aroma seemed to imbue her skin. It had caused a visceral reaction, tugging on something warm and tender deep inside him.

But that was just a momentary flight of whimsy brought on by his clamoring taste buds, he rationalized.

Of course Abby would smell like peach cobbler after spending time baking one. There was no great mystery in that. It had no bearing on any profound emotions beneath the surface. Even a peach-filled treat wasn't enough to get past the scar tissue surrounding his heart. So, there was no logical reason not to sample Abby's offering as soon as possible.

He didn't allow an opportunity to second-guess himself. "I'm going to try a bite. Would you care to join me?"

At her nod, he stepped aside to let her enter, then he closed the front door and led the way down the hall.

"Where's Emma?" Abby questioned at his back.

"Upstairs, taking a nap," he replied, as he walked into the kitchen. "I expect she'll be awake before too long, but we should have enough time to enjoy a heaping helping of cobbler first."

She arched an eyebrow at him. "What happened to having 'a bite'?"

He waved that aside. "Merely a figure of speech. I wouldn't want you to think I didn't appreciate your efforts."

Soft pink color bloomed on her cheeks, indicating his remark had brought her pleasure. Which pleased him, in turn.

He set the tin on the table and moved to collect two plates, a pair of forks and a large wooden serving spoon. Once he'd placed the items beside the peach cobbler, he pulled out one of the chairs and gestured toward it. "Please, have a seat." As soon as she was settled, he stepped back away from her. "I made a fresh pot of coffee shortly before you arrived. Would you like a cup?"

"That would be lovely. Thank you."

While he occupied himself pouring coffee into two

mugs, Abby dished out the cobbler. She filled one plate with a generous serving, which he guessed was for him, and then deposited a much smaller portion on the second plate for herself.

Placing a mug in front of her, he carried his coffee to the end of the table and sat down in front of the larger helping of cobbler that she'd set aside for him.

He picked up his fork and speared a chunk of spiced peach topped with a sweetened crust. The bite hadn't yet made it to his mouth, however, when there was a knock on the front door.

Abby paused with her coffee mug halfway to her lips. "I wonder who that could be."

"I haven't the slightest idea." He didn't get many callers nowadays, apart from Abby and his family, who would be miles away at their ranch right now.

Then again, he *had* just recently ventured out for the first time in months. One of the townsfolk at church, or more likely the preacher and his wife, might've taken that to mean Elias would welcome visitors.

He lowered his fork to his plate and started to push back his chair. Catching the sound of the front door opening, he paused.

The corners of Abby's mouth turned down slightly and her eyes narrowed. "Who would be so ill-mannered as to enter your home without waiting to be admitted?" she demanded, plainly affronted on his behalf.

Elias could think of only one person in town with enough nerve to walk in uninvited, believing she had the right.

He didn't bother to get up to greet her. Settling back

into his chair, he listened to the footsteps crossing the foyer.

Abby made a move to rise, doubtlessly intending to see who was in the front hall, but he stayed her with a hand on her arm. She looked at him, a question in her eyes.

Before he could answer, he heard a stair creak as his unwanted guest headed up to the second floor. "If you're looking for me, I'm in the kitchen," he called out to the woman intruding upon his peace.

There was a moment of silence, then the clatter of shoes against the wooden treads, backtracking to the bottom of the staircase before heading down the hallway toward him. The footfalls grew louder as she neared the kitchen.

His former mother-in-law appeared in the doorway, her face pinched up in an expression of irritation. Her eyes widened when she sighted Abby sitting at the table with him. "I didn't expect to find you here, Abigail."

Abby seemed likewise taken aback by her mother's unanticipated presence, but she recovered quickly. "Business at the mercantile was slow this afternoon, so Papa sent me home early. When I stopped in here and inquired about Emma, Elias told me she's napping. He invited me to have a piece of cobbler while waiting for her to wake up."

Elias noticed Abby had failed to mention the fact that she'd made the peach cobbler for him or that she must have left the mercantile a while ago in order to have time to bake it.

Clearly, she didn't want her mother to know the true details.

Which was fine by him.

Mrs. Warner had doubtlessly come with a purpose, and he didn't care to prolong her stay any more than necessary.

Though he deemed it unlikely that she would take him up on an invitation to join him and Abby at the table, he wasn't willing to risk it. Instead, he stood to face her. "To what do I owe this visit?" he asked.

"I've just come from a meeting of the Silver Springs Ladies' Benevolence Society. Lydia Freedmont has asked me to inform you of a recent development."

"By all means." He waved for her to continue.

"We've just received word that another doctor is on his way, coming from back East, along the wagon trail. He's agreed to take over the position here in Silver Springs, seeing to duties that have been sadly neglected for so long. Once Dr. Hiram Michner arrives in late September or early October, he'll have the use of this clinic and residence. Therefore, it's been decided that you can remain here for another month or two only, then you must vacate the premises."

"You're evicting Elias?" Abby gasped.

"I'm merely relaying the decision that was reached through a democratic vote," Mrs. Warner retorted. "Besides, he has no claim on the property. It was only Christian charity that allowed him to stay here in the first place once it became clear he hadn't any intentions of living up to his obligations to see to patients in the community. Since this town's still in need of a doctor, and Dr. Hiram Michner has accepted the job, this building belongs by rights to him now."

Elias had known for some time that if he wasn't able

to fulfill his responsibility to the townspeople, they would seek out someone who could. The town's generosity had its limits, and he'd reached them. It came as no surprise that he'd been supplanted. However, it did present some problems for him.

"Where does the *Benevolence* Society expect Elias and Emma to go after being forced from their home?" Abby's tone made it plain she felt the group's actions were contrary to its name.

"Where we go isn't their concern," Elias responded.

That didn't stop Mrs. Warner from voicing her opinion on the matter. "Elias will have to find other accommodations." She turned to address him directly. "Perhaps a room in Mrs. Wheeler's boardinghouse. However, I don't believe a public rooming establishment is a proper place to bring up a child. It would be better for Emma to stay with me and Mr. Warner at our house once you leave here."

Elias's mind instantly rejected the idea. Though he'd been willing to consider it not too long ago, he had since then experienced some grave doubts about agreeing to such an arrangement.

Abby had warned him of her mother's determination to wrest Emma from his care. Apparently, his attendance at church hadn't been sufficient to put a stop to the older woman's plans.

He wondered how much his former mother-in-law had to do with the current situation regarding his imminent eviction. Had she actively worked to see him pushed out in favor of another doctor, manipulating the circumstances toward her own ends? Or had she simply taken advantage of an opportunity when it had presented itself and used it for her own purpose?

Either way, he couldn't let her achieve her aims. Not without a fight.

"I wouldn't want to impose on your good nature." Especially seeing as she seemed to be somewhat deficient in that regard, most particularly when it came to him.

"It's no imposition," she assured.

He opened his mouth to decline in no uncertain terms, but Abby spoke first.

"I'm sure Elias would prefer an arrangement that doesn't require him to be parted from his daughter."

Catching Abby's eye, Elias silently communicated his gratitude for her steadfast support.

She sent him a small smile in return and then continued, "There's plenty of time to make plans before the new doctor's arrival. Prudence dictates that this decision shouldn't be rushed."

Mrs. Warner appeared vexed by her daughter's subtle opposition, but she could hardly argue against the wisdom of Abby's words.

"Lydia Freedmont has asked me to join her for afternoon tea after I've finished here, so I must be off now." With a curt nod to him, his former mother-in-law pivoted on her heel and headed down the hallway toward the front of the house.

Though she'd dropped the matter for the time being, Elias didn't fool himself that she had given up her campaign to gain custody of Emma. He was certain this wasn't over yet, not by any means. But that was a battle for another day.

"Doubtlessly, Mrs. Freedmont wants a full report on your reaction and whether or not the Ladies' Benevolence Society should expect any trouble from you," Abby remarked, once the front door had clicked shut behind her mother. "What *are* you going to do, Elias?"

"I'm not looking to cause further problems for the town. Nor do I intend to hand my daughter over to your mother without any protest. Beyond that, I don't know," he admitted. "But like you said, I have time yet."

If nothing else, he knew Josiah and Mattie would welcome him and Emma in their home at the ranch, despite the tight quarters inside the log cabin once their own baby arrived. Knowing he and his daughter wouldn't be homeless, he couldn't see much point in worrying a great deal beyond that.

But if he and Emma were living five miles from town, then Abby would no longer be able to visit them whenever she pleased. That definitely gave him serious pause.

Abby chewed the corner of her bottom lip, her brow creased with concern as though her thoughts had run along the same lines as his. She didn't comment further, however.

The encounter with his former mother-in-law was enough to give most men indigestion, but it would take more than that for Elias to willingly forgo the treat Abby had made especially for him.

Returning to his seat at the table, he picked up his fork and finally took a bite. The taste of cinnamon-spiced peaches and sweetened dough filled his mouth. He hummed in pure enjoyment as he savored the delectable flavors.

Abby's face lit up with pleasure at his obvious appreciation for her baking efforts. "I'm glad you like it."

"This is better than Mattie's peach pie," he stated without thought. Then his brain caught up with his mouth, and he felt a twinge over his disloyalty toward Josiah's wife. "But please don't tell her I said that. I don't want her to feel slighted. And I'd surely not like it if she stopped bringing pies for me."

"Your secrets are safe with me."

He wondered if that was strictly true. Oh, not about her telling Mattie that he preferred this cobbler over her peach pie. He trusted Abby to keep that confidence. Rather, he questioned whether he could be as open with her in other respects. About *everything* inside of him.

Over the past two weeks, he had come to feel as though he could talk to Abby about certain private aspects of himself without fear that she would judge him harshly. But he hadn't revealed all the darkness deep within him.

She didn't know what lurked in the depths of his damaged heart. He'd not allowed her to see that part of him. Not fully. If Abby ever caught more than brief glimpses… He doubted she'd be as sweetly sympathetic if she saw the true condition of his heart, knew about every last bit of ugliness he'd locked away out of sight. Would she turn away from him then?

He'd grown used to Abby backing him, even against himself. He didn't think he could face losing that.

Because it would surely mean losing Emma, too.

Should Abby suddenly decide that he wasn't the person to care for his daughter, then all the fight would go out of him. Her faith in him was what had sustained him thus far, what he knew would continue to sustain him whenever his doubts crowded in on him. Without it, he feared a return to his former state—the one he'd inhabited for the better part of a year following Rebecca's death.

And thus, rendering him unfit to be in his daughter's life any longer.

God help him if he ever came to that end.

Chapter Nine

The Prescotts arrived in Silver Springs midway through the following week. Elias had chanced to spot them through his sitting room window as their carriage rolled past on the way to Mrs. Wheeler's boardinghouse just after noon. A short time later, Adela, Mattie's younger sister, appeared on his doorstep for a visit with Emma while her aunt and uncle got settled in their rooms and rested up from their long journey.

Adela greeted her honorary niece with enthusiasm, showering the baby with hugs and kisses, much to Emma's delight. Elias felt like a third wheel, decidedly extraneous to their happy reunion.

A feeling that didn't abate any as the afternoon passed.

Adela took sole charge of Emma, feeding and changing her, and then spent more than an hour playing games with the baby and telling her stories. Elias might as well have not been there, for all the notice either of the two females paid him.

He'd imagined that he would welcome a respite after

the past three weeks when he had tended to his daughter's needs with a minimum of assistance from others. But curiously he found that he didn't. Left at loose ends, he wasn't quite sure what to do with himself.

It was a bit of a shock to realize just how accustomed he'd become to his altered circumstances in such a brief span of time. He and Emma were dealing somewhat better with each other than they had at the start—doubtlessly helped along by copious amounts of peaches.

Though Elias still harbored a fair share of doubts concerning his capabilities as a father, he was certain on one essential point, at least. He didn't want to go back to the way things had been, with his daughter on the periphery of his life.

Emma had brought color and vitality to an existence that had been sadly grim before. Caring for her gave his days purpose, a reason to focus outside himself and his own tumult. Something that had been sorely lacking since he'd quit doctoring.

A knock on the front door pulled Elias from his musing. After descending the staircase, he opened the door and found Abby waiting on the other side.

She wore a simple cotton dress the exact blue-gray shade of her eyes. Her light brown hair was pulled back in its customary fashion at her nape, but several curling tendrils had escaped their restraints and framed her face.

Elias moved back in silent invitation for her to enter.

She stepped over the threshold, her ever-present canvas bag of sketching supplies in hand. "It's a fine afternoon for an outdoor excursion. I wondered if you and Emma might care to come with me again."

"I wish we could, but Adela's here right now, visiting with Emma upstairs in the sitting room, and it doesn't look as though she plans to shift any time soon."

"Oh, I wasn't aware that the Prescotts had arrived in town. Well, perhaps another day then." Despite her nonchalant tone, disappointment showed plainly on her features.

"Why don't you join us instead?" Elias suggested, sweeping an arm out and gesturing toward the stairs.

Her expression brightened, and she acquiesced at once. He followed behind her as she started up the staircase.

After she reached the second floor and greeted Adela and Emma, she settled next to the pair on the settee. Abby was a few years older than Mattie's sister and had had only a handful of opportunities to spend time in her company, but both young women loved Elias's daughter. Emma acted as a link between the two, bringing them together whenever Adela came to town for a visit.

Elias resumed his previous position, seated in an armchair, with one boot-clad foot crossed over the opposite knee and a hand resting on his bent leg.

Meanwhile, Adela launched into a lengthy explanation about how she'd been kept apprised of the goings-on in Silver Springs through letters from Mattie and had known just where to find Emma when the Prescotts arrived in town.

He paid scant heed to her words as she chattered on, since he'd already heard the entire story once before.

Instead, his eyes were drawn to Abby. He took the opportunity to look his fill while her attention was focused squarely on the younger girl. Abby's coloring might not be as striking as her sister's had been, but her loveliness was no less appealing for its subtlety.

He took care not to fall into the trap of judging the two siblings based on comparisons to one another, as their mother had done for years. That wasn't fair to either Abby or Rebecca. Each woman was her own person, unique and special in her own right.

Watching Abby's lips move, he realized he'd missed whatever she had said. He directed his mind back to the conversation at hand in time to hear Adela's reply.

"I think Mattie will be pleased to learn that Uncle Ephraim's considering building a hotel here in Silver Springs," she remarked, as she deftly shifted Emma in her arms and began to rock her when the baby made a fussing sound. "Of course, it won't be anything near as grand as The Prescott Hotel in Oregon City, but it will provide us a more comfortable place for an extended stay than the boardinghouse affords. Aunt Lavinia and I want to be nearby to help Mattie when the baby comes in December and for several weeks afterward, as well."

Though she didn't glance at Elias, he wondered if she harbored any ill will toward him that he had given up doctoring and would not be aiding Mattie through her labor. He offered the only reassurance he could. "I've been informed that a Dr. Hiram Michner will arrive well before winter. He'll be on hand to oversee the birth."

Adela greeted the news with visible relief. "I'm certain that will ease Mattie's mind as her time grows near. Neither my aunt nor I have any experience as midwives."

Guilt assailed Elias that he wouldn't be there for his brother's wife—or for the niece or nephew soon to enter the world. That he couldn't be what his family needed. Yet again.

Circumstances may have changed, but he hadn't. Not truly. Despite his earlier thoughts.

He was still broken. And he feared he would always remain so.

Worry for Elias filled Abby's heart at the small glimpse he'd revealed of his present state of mind, but she didn't despair. She was hopeful of the progress he'd made thus far—no matter the distance yet to overcome before he was healed and whole once again. And until then, she would continue to seek the Lord's guidance.

Right now, however, it seemed that a shift in the current conversation was called for, and she steered them toward happier things. "You must be excited for the arrival of your sister and Josiah's baby, Adela. A niece or nephew for you, and a playmate for Emma."

"I can hardly wait to meet the new little one. I've already finished stitching two infant gowns as a special gift for Mattie and Josiah in anticipation of the blessed event. I've brought them with me from home. They're packed in one of my trunks over at the boardinghouse. I don't remember where exactly or in which one, so it will take some time for me to locate the garments. But once I do, I'd be pleased to show them to you."

"I would enjoy seeing them. I've often admired

the embroidery you stitched on a number of Emma's clothes." Abby fiddled with a loose thread trailing from the gathered waist of her dress. "I'd like to present Mattie and Josiah with a handmade gift for the baby, as well, but I don't have much skill with a needle."

All Abby's clothing had come ready-made from her father's mercantile, with the exception of her two nicest gowns, which had been procured from the dressmaker's shop on Main Street.

"You have other talents," Elias interposed. "Why don't you frame one of your sketches to give to them? I'm sure they'd appreciate a picture they could hang next to the baby's bassinet."

Though Abby wasn't entirely convinced on that point, she didn't argue against it. "Maybe. But I was thinking more along the lines of something that would be of practical use for the baby rather than merely ornamentation."

"What sort of things do you sketch?" Adela questioned, her hazel eyes bright with interest.

"Nothing very exciting," she hedged, attempting to downplay it. "I prefer to draw landscape scenes for the most part. Besides those, I've tried my hand at depicting some of the buildings around town."

"I'd love to see them." Adela shifted on the settee, her dark reddish-brown curls catching the light as she moved.

The younger girl's hair was tied back with a length of the same green satin ribbon that edged her elegant cream gown. Although not terribly practical for tending to a baby, Adela's attire provided a lovely foil for her gleaming tresses.

With her beauty and graceful demeanor, Adela was

the embodiment of everything Emmaline Warner most desired in her daughter. The older woman was forever doomed to disappointment on that score, however.

Feeling quite inadequate in comparison to Mattie's sister, Abby hesitated to expose herself and her drawings to possible judgment from the younger girl.

As she dithered in indecision, she noticed Elias's gaze focused on her.

He eyed her speculatively for several long seconds before turning to address Adela. "I reckon Abby has her sketchbook tucked away in there." He indicated the canvas bag she'd set on the floor at her side.

Adela leaned forward in apparent anticipation.

Despite unabating reluctance, Abby found she didn't have it in her to refuse in the face of Adela's eager expression.

Retrieving her sketchbook, she passed it to the younger girl.

Emma displayed a keen curiosity in the proceeding and tried to grab at the pages, but Adela kept them out of her reach.

Fearful that the baby might yet tear the drawings, Abby lifted her niece from Adela's hold. Once Emma was safely settled on Abby's lap, she returned her attention to the younger girl.

A fair bit of trepidation filled Abby as her work was scrutinized for the second time in the space of two weeks.

Adela twirled a lock of hair between her fingers while she perused several sketches. "You've captured a good likeness of the countryside and various town facades, even without the use of color. It would be incredible to see some of these scenes in their true hues."

Abby expected the other girl to hand the sketchbook back after that, but Adela evidently wasn't finished with it yet.

"Any one of your drawings could serve as a pattern to embroider on fabric," Adela mused. "And imagine how thrilled Mattie and Josiah would be to receive something such as a baby quilt with pictures of their ranch stitched on it." Her eyes gleamed at the prospect.

It *was* a wonderful idea, in the abstract. Putting it into practice was another matter entirely.

"It's a shame I'm so useless at needlework, but the Good Lord didn't see fit to bless me in that respect," Abby sighed.

Adela dismissed the comment with a wave of her hand. "That need not be a problem."

"But how—?" Abby shook her head in bewilderment.

A broad smile lit Adela's face. "I have just the solution. If you sketch directly onto squares of pale cotton cloth, it would be a simple matter for me to go over the lines with colored threads. That's assuming you don't mind me taking a part in this, of course." She didn't give Abby a chance to reply one way or the other before continuing, "You could choose three or four vistas to draw. Once complete, the picture blocks could be interspersed with other squares of coordinating fabrics and sewn together to form the quilt."

Even though Abby was envisioning it already, she mustn't get ahead of herself. What Adela had described hardly seemed an equitable division of labor, leaving the younger girl to shoulder the greater burden in terms of time and effort.

"Won't it be too much work for you?" Abby questioned.

"Not at all. I'll enjoy it, in truth. And I'd count it as an honor to have a hand in such a special gift."

Adela's enthusiasm proved catching.

Excitement bubbled up inside Abby as she considered the possibilities. "I'll need to visit Mattie and Josiah's ranch in order to do some rough sketches."

And the sooner the better if she hoped to have several embroidery patterns ready before the Prescotts returned to Oregon City in twelve days' time. That would afford Adela almost four months in which to finish the quilt before she and her aunt journeyed here again for the baby's expected arrival.

"You can come with us to their ranch tomorrow," Adela invited. "There's plenty of room in our carriage for an additional passenger. My aunt and uncle and I plan to head out midmorning to see Mattie and Josiah. We'll spend the afternoon visiting with them at the ranch and then return to town before dusk, so you won't miss supper. That should give you enough time to complete a number of sketches."

"Thank you for the kind offer, but I don't want Mattie and Josiah to have so much as an inkling about what I'm up to. That way you and I can surprise them with the quilt once it's done."

"Well then, what if you came along with us, and

we let you out a ways off, before we reach the cabin?" Adela suggested instead.

Abby opened her mouth to answer, but the voice that spoke wasn't her own.

"No, definitely not." Elias's hard tone brooked no arguments.

Elias had felt his eyes starting to glaze over as Abby and Adela's discussion progressed—not surprising given the topic had centered on sewing and what-have-you. However, Adela's last remark had snapped him out of his stupor and back to attention right quick.

He straightened in his chair. "It isn't safe for Abby to be all on her own, away from the cabin, without any means of protection. Especially not for the whole of the afternoon. Josiah mentioned to me that he's spotted signs of a mountain lion prowling around the ranch over the past few weeks."

Abby gasped, her eyes widening in alarm. "Mattie must be terrified. I hope she and Josiah are sticking close to the cabin to stay safe. Has he seen the animal during the day?"

"They're both fine," he assured her. "Josiah's alert to the danger, but he didn't seem overly worried by it, other than the risk it poses to his horses. He hasn't actually seen the mountain lion at all. Only its tracks. But make no mistake—that's no guarantee you won't encounter an angry cat, even in the daylight hours. Although I'll admit the chances are slim." Elias added the last, not wishing to frighten Abby out of her wits.

He should have worried more about the opposite, he

realized, as resolve firmed her expression. "I'm sure I'll be fine, then," she said.

He met her intent gaze head-on. "So am I, because you're not going alone. I'll be coming with you to make certain of it." He wouldn't back down on that.

Abby's lashes lowered as she glanced at the baby in her arms. "What about Emma? Who will look after her while you and I are gone? You're not thinking of leaving her with Mother, are you?"

"No. We'll take Emma with us."

Abby's eyes returned to his, her delicate eyebrows pulling together. "Aren't you concerned for her safety with a rogue mountain lion roaming the area?"

"Of course. That's why we'll have to stay within shouting distance of Josiah's cabin, and I'll bring my rifle along as an added precaution. I don't expect to run into any trouble. Still, it's wise to be prepared for any eventuality, just in case."

The thought of anything happening to his daughter, or to Abby, was like a hot poker to his innards. He vowed to remain vigilant, ensuring no harm came to either one of them.

Chapter Ten

"I don't believe I could find a more beautiful setting to sketch if I searched the whole world," Abby reflected the next day, reverence filling her voice.

Elias stared out across land he'd never set eyes on before today. His brother's horse ranch.

"This is the first time I've been out this way," he admitted.

He and Abby sat on a hill overlooking the small log cabin and outbuildings. Emma napped at their side in the shade, the remnants of a picnic dinner scattered on the ground around them.

Several hours remained yet, before the Prescotts were due to come back for them and make the return journey to town.

Elias scanned the surrounding area for any signs of trouble, but all appeared peaceful. He breathed in the fresh air scented with pine and sun-warmed earth.

The vast grass-covered countryside dotted with trees was awe-inspiring. And it belonged to Josiah. It was the realization of a dream, his reason for leaving his old life behind and traveling to Oregon Country.

Seeing everything Josiah had achieved filled Elias with pride for his brother. But it also brought a large dose of guilt that he'd had no part in aiding the younger man in turning that dream into reality.

Elias had never journeyed to his brother's ranch. Not even to help build the cabin when winter was fast approaching and Josiah and Mattie needed shelter before the first snowfall. Not a single trip during the past year.

He'd never once been inside his brother's home in all the months they'd lived here.

It shamed him to admit how badly he'd behaved after his wife's death. Even if it had seemed as though he could do nothing else at the time. Besides leaving his brother and sister-in-law to get by on their own without his assistance, he'd heaped additional responsibilities on their shoulders. He'd forced them to act as parents to his child on top of tackling the backbreaking work required to build a horse ranch from nothing.

Elias had taken advantage of their generous natures without so much as a word of thanks in appreciation or acknowledgement for all the trouble he'd put them to throughout the last year.

"Mattie and Josiah were caring for my child, yet I couldn't even scrape up the will to visit. Not once. From the day she was born, they did everything for her."

"I know."

He glanced at Abby and saw understanding shining in her gaze.

It warmed the frozen places inside him, though he knew he wasn't entirely deserving of her compassion.

The people she should feel sympathy for were the ones he had wronged. His family.

"I left it to others to name my daughter. Did you know that?"

She didn't appear shocked by his words, though she shook her head, indicating she'd been unaware of that fact. "I had wondered if perhaps Rebecca decided on it before her passing," she said, "since it seemed an odd choice for you to have made on your own. Although you and Mother used to get on better, you never had a particularly close relationship with her."

That was true enough, due largely to the number of times when he'd felt that Emmaline Warner was coming between him and his wife. No man cared for that.

Even before open disapproval had replaced the older woman's previous unfortunate tendency to fawn upon him, Elias had merely tolerated her—and that only for Rebecca's sake. He hadn't been accustomed to a maternal figure in his life, and especially not one as overbearing as his former mother-in-law had proved to be during the early days of his marriage. But she'd been family, so he'd forced himself to get along with her as best he could.

Though Rebecca was gone, he and Mrs. Warner would remain bound together forever through Emma. Another situation that, though not to his liking, he was forced to accept.

"Mattie and Josiah chose the name without any input from me," Elias recounted.

His eyes sought out his daughter, lying sprawled on her back fast asleep with one small fist tucked against her bonnet-clad head. She made an adorable picture.

The warmth of the summer afternoon had given her cheeks a faint rosy glow, and her miniature features were relaxed in a serene expression.

Though her name had been derived from his former mother-in-law's, it didn't bring the older woman to mind when he spoke Emma's name.

The name suited her, and he'd never had a notion of changing it. In the beginning, however, that had not been a conscious decision. He hadn't given much thought for Emma at all during those dark days, truth be told. Which seemed like the worst transgression a father could commit.

He judged himself harshly for it, but Abby never had.

Just as she wasn't judging him now, he discovered when he turned his gaze back to her. Despite what he'd revealed a moment ago.

What was it about Abby that impelled him to confide in her about the worst in him? Was it because she'd never condemned him? Was that what made it so easy to bare his soul to her?

He felt a desire to open up to her further, to tell her things he'd never told another person. He was driven by a need to unburden himself, and he gave in to the urge.

"After Rebecca died, I distanced myself from everything and everyone. Emma, most of all. In a bid to protect *myself*. She came weeks early and seemed so tiny and fragile in my hands when I delivered her." He curled his fingers into fists, as though by hiding his palms from view he could wipe out the memory of his wife's blood staining them. "Outwardly, Emma looked healthy, but I couldn't know whether there might be something wrong with her that wasn't readily apparent. And even the healthiest of babies can succumb to the hardships on the trail. I feared she wouldn't survive. Especially since she was without her mother to nurse her. I couldn't face the agony of having another person I cared about ripped away from me. I didn't want to get attached. My heart couldn't have taken another loss so soon on the heels of the first. That's why I kept myself apart from Emma for so long."

Shutting himself off from his daughter had been his coping mechanism, the only way he'd believed he could make it through each day without his wife. "It became a habit I couldn't seem to break. Didn't want to break, if I'm honest with myself. Because even after I'd accepted that Emma wasn't going to sicken and die within a few days or weeks, she remained a constant reminder of what I'd lost. Her appearance grew more and more like her mother's as time went on, and I couldn't look upon her face without seeing Rebecca's." And remembering that he'd failed her.

Which had only strengthened his determination to not repeat those mistakes—in the misguided belief that he was protecting his child as much as himself. "The one way I knew to ensure I wouldn't feel that pain again was to never let my daughter close to me."

"But you loved Emma anyway." Abby didn't phrase it as a question. Sometimes, it seemed that she knew him better than he knew himself.

A slight smile curved his lips in response. "Yes, I do love her." Now it would be like slicing out his insides to cut her from his life. "She worked her way into my heart without me recognizing it. Even though I did my best to keep it from happening. I'm not proud of that fact, but it's the honest truth."

Abby laid her hand over his clenched fist. "You suffered a terrible loss a year ago. You were grieving. Only God knows how any one of us would react if we had to walk in your shoes. But you're in a different place now than you were then. You've opened yourself up to experience love for Emma, and that's what is important."

He realized it was true. Largely due to Emma. But Abby had played a significant part, as well. Turning his hand over, he linked his fingers with hers.

Between her and Emma, the two had brought him back to life by giving him moments of joy such as this one, which helped to alleviate the sadness of the past.

That wasn't to say he was ready—or ever would be ready—to open his heart to another woman. He didn't plan to marry again. Not even to provide a mother for Emma.

He'd survived growing up without his own mother. It would be the same for Emma. Though the situation presented different challenges for a girl child, his daughter was fortunate in having no shortage of female relatives, any of whom would be willing to step into the breach in Rebecca's stead as Emma grew older.

There was no good reason for Elias to risk the devastation and pain of heartbreak and loss for a second time.

Abby tried to concentrate on her sketching, but it had proved difficult as the afternoon hours slipped by. Her eyes were constantly drawn to Elias and his daughter. Emma now sat upright on the blanket spread over the ground.

Since waking up from her nap, she had been intent on investigating her surroundings. Which meant Elias was kept busy rescuing the baby from mischief.

When Emma had picked up a pine cone and moved to put it in her mouth, Elias had taken it away from her. Then she'd reached toward a large bumblebee in the grass, and he'd captured her hand before she could make contact.

Now the baby's interest centered on a squirrel hopping across a patch of dirt beneath the trees.

The furry critter paused to collect something, tiny forepaws wrapping around the object and bushy tail twitching.

Emma giggled in glee and patted her palms against her legs.

The squirrel's head came up at that. It looked in their direction, then turned to scamper up a pine tree.

Emma shifted onto her hands and knees and started crawling after it.

Elias pushed to his feet, catching up with his daughter in two steps. "I think that's quite enough of that," he admonished. "Up you come." He lifted Emma into his arms and walked away from the stand of evergreens, heading toward the crest of the hill.

The sun glinted on his dark russet hair, turning it the color of flames. Lines fanned out from the corners of his eyes as he squinted against the glare. He had not brought a hat, though Emma was protected from the strong rays by the bonnet tied under her chin.

The sky was a brilliant blue, without a cloud in sight to mute its intensity. A slight breeze rustled the leaves and sent a few fluttering to the ground. The twitter and chirping of birds in the trees filled the meadow with a joyous melody.

Elias spoke to Emma in a low voice as he indicated various landmarks spread out before them in the valley below their vantage point. He pointed out his brother's simple log home, where Emma had lived through the winter, spring and the beginning of summer. A bedroom had been recently added on to the original one-room structure, to accommodate the growing family. Josiah had completed the new section soon after learning of his coming child.

Next, Elias pointed to a sprawling birch tree a dozen yards from the cluster of outbuildings. Then to horses of every color, grazing on sage-green grasses in the far pasture. The road that was barely more than wagon wheel ruts leading from the ranch back to town. A wooden bridge that spanned the sparkling stream, which was lined with cottonwoods. Towering mountain peaks in the distance, silhouetted against the vast sky, stretching toward Heaven.

This was God's own country, and Abby could see His hand in everything around them. But most of all, in the father and daughter standing before her.

With an effort, she returned her attention to her sketchbook.

A short while later, Elias ambled back toward her. "It looks as though the Prescotts are saying their goodbyes to Josiah and Mattie and getting ready to leave. Everyone has come outside the cabin and gathered around the carriage. I figure Adela and her aunt and uncle will be here within a quarter hour to collect us. Are you about done with your sketches?"

She took a moment to scan the pages she'd filled with rough drawings. "I believe so. I've made a good start on several different scenes. That ought to be sufficient to use as references for the final sketches I'll draw directly onto the fabric, which I'll do at home. I shouldn't need to make a second trip out here."

Elias bent to set Emma on the quilt, then he sat down at Abby's side, one leg stretched out in front of him and the other drawn up toward his chest, with an arm hooked around his bent knee. "That's probably best. Less chance of the cloth getting soiled that way."

"And less chance for Mattie or Josiah to spot me on their property and demand to know what I'm about," she added. "They didn't see you and Emma just now, did they?"

"No. Nobody glanced in our direction," he assured her.

"Good. Because it might've raised questions that would be difficult to answer without ruining the surprise."

"There's no cause to worry on that score. Josiah and Mattie remain none the wiser."

"Well, that's a relief." She tapped a finger against her chin as she contemplated the series of drawings filling the pages of her sketchbook. "Since we have a few minutes yet before the Prescotts arrive, perhaps you could help me choose which scenes to use for the quilt. I've sketched a half dozen possible options. Since Adela can't stitch them all, I must decide on just three. Only I'm finding it difficult to work out which ones are my favorite."

Elias rubbed a hand along his jawline. "I don't know

how much help I can offer to you—deciding on quilting designs is not one of my strong suits. You'd be better served to wait until Adela and her aunt get here and ask them instead of me."

"I'd value your opinion. You know Josiah better than anyone, and this gift's as much for him as for Mattie. I'd like the pictures to have as much meaning for him as I hope they will have for Mattie and the baby."

Elias's gaze warmed at her words. "In that case, I'd be pleased to take a look."

He shifted to get a closer view, his shoulder bumping against Abby's.

Her arm heated where it pressed up against his, even through the layers of clothing separating them. It was a pleasant feeling having him near, but she couldn't let it distract her. She mustn't forget the reason he'd moved close—and it wasn't due to tender emotions for her.

Clearing her throat, she focused on the task at hand and directed his attention to a particular drawing. "What do you think of this one?"

His answer came immediately, without an instant's hesitation. "There's no question you should include that picture of the cabin. It's their home, the heart of the ranch."

She turned to smile at him. "And you thought you wouldn't be any good at this."

A slight flush stained his cheekbones. "Well, I imagine it was probably just a fluke. Don't expect to see me at a quilting bee any time soon."

"I don't know why not. If you can sew a wound closed, you should have no trouble stitching fabrics together," she pointed out, her lips twitching at the image her words had brought to mind—of him sitting in a circle with a bunch of women, trading gossip while he plied a needle to sew a seam.

His expression turned disgruntled in response to her teasing. She couldn't hold back her mirth, and he scowled at her.

"If you're quite through—" he raised his voice to speak above the sounds of her laughter "—I suggest we get back on track. That is, if you still want my help. We haven't got all day here, and we've veered far off course."

It took her a moment to regain control of herself. "You're right." Clearing her throat again, she bent her head to her sketchbook once more and asked for his thoughts on their next choice.

"Horses should feature on the quilt, as well," he recommended, snagging Emma before she crawled out of reach and settling the baby on his lap. "They're an important part of Josiah and Mattie's lives. Their days revolve around caring for the horses."

Abby flicked through a few pages. "I drew two scenes with horses in them. One shows some of the horses near the barn and outbuildings, and the other has a group grazing farther off in the pasture." She showed Elias the pair of drawings in question.

She noted that Emma had pulled his left hand to her mouth and set to chewing on his thumb. He didn't appear to mind his daughter using him as a teething aid, or the drool that coated his fingers.

He studied both pictures in silence for several seconds before replying. "The foals in the pasture are mighty cute—and seem appropriate for a baby quilt."

She tilted her head to the side and considered the matter briefly, then nodded. "I agree. The pasture scene it is, then. That's two done. We need one more." She moved on to the remaining sketches. "Which of these other three do you prefer? There's the wagon road cutting through the valley. The stream bordered by trees. Or the snow-capped mountains." She paused for a moment on each one as she spoke.

"Hmm. That's a tough choice. I'm partial to both the stream and the mountains." Elias mulled over it for a bit. "How about combining the two into one drawing?"

Once he'd mentioned it, the solution seemed obvious.

"That's a wonderful idea. I can't believe I got so wrapped up in the little details that I missed it." She flipped to a fresh page as ideas filled her head. Using broad strokes, she quickly began on a vague outline to figure out the placement of certain elements. "This will be perfect. A panoramic view comprising acres of ranch land. Thank you for the suggestion."

She glanced up at Elias, a smile curving her lips, and was met with one from him in return. His entire expression lightened, making him appear younger, the lines on his face less pronounced.

He reached out his right hand toward Abby, and her heart missed a beat, then picked up speed.

His fingers touched the side of her head. "Hold still for a moment. You have something in your hair."

She froze. "It's not a bee, is it? I got stung once when one landed in my hair and I tried to brush it away, not realizing what it was."

"Don't worry. It's just a leaf this time." His wrist grazed her cheek as he sifted through the strands of her hair, working the leaf loose. "There, I got it." He released the offending object, and it fluttered to the ground.

When he moved away, Abby felt the loss of his nearness, like a cloud had blocked out the warm rays of the sun.

With one arm encircling Emma, Elias used his free hand to begin stowing items in the wicker basket. After Abby had added a few last details to her drawing, she tucked her sketchbook and charcoal into her bag and then assisted him in packing up the remains of their picnic.

She couldn't help thinking that she and Elias made a good team. It was a thought that led down dangerous paths, however.

Even as she felt an increased closeness to him, she couldn't let it develop any further, or her heart would surely suffer for her foolishness.

She could never take Rebecca's place in his life.

Abby accepted that he would never care as deeply for her as he had for her sister. She couldn't foresee a happily-ever-after for her with Elias.

If she let down her guard, started wishing for impossible things, it would lead to nothing but heartbreak when those dreams never came to be. She had to protect herself from the pain of disappointment and shattered illusions.

Chapter Eleven

"I'm sorry if I'm intruding, but I had to come see you today." Concern shone in Abby's pale blue gaze as she sat on the settee in Elias's upstairs sitting room with Emma on her lap. "This must be a difficult day for you." She worried her bottom lip between her teeth. "How are you doing?"

"I'm fine," he replied, hoping that would put an end to it. He didn't want her probing the festering wound he'd done his best to turn a blind eye to.

He had expected to be left alone today, on the anniversary of his wife's death. Would certainly have preferred it that way. Then, he could've tried to pretend it was like any other day.

The Prescotts had returned to Oregon City the day before yesterday, after a week-and-a-half visit in Silver Springs. Prior to their departure, Mattie had insisted on marking the occasion of Emma's birthday with the entire family in attendance. The celebration—a special supper—had been held on the previous Sunday, ostensibly, for the Prescotts' benefit, in order to include them.

However, Elias suspected that Mattie's reasoning almost certainly had just as much to do with the fact that she'd surmised Elias wouldn't be in a celebratory frame of mind on the actual date of Emma's birth. For obvious reasons. And she was correct in that assumption.

"How can you say you're 'fine'?" Abby questioned, bewilderment clouding her expression. She tightened her hold on Emma. "It's impossible not to be affected when today's the one-year anniversary of Rebecca's tragic passing."

Elias didn't need her to remind him of that. He wasn't likely to forget. And it was true that he was affected by it. That didn't mean he wanted to think about it. He didn't care to lay himself open and dissect the state of his heart at present.

It was almost two weeks since the afternoon he and Abby had spent out at Josiah and Mattie's ranch—when Elias had revealed certain things to her. If she imagined that gave her some sort of insight about what went on inside of him, she was wrong.

He doubted whether she could even begin to understand the maelstrom of emotions he had to battle just to function. They formed a roiling, tangled mass in the pit of his stomach, which he had trouble making sense of himself. Revealing any part of it to Abby was most definitely not in his plans.

Plainly, she was of an opposing mind on the matter. Though maybe she was seeking some solace for herself as much as she was trying to offer it to him.

Elias should have realized that today would be trying for Abby just as it was for him, only for different reasons. She had lost her sister in the same instant when he'd lost his wife. No matter that Abby hadn't learned of it until weeks later.

And after everything she had done for him in the months since then, all the times she'd been by his side supporting him, he could do no less for her now.

He sat down next to her on the settee. "Today must be difficult for you."

"Yes, it is," she readily acknowledged, her pale blue eyes glistening with unshed tears. "And there's no shame in admitting it. Though we have a piece of Rebecca with us still in Emma, I miss her terribly. And it breaks my heart to think that Emma will never know her mama."

"She has you," he replied.

"It's not the same thing." Her head lowered, as she looked down at his daughter, who remained blissfully unaware that she was central to their discussion. "I can't possibly replace Rebecca in Emma's life. No one can. And the pain of missing her is always there for me. Will always be there. But it feels more intense on this particular day than it has for some time."

A teardrop rolled down Abby's face, and he wrapped an arm around her shoulders, pulling her into his side. He leaned down to place a kiss on her cheek, but she turned her head unexpectedly at the last moment, and he missed the mark. His lips wound up pressed to the corner of her mouth, rather than the spot where he'd been aiming.

He drew back hastily, trying to convince himself that the kiss was of little consequence. Yet it had affected him in ways he didn't care to examine. He wasn't sure how he felt about it, to be perfectly honest. He opted not to dwell on it.

Abby raised a hand to touch her lips. She looked at him with shining eyes, and he feared the brightness was no longer from her tears alone.

Had she misconstrued his intent? He hoped not. He didn't wish to see her hurt by his hand, didn't want to fail her and be the cause of further heartache for her.

Though he admired and respected Abby, his feelings for her could never go beyond that. He had nothing to offer her.

He cleared his throat and pushed to his feet to put some needed distance between them. "It's to be expected that thoughts of the past have stirred up emotions for you and brought them to the surface."

Abby wiped the tear track from her cheek. "But not for you," she replied, referring to the claim he'd made earlier that he was fine.

Despite his previous determination to avoid the subject, talking about how the past had twisted and changed him was far preferable to a discourse focused on that almost-kiss.

The trouble was, he didn't know where to start, how to adequately explain to Abby the confusion of his conflicted feelings in regards to himself…and his late wife. He'd loved Rebecca, but he hated what she'd done. Hated what her actions had wrought and what it had done to him—what he had become as a result. A man he didn't want to be.

The shock of her death had dulled with the passing of time, but his guilt hadn't diminished any. It remained as piercing as it had been a year ago, on the day Rebecca had breathed her last. Self-recriminations acted as countless jagged shards impaling his heart.

He shook his head. "Sometimes it's easier to discount certain things than to face them. For a long time, I've done my best to numb my emotions in order not to feel."

"But you can't ignore them forever."

"No." He couldn't, though the Lord knew he'd tried. "But it seemed the only way to get me through each day. And it also felt like a better choice than the alternative." Releasing a weary sigh, he recalled the event that had altered the course of his life irrevocably. "After Rebecca died, I was consumed by anger born out of pain. Most of it directed at myself. But a large portion was aimed at her, too."

"For leaving you?" Abby guessed. Her brow furrowed. "But surely, you must see that she didn't have any say in the matter."

"Perhaps not in that moment," he acknowledged. "But before that, she…" He searched to find the right words. When they eluded him, he pressed ahead anyway, hoping that Abby's gift for understanding him would hold true here, too. "Rebecca kept the news of our coming child from me until we were too far along the trail to turn back."

"Would you have turned back if you'd known sooner?"

"We wouldn't have left Tennessee in the first place, if she had seen fit to tell me right when she'd begun to suspect her condition. She used subterfuge in order to keep it from me, since as a doctor, she knew I would have recognized certain signs." He moved to the window and laid his forearm along the top of the wooden frame. Though he stared out at the street below, his mind focused inward.

Had he and Rebecca stayed in Nashville, he would've cosseted her, wrapping her up in cotton wool during the months of her confinement.

Instead, she'd faced endless chores from sunup to sundown and harsh conditions on the trail. When the baby came too soon, she'd been forced to deliver Emma inside a cramped covered wagon in the middle of nowhere, far removed from civilization.

He clenched his jaw, and his hand formed into a fist. Pushing away from the window, he turned to face Abby. "If I'd been given any say in the matter, I wouldn't have risked her safety and the health of our child."

"Rebecca must have realized that—and she lied to you and used it to manipulate you?" Abby's expression clouded over with disbelief.

Whether that was due to her doubting his word or because she didn't wish to believe that her sister had committed such a deed, Elias refused to speculate.

Emma struggled in Abby's hold, plainly wanting to get down from her lap. Abby placed the baby on the floor, and Emma crawled across the rug, straight toward him. Once she reached him, she latched on to the leg of his trousers and used it to pull herself into a standing position.

He bent and lifted his daughter into his arms, then walked over to his armchair and sat down with her on his lap. Her tiny fingers wrapped around his thumb, her grip surprisingly strong. It seeming to squeeze his heart, as well, as though connected by invisible cords.

His gaze returned to Abby. "Rebecca had her heart set on making the trip, and she let nothing and no one—least of all me—stand in her way." To her own detriment.

She'd paid the price with her life. Though he guessed she had never thought for even a moment that it would come to that end.

Understanding dawned in Abby's gaze. "You lay a share of the blame for what happened on Rebecca."

"Rightly or not, I do." And he felt guilty for it.

He recognized that he needed to forgive her in order to move beyond that. It was necessary for his own sake as much as for Emma's. He had to let go of his bitterness for the part he believed Rebecca had played in what happened.

But he didn't know how to find his way clear of it.

Abby's heart bled for Elias that he had been carrying around such a heavy burden for so long alone. It was clear to her that he'd never shared it with anyone. Until now, when he'd revealed the truth to her.

She didn't condemn him for the way he felt. Emotions weren't something that could be commanded at will. And she had empathy for him, gained through her own experiences butting up against her sister's willful nature—her actions motivated by the best of intentions, of course.

Growing up, Abby had seen first-hand Rebecca's penchant for having things her own way, which was a character trait their mother had fostered in her elder daughter. Rebecca's kind and loving heart had tempered the worst of the effects—but it had been a trial at times, all the same.

Rebecca hadn't been perfect. And it seemed her marriage to Elias hadn't been perfect, either. The latter was a revelation to Abby.

For years, she had viewed the romance between Elias and her sister as some sort of fairy-tale ideal that was far beyond her own reach. But now she realized that even their seemingly rosy union had not been without thorns.

"I loved my sister, but that didn't blind me to her faults. She could be selfish in pursuing her own aims. On occasion, she failed to give proper consideration for others when their wishes ran counter to hers. Still, I'm a bit astonished that she would seek to keep such a significant event a secret from you."

"She wanted to be near your mother when her time came." Elias's knuckles showed white as his grip tightened on the chair arm. "Despite the fact that, as a doctor, I was in a unique position that allowed me to remain by her side the whole time and assist her through the birthing. Apparently, that wasn't enough for her, having only me to rely upon. She ordered circumstances in a bid to make them more to her liking."

"She had no right to take the decision out of your hands by staying silent, no matter how she may have justified her actions to herself. The choice wasn't hers alone to make."

"Well, she was right to doubt my doctoring ability. Events proved that much when I failed her."

Abby wanted to go to Elias, to wrap her arms around him and offer comfort, but he seemed to hold himself apart from her, despite the baby sitting in his lap, his demeanor displaying clear signs warning Abby not to trespass.

"You didn't fail Rebecca," she denied. "You were there with her through it all, until the end. Her death was tragic and heartrending, but no one's at fault for what happened. Certainly not you. I know in my heart that you did all you could. It was not in any man's power to save her." Blinking to stem the tears that threatened to fall once more, she prayed that Elias would believe her words.

"Your mother doesn't hold me blameless. She's made that plain countless times before." He shifted Emma on his lap. "Frankly, I'm surprised she's not here now to remind me that it's my fault her daughter isn't with us any longer."

Not for the first time, Abby wished that her mother would have made some effort to temper her animosity toward Elias. Or at least shown enough fortitude to refrain from airing her grievances in his hearing at every opportunity.

"Pain and regret have clouded her thinking. She became so overset this morning that she took to her bed only a short time after she had risen, claiming she couldn't face this day." Abby chose to remember the good, finding solace in fond memories of Rebecca rather than dwelling on her untimely demise. Not so, their mother. "Why would you give a moment's credence to her grief-fueled vitriol?"

"Because I've thought the same thing myself."

A shocked gasp escaped her, stealing all the air from her lungs. "Well, you're wrong to think that," she insisted as soon as she had breath to speak. "Just as Mother is. You couldn't be more wrong. So, stop it this instant."

His eyebrows arched toward his hairline. "*Stop it? Just like that?*"

"Yes," she persisted, and then felt foolish. Only a few minutes ago, she had acknowledged that emotions couldn't be willed, yet now she'd demanded that he do exactly that. "Of course, praying for the Lord's help to alter your perception would aid the situation a great deal at this juncture," she tacked on to correct her blunder.

"I suppose so."

He lapsed into silence, and it seemed as though he didn't wish to discuss the matter any further.

Emma patted her palm against Elias's mouth. He snagged her hand to still its movement and pressed a kiss to her tiny fingers.

Abby's thoughts were drawn back to the kiss he'd bestowed on her a short time ago. What were the reasons behind that action? Why had he done it?

The gentle touch of his lips had left her with a feeling of warmth radiating through her along with hope that he held her in some esteem, that he looked on her as more than Rebecca's little sister. Perhaps he saw her as a friend—or something even more than that.

She cautioned herself not to read too much into the kiss. His embrace had lasted but a moment, and he hadn't sought to prolong the closeness between them. Neither of which indicated much in the way of romantic feelings toward Abby.

Elias had loved Rebecca. And the anger he harbored toward her at present didn't erase that.

She couldn't ignore the possibility that he might

never love any woman besides his late wife. Any amorous sentiments in Abby's direction still seemed rather unlikely.

Yet, he had opened himself up to her, revealing his innermost self. Thus, a tiny seed of optimism had been planted deep within her. It needed only a small ray of sunshine and a bit of tender care to burst forth into flowering life.

Chapter Twelve

"The Lord is with us always." David Linton's voice filled the small church as he addressed the gathered congregation on the following Sunday.

Elias sat on a pew with Josiah and Mattie situated to his left, and Abby seated on his right side. Emma was a warm, comforting weight on his lap. The elder Warners had positioned themselves on the far side of their daughter.

"Seek Him out, and He is there," the preacher continued. "Cry out to Him, and He hears."

The message struck a chord with Elias as he recognized the truth of those words.

He had stopped praying long ago, on the day after his wife died, when it seemed that the Lord hadn't heeded his cries to spare her life.

But the preacher's sermon served as a timely reminder to Elias. Even though he hadn't received the answer to his desperate prayers that he'd been searching for, that didn't mean the Lord had not been listening.

"Though we may turn our backs on Him for a time,

He will never turn away from us. 'And the Lord, He is the One who goes before you; He will be with you, He will not leave you nor forsake you; do not fear nor be dismayed.'"

The preacher's gaze swept across the rows of pews filled with worshipers. "Lift yourself up to Him, and He will welcome you with open arms once more. The Lord forgives our transgressions, but we must have the courage to confess them to Him. Holding on to anger and resentment acts as a poison, eating away at the core of our righteousness."

Elias felt as though the Lord was speaking directly to him through the preacher, providing wisdom and guidance at the very moment when he needed it most. God's perfect timing was made more remarkable by the fact that it could not be explained except by faith alone. The Lord had delivered the specific message necessary to strengthen and encourage him.

Elias had needed only to open his heart to the Lord to hear.

He would never know peace by turning from God. It was only through Him that Elias would find healing. The Lord alone had the means to offer absolution for him.

Although he'd lost his way after Rebecca's death, the Lord hadn't given up on him. Just as Abby never had. In the face of that faith and support, Elias couldn't give up on himself. He couldn't refuse the blessings he'd been offered, whether he felt he deserved them or not. He called on God's mercy from above.

Lord, please, forgive me for questioning Your will. Forgive me, O Lord, for holding myself apart from You.

I allowed anger to take the place of love in my heart, and now I seek to put that right. I ask for Your help in letting go of destructive emotions that bring nothing but further misery, so that I may be the kind of father my baby girl deserves—a father worthy of her, and a father of whom she can be proud.

He pressed a kiss to the top of Emma's downy head and then smoothed a soft curl between his fingers, experiencing a measure of peace for the first time in a long while.

He never wanted to let Emma down. For far too long, he'd mistakenly thought that by not trying to be more than he believed he was capable of, he wouldn't run the risk of failing her. Only now did he see that to not try at all *was* to fail her. She deserved his very best efforts, even if he sometimes fell short.

The Lord had placed Emma into his care, entrusted her to him. That counted for much. And he didn't take it lightly. The Lord could see inside him; He knew Elias's heart. Better than Elias knew it himself.

This—Emma resting secure in his embrace, his to love and protect for all the days of his life—was God's will. He gained courage from that simple truth.

Elias would always miss Rebecca—that would never change—but when he stopped fighting it and let the memories of her come, they didn't bring the sharp twinge of guilt and unwarranted anger toward her that they had for the past agonizing year. The raw pain of her loss had diminished to a dull ache in his chest.

He vowed not to dwell on the past and what was gone. Instead, he'd look toward the future, focusing on the things that were within his control.

Abby shifted next to him on the pew, drawing his gaze to her.

She, like the Lord, had never forsaken him. It was for Emma that he had come to church initially, but Abby had been the one to encourage his attendance and urge him to seek the Lord's aid. He recognized that he had reached this place, at last, in no small part because of her steadfast support.

He reached for her hand and squeezed it in gratitude. She graced him with a warm smile in return.

Mrs. Warner noted the exchange and sent him a sharp look from across Abby. He removed his hand hastily.

As little as he liked the older woman's meddling, he was grateful for it in that moment. Despite his fondness for Abby, he wouldn't allow emotion to lead him along a precarious ledge. He couldn't risk leaving his heart vulnerable to the dangers of a misstep that would leave him broken, his lifeblood pouring out.

Because he wouldn't survive a second time. Would not have the strength to climb back out of that dark place if he fell so far down again.

Abby watched Elias out of the corner of her eye as he cuddled his daughter, his intent gaze focused on the preacher sermonizing from his pulpit.

More and more, she saw signs of positive changes taking place in Elias. She'd caught glimpses of the man he used to be, the one she remembered from years past, before tragedy struck and brought him low.

He had appeared less closed off and remote over the last few weeks—not only from her and Emma but toward others, as well. It seemed that he'd begun to find small moments of joy in his daily existence once again.

She didn't want Elias to mourn Rebecca for the rest of his life, and she prayed that God would grant him peace. That he would embrace the opportunity to feel love again.

Perhaps he might even find it with me, Lord, she silently beseeched Him.

Was she foolish to harbor such hopes in the depths of her heart? Or would her courage be rewarded if she opened herself up completely to the possibility?

When fears threatened to overwhelm her, telling her to give up, she reminded herself that all things were possible in the Lord, for those who believed. She firmed her resolve.

She no longer assumed that she could never measure up to the perfect image of his beloved wife in Elias's eyes. She'd been judging herself against an ideal that wasn't real—that had never existed except inside her own mind. An ideal which nobody could live up to. Not even Rebecca.

There had been a time when Abby had believed that Elias and her sister had a perfect marriage, that Rebecca was the perfect wife for him and Abby could never come close to equaling her. She knew now that it might not be so cut-and-dried.

Emma let out a squawk of complaint as she dropped her rag doll and it tumbled to the floor. She lunged forward, trying to reach her lost toy.

Elias held her in place with one arm hooked around her waist. Twisting his torso in an awkward fashion, he stretched his other hand down toward the floorboards.

His efforts to retrieve the doll were hindered by a lap-ful of squirming, unhappy baby.

Abby laid her hand on his shoulder to gain his atten-tion. "Let me get it for you," she whispered close to his ear, trying not to disturb those around them.

"That would be much appreciated," Elias replied in a low voice as he straightened. "Thank you."

She bent to pick up the rag doll and presented it to Emma. "Hush, sweetness. Here's your doll."

The little girl crowed in delight at its sudden reap-pearance, her arms outstretched. She wrapped chubby fingers around the toy and clenched it against her body.

"Is that better?" Abby asked, stoking her niece's soft curls back from her face.

Emma responded with a grin that displayed two tiny front teeth. A driblet of wetness escaped from the cor-ner of her mouth.

Elias shifted in order to slide his hand into the pocket of his trousers. He extracted a pressed, snowy white cotton handkerchief and used it to wipe Emma's chin.

"I'd say you're getting the knack of this, Elias," she remarked, pleased for him and Emma that the situation had improved noticeably for the two of them in the last several weeks.

A loud throat clearing sounded on Abby's right, snagging her attention. When she glanced over at her mother, she found the older woman shooting a barbed stare at her.

"Shh," her mother hissed in reproach.

Abby turned to face the front once more and but-toned her lip for the remainder of the church service.

A short time later, when the preacher's sermon had

ended and the congregation had begun to make their way to the door of the church, Abby's thoughts returned to her earlier reflections. They took up right where they had left off a while ago, musing over the possibility of romantic feelings developing between her and Elias. Perhaps they'd started to grow in his heart already, just as she suspected they had in hers.

Though she didn't want to attribute greater significance to his actions than was warranted, her heart looked for evidence that he felt something more for her—and she imagined that she had found it. Just what emotion it was—whether simple fondness and admiration, or the first stirring of lasting love—she didn't know for certain. But there were an ever-increasing number of instances that seemed to serve as proof. Recalling them in her head gave her hope to cling to.

Gestures such as his kiss the other day or the touch of his hand on hers during Preacher Linton's sermon. Or even simply the conversations between them, when he recounted difficult memories from his past or shared what he was feeling, revealing pieces of himself to her that she knew he had never shared with anyone else.

All that combined to lend weight to her belief, offering her some assurance that it wasn't merely an insubstantial dream with no chance of ever becoming real.

Would love blossom between her and Elias if she gave it an opportunity to flourish? Might he wish to have her as his wife one day?

All too easily, she could envision marrying Elias, starting a life with him and serving as a true helpmate to him. Sharing in the Lord's blessings and supporting each other through the rough patches as they journeyed together. Helping him raise his daughter. Acting as a mother to Emma, spending every precious moment with her. And, perhaps, bringing other children into the world, as well—younger brothers or sisters for Emma.

Abby tried to rein in her imaginings, determined not to get too far ahead of herself.

Even though it presented a beautiful and joyous picture, it might not come to pass. And she didn't wish to be left brokenhearted by that reality, if a life with Elias wasn't God's will. All the prayers in the world couldn't alter what would be, and her heart could be shattered if her desires ran counter to the Lord's plan for her. She had learned that much from Elias's tragic situation.

However, she took comfort in knowing that no matter what the Lord had in store for her, it would happen according to His purpose. She didn't need to understand His reasons to recognize and accept that truth. God granted understanding in time; one only had to hold fast to courage and patience in seeking the meaning.

Abby placed herself in the Lord's hands willingly, her heart filled with hope for what may come.

"You gave a wonderful sermon today," Elias praised the preacher as they stood on the front steps of the church. He extended his arm in order to shake the other man's hand. "Thank you. I mean that genuinely."

"You're welcome. Most sincerely." David Linton laid his left hand over the top of their clasped hands, his gaze full of compassion and understanding. The moment stretched out for a number of seconds before he let go.

Elias shifted his daughter in his arms. She had fallen

asleep near the end of the service, during the hymns. Her small body was a warm weight against his chest, her head resting heavy on his shoulder while Josiah and Mattie stood at his side.

A slight breeze teased strands of Mattie's brown hair that had slipped free from the bun anchored at her nape. "Would you and Tessa and your children care to join us at Elias's house for Sunday dinner today?" she invited the preacher. "We'd welcome your family's company."

"It would be our pleasure," he accepted. "Tessa has been meaning to find an opportunity for a lengthier visit with you for a few weeks now. Unfortunately, Henry and Lizzie keep her too busy to make more than the occasional trip out to your ranch, and she didn't want to intrude while your relatives were visiting with you."

"I can quite understand about the children." Mattie placed one palm against her stomach. "This little one has yet to put in an appearance, and still I'm only able to come into town but once a week."

The preacher smiled at her words. "I trust both of you are doing well."

Mattie beamed in response. "Yes, I'm pleased to say."

"And I aim to see it stays that way," Josiah added, wrapping an arm around his wife's waist.

Mattie placed her hand over Josiah's as she addressed the preacher. "Please tell Tessa that I look forward to chatting with her. And we'll see you and the children at Elias's house about one o'clock, if that's convenient for you."

The preacher folded his hands before him and nodded. "We'll be there then."

Elias descended the short flight of wooden stairs, Josiah and Mattie following behind him, making way for the next family waiting in line to greet the preacher.

Elias turned his head to the left and then the right, searching the churchyard for Abby, who had exited with her parents ahead of him and his family.

He found her among a small group standing a dozen yards away. He'd started toward her before he took note of the people with her. But as soon as the others entered into his awareness, he pulled up short.

His former mother-in-law had cornered Mr. and Mrs. Freedmont and their son, Augustus. She was speaking to them rather animatedly while Abby remained silent at her side.

Elias had no wish to interject himself into that particular gathering, no matter the curious desire that had overtaken him a moment ago, compelling him to seek out Abby. He'd acted without conscious thought and wasn't of a mind to puzzle out the reasons behind his sudden impulse. Resolutely, he changed course, putting his back to the scene.

After exchanging greetings with a few acquaintances—parishioners who had slowly warmed to him as he'd become a regular attender of Sunday services—he and Josiah and Mattie started back toward the main part of town, heading to Elias's home.

As they walked down the slight hill, he noticed Mattie glancing in his direction. Her gaze settled for a handful of seconds on Emma, snuggled against his chest, before her eyes came up to meet his.

Lines marred her forehead as her eyebrows drew

together. "I'm sorry Josiah and I weren't with you and Emma on Wednesday."

On Emma's birthday—and the anniversary of Rebecca's passing. That was what Mattie had meant, though she hadn't said it directly.

He hated to think that she or Josiah might have been made to feel any regret for not being with him. Until Abby had arrived on his doorstep, affording him little choice but to accept her presence, Elias had believed he wanted to be left alone with only his daughter, who was incapable of bringing up uncomfortable subjects he'd done his best to forget. And he'd made that clear to his brother and sister-in-law the previous Sunday, in no uncertain terms. They'd offered to come to town—had tried to insist on it, in fact—but he had refused.

"You only agreed to stay on the ranch because I asked it of you," he replied, hoping to ease Mattie's pinched expression. "I'm the one who wanted it that way. I saw no call to upend your usual routine and disrupt the whole of your day with a needless trip all the way into town on my account, merely to keep me company."

"Necessary or not, I wish it were possible for me to see you and Emma more than once a week." Sadness lurked in her light brown eyes.

A sadness Elias suspected had been there for some time. Yet he'd not bothered to notice it before now, too wrapped up in his own troubles to see the truth. His eyes sought his brother's and found the emotion in Josiah's blue gaze a mirror to his wife's.

How could Elias have blinded himself to the toll recent events had taken on Mattie and Josiah? He'd been heedlessly ignoring the magnitude of the sacrifice they'd willingly made in giving up Emma, whom they had raised as their own child for almost a year. Near a dozen months of seeing her every day, caring for her and loving her. It must have been a terrible wrench to go from that to having only a few short, precious hours with her each week.

Despite their excitement about their coming baby, Elias could well imagine the sizable hole Emma must have left in their lives upon her departure from their home.

Remorse flooded his heart at his shameful failure to consider their feelings in this and the utter selfishness he'd displayed toward his family. He'd taken his brother and sister-in-law for granted on occasions too numerous to count.

He searched for a means to redress the situation, to make amends to Josiah and Mattie.

A few days later, Elias had hit upon a solution to fix things, at least in part.

"I thought I'd borrow a horse and wagon from Mr. Rothmeier's livery stable and drive out to my brother's ranch one afternoon this week," he announced, sharing his plans with Abby when he and Emma stopped by the mercantile on Tuesday morning.

Since breaking his self-imposed isolation inside his home nearly a month ago, he'd taken to venturing out on a weekly basis in order to get his own supplies rather than continuing to leave it to Josiah and Mattie to shoulder the responsibility in his stead.

Josiah still settled the tab for the items Elias ordered, however, and that didn't sit right with him. But as things stood at present, he had little choice in the matter. Without a source of income, he had no other option but to accept his brother's charity. Humbling his pride was nothing compared to ensuring his daughter had all she needed.

Emma was his primary consideration in everything he did now, every decision he made. That wasn't to say he meant to allow the current situation to continue on indefinitely, only that his daughter factored into this, too.

Not for the first time, he contemplated the necessity of looking for work—something other than doctoring since he had no intention of returning to his former profession. But undertaking any job around town presented some problems not readily dismissed or easily dealt with.

Emma spent her days with Elias—or more accurately, he spent his days with her, caring for her. He couldn't help but worry over who would have charge of his daughter while he went off to some job. This was the reason why he hadn't yet put in a serious effort to approach some of the local business owners in a bid to obtain gainful employment.

He looked to the Lord to guide him in this, as in all else—to light his path and show him the way. After a year of refusing to speak with God, Elias now prayed constantly for Him to provide answers to the multitude of questions arising from the altered trajectory of his life, which had changed so suddenly over the past several weeks.

With his decision to visit his brother and sister-in-law, Elias felt as though he was moving in the right direction at last, after veering so sharply off course a year ago.

Abby had paused in the middle of filling his order and regarded him with a warm smile. "Mattie and Josiah must be looking forward to seeing you and Emma."

"They don't know we're coming, actually," he admitted. "But I figure they won't mind if we show up unannounced."

"I have no doubt that it will be a wonderful surprise for them. They've been missing Emma."

A fact that had taken Elias entirely too long to recognize. "It's time I made an effort on their behalf, as they did for me for the last year. Over the course of the past spring and the first part of this summer, they brought Emma to visit me two or three times each week, despite their responsibilities at the ranch." He adjusted his hold on his daughter and rubbed his hand up and down her back. "I should have done this much sooner, especially seeing as there was no good cause that prevented it."

Abby's gaze shifted to the baby in his arms. "It's not as though you've sat around twiddling your thumbs and doing nothing all day for the past month. You've been occupied with looking after Emma. That isn't something to be discounted."

"Neither is it something that obliged me to stay away from their ranch and remain in town," he pointed out. "And she hasn't been in my care for very long—I have even less excuse for my absence when Emma was living on the ranch," he admitted, owning up to the consequences of his actions rather than attempting to justify or excuse them. "But I thank you for your stalwart defense of me." Even though he hadn't always deserved it.

Abby's faith in him had never wavered. All the more reason to make some long overdue changes.

Starting with the trip out to Josiah and Mattie's ranch. Elias vowed that this would be only one of many transformations to take place in his life—and inside himself—in the days ahead.

"You're welcome to come along with me and Emma," he invited Abby.

She hesitated in indecision for a moment before replying. "I shouldn't horn in on a family gathering." Her disappointment was palpable, indicating she'd answered as she thought she should for courtesy's sake rather than according to her true desire.

"Josiah and Mattie look on you as family," he assured her. "I'm certain they would enjoy the opportunity to visit with you." And Elias would enjoy her companionship during the five-mile drive from town. He liked spending time in Abby's company and talking with her, no matter the occasion.

But he realized that he wanted her with him for this especially. Though he didn't care to look too closely at his reasons, he found himself praying that she would accept his invitation.

She nibbled on the corner of her bottom lip until she appeared to come to a decision. "If you're sure I won't be intruding, then I'd love to join you. I'll be free tomorrow afternoon."

His heart felt lighter in his chest, and he didn't give her a chance to fall prey to any second thoughts. "Emma and I will stop by and pick you up at your house shortly after noontime tomorrow, if that suits you, and we can head out of town from there."

Her light blue eyes sparkled in anticipation as she nodded her agreement. "I'll be ready and waiting."

Elias looked forward to the next day with a feeling of profound satisfaction.

And he acknowledged that it had just as much to do with the prospect of time spent in Abby's company as it did with gaining an opportunity to make amends for his regrettable behavior toward his brother and sister-in-law.

Chapter Thirteen

Abby breathed in the fresh air redolent with the scent of pine, as Elias guided the horse and buckboard toward his brother's ranch. Birds chirped in the trees on either side of the rutted dirt track they followed. Though the wildflowers of spring were long gone and the grass had begun to turn brown in places, the bounty of nature was breathtaking nonetheless.

Emma sat perched on Abby's lap, a floral sunbonnet shading her delicate skin from the bright rays of the sun. The baby chewed on her fist while her curious gaze took in the sights all around her.

Abby had elected to go without a hat, and the sunshine felt pleasantly warm on her face. The breeze teased a lock of her hair free from the pins secured at the back of her head. Tucking the loose strands behind her ear, she sighed in contentment at the fine summer day, perfect for paying a visit to Elias's relatives.

She had been out this way on only a handful of occasions. She would have liked to journey to the Dawsons' ranch more often, especially while Emma had been staying with them, but Abby's parents hadn't allowed her to travel the five-mile distance on her own. With her father occupied with the mercantile and a good deal of her mother's time spent on her various social commitments, there had been few opportunities for the Warners to make the trip from town out to the ranch and back.

"Thank you for asking me to join you," she said, breaking the companionable silence that had descended upon the wagon.

Elias adjusted his hat to shade his eyes. "It's my pleasure. I like having your company."

His words warmed her, and she hugged them close to her heart.

When the wagon reached the crest of a hill, the ranch buildings and fenced pastures of sun-browned grasses came into view, stretched out in the valley below them. Wispy smoke rose from the chimney of the log cabin, indicating they would find someone at home. Mattie, most certainly, and Abby suspected that Josiah wouldn't stray far from his wife's side. From what she'd seen of them in town, Josiah was diligent in ensuring Mattie's safety and comfort while she was in a delicate condition.

Elias clucked to the horse, steering the wagon down the hill. A few minutes later, they reached the stream and clattered across the wooden bridge that spanned the water. As they neared the cabin, the front door opened and Mattie appeared in the doorway. She stepped out onto the porch, watching their approach.

"Josiah and I weren't expecting you today, but this is a pleasant surprise," she remarked when Elias drew the buckboard to a halt near the bottom of the wooden stairs leading up to the porch. A slight frown marred her brow. "There isn't anything wrong, I hope."

"Nothing except Emma missing her aunt and uncle. I should have brought her for a visit much sooner," Elias replied with a sheepish grin.

A smile wreathing her face in return, Mattie came down the porch steps and moved toward Elias's side of the wagon. "I'll not argue with that." Once Elias had climbed down from the buckboard, she greeted him with hug. "I appreciate you bringing Emma out here to the ranch to see us." She turned toward Abby. "Did you perchance have a hand in it?"

"Not at all. It was entirely Elias's idea. And he was kind enough to invite me to accompany him and Emma."

Mattie appeared surprised by the revelation—but obviously pleased by it, as well.

Abby stood, preparing to make her way to the ground from the high wagon seat, only to be brought up short as she searched for a safe method to disembark with a baby in her arms.

"Wait for me to come around and help you down," Elias insisted, plainly having noted her dilemma.

He tied the horse's reins to the hitching post and rounded the wagon to reach Abby's side. Mattie followed a few steps behind him.

Elias reached up and lifted his daughter from Abby's hold. He passed the baby into Mattie's outstretched arms and then extended his hand toward Abby to assist her down from the wagon.

She laid her fingers across his palm, and warmth

suffused her skin as his hand curled around hers. All too soon he released her, the moment after her feet had touched the ground. She felt a chill of loss when he moved away from her, but she quickly pushed the disquieting sensation from her mind.

Turning her attention to Mattie, she noticed the other woman looking at something behind Abby. She glanced over her shoulder, trying to follow the direction of Mattie's gaze and figure out what had caught her attention.

She expected to perhaps see Mattie's husband walking toward them, but there was no sign of him. Abby spotted nothing of particular interest apart from the barn and other outbuildings.

"Is Josiah in the barn, working with his horses?" Elias questioned.

"No. He's tracking the mountain lion that has been stalking our livestock and threatening the horses," Mattie replied. "He should be back soon, though. Come on inside." She shifted Emma on her hip and started toward the cabin.

Abby fell into step beside her, with Elias trailing behind them.

They reached the porch and ascended the short flight of stairs, but Mattie didn't move to open the front door. Instead, she stopped and turned to scan the surrounding countryside once again, worrying her bottom lip between her teeth. "Where is he, Lord?" she murmured under her breath. "He should've returned by now."

Abby suspected that the other woman hadn't intended for her words to be overheard, but Abby had caught them nonetheless. She couldn't let them pass by without a response. "Do you think Josiah has run into trouble?"

"I pray not. I'm probably making much ado about nothing." Though Mattie attempted to downplay the issue, forcing a smile into place, her concern over her husband's continued absence was readily apparent in the dark shadows dimming her eyes.

Abby feared that such worry wasn't good for the mother-to-be and her unborn child, but she didn't know how to lessen Mattie's anxiety for Josiah.

"How about I just go and look for him?" Elias volunteered.

Mattie hesitated for a moment before replying. "I don't want to put you to any unnecessary bother due to my fretting. I'm sure he's fine."

"It's no bother," he assured her. "If it will help put your mind at ease, I'll gladly go. Did you notice in which direction he went?"

"I watched him walk out past the barn and head toward the trees on the far side of that pasture." She pointed to the south.

Elias nodded in acknowledgement, then backtracked to the wagon and retrieved the rifle he'd brought along as a precaution.

Abby breathed a small sigh of relief that he wouldn't be setting off into possible danger without a means of protection.

She wondered whether Elias felt as much concern over his brother's well-being at this moment as Mattie did. If that were the case, he certainly hid it better than Josiah's wife.

Abby prayed that nothing dire had befallen Josiah.

"Try not to worry too much, Mattie," Elias said. "Josiah's most likely just lost track of the time. I'm sure that we'll both be back before you know it." But the impact of his comforting words was somewhat dampened when his next move was to check that his rifle was loaded—an action that probably had done nothing to quiet Mattie's worry for her husband.

Abby couldn't suppress a pang of apprehension for Elias's safety as he set out alone along the route his brother had taken.

"Be careful," she called out to him.

"I will." The wind carried his promise back to her.

She stood motionless on the porch, her gaze locked on his retreating figure. All she could do was send a prayer Heavenward for the Lord to watch over him and keep him from harm.

Elias had traveled a mere hundred yards from the cabin when he saw movement out of the corner of his eye, at the edge of the tree line off to his right.

Swiveling his head in that direction, he experienced a rush of relief at the sight of his brother and changed course to meet him.

Almost immediately, he realized something was very wrong.

Josiah's unsteady gait—combined with the awkward way he held his rifle, the gun barrel nearly dragging along the ground—set off warning bells in Elias's head. And as the younger man moved closer to Elias, he discovered much more cause for alarm.

Beads of sweat covered Josiah's brow, and his skin

had a gray undertone. His normally bright blue gaze was glassy and unfocused.

"Josiah? What happened to you?" He didn't see any visible injury.

Without uttering a single word, Josiah slowly sunk to his knees and then pitched forward. Elias barely got to his brother in time to prevent him from sprawling face-first into the dirt at his feet.

He sucked in a shocked breath when he got a look at Josiah's back. His shirt was ripped into shreds and soaked with blood. The waistband of his dark trousers was likewise wet with blood.

It seemed to be everywhere—so much blood that it obscured Elias's view, blotting out everything else. There was too much of it to properly gauge the extent of the damage—beyond knowing that it had to be bad.

Bile rose in Elias's throat. He'd seen his fair share of wounds during his time as a doctor, but this was his baby brother. It wasn't the blood and torn flesh that caused the sick feeling in his stomach—it was the fact that it was Josiah who had been savaged. Josiah who could all too easily die from his injuries. Even if he survived the loss of blood and possible internal damage he might have suffered, there was always the danger of infection setting in later.

Lord, please, don't take him from me, too, Elias pleaded.

He didn't think he could bear another loss on top of the grief he'd already endured, the pain he'd barely survived—*couldn't* have survived without his brother's loving, unending support.

One thought pushed all others aside. He couldn't permit his brother to die. He couldn't let it come to that. He had to get Josiah back to the house and tend to him as quickly as possible.

"Hang on, little brother. Stay with me. I've got you. Don't give up on me now, you hear?" Placing his shoulder under Josiah's arm, Elias lifted his brother to his feet and wrapped an arm around his waist, supporting most of his weight.

Josiah grunted at the movement, which had likely caused further agony to the ravaged muscles in his back. He swayed, even with Elias's assistance, as though fighting to stay conscious.

The progress was agonizingly slow as they made their way back toward the cabin. Elias felt Josiah's precious lifeblood seeping through the material of his shirt-sleeve, warm and sticky against the arm he had locked around Josiah's waist, its coppery scent heavy in the air surrounding them.

His heart was filled with urgency to move faster, but he had to stick to a pace that Josiah could manage or risk doing even more harm to him. Elias glanced ahead and felt daunted by the vast distance remaining.

He saw Abby running toward him and Josiah. She'd left Mattie standing on the porch, holding Emma.

Mattie hugged the baby close to her, as if drawing comfort from the little one.

When Abby reached them, she ducked under Josiah's free arm on the side opposite from Elias, offering her support.

"Be careful of his upper back," Elias cautioned her.

Heeding the warning, she placed her hands gingerly

and then helped Elias more or less carry his brother across the expanse of grass-covered ground.

They were able to move faster with her help. Still, it seemed to take an eternity before they neared the log cabin.

Elias noticed the ashen cast of Mattie's face and the agonizing fear that filled her eyes. Despite her obvious distress, she didn't hesitate in the face of crisis and opened the front door wide as the trio climbed the porch steps.

She gasped when she got a look at the dark red blood staining the back of Josiah's once-white shirt, and her hand flew to cover her mouth. Tears rolled down her cheeks unchecked.

"We need to stop the bleeding and clean the wounds," Elias stated as calmly as he was able in an attempt to focus her attention away from her terror and toward practical matters instead.

Mattie scrubbed the tears from her face with her free hand. Though more fell to take their place, she obviously fought to regain control of her emotions. "Take him into the bedroom and lay him on the bed," she directed.

Josiah voiced a weak protest about ruining the wedding-ring quilt that had belonged to Mattie's late parents.

"Never mind about the bedding!" she cried, and then repeated her order for Josiah to be laid down, brooking no further arguments.

Once he'd been settled on his stomach atop the quilt, she passed Emma into Abby's arms and sunk to her knees on the floor at her husband's bedside.

Grabbing hold of Josiah's hand, she clung to it and turned an imploring look toward Elias. "You have to help him. Please."

I don't know if I can. Elias lowered his gaze to his brother's torn and bloodied back. Would this grievous wound prove to be beyond his ability to mend?

"You must try," Abby insisted, as though sensing his doubts.

There had never been a thought in his mind that he wouldn't do all he could for his brother. "I will." But he left it unsaid that his efforts might not be enough. Though he'd do everything in his power, he feared that he would still fail—that he wouldn't be able to save his brother and Josiah would die.

Just as all his efforts hadn't been enough to save Rebecca.

A dull pain throbbed above Elias's left eye. His heart thudded heavily in his chest.

He wasn't ready to hold another life in his hands. But neither could he stand by and do nothing when his brother was in desperate need of Elias's medical training and knowledge.

Josiah had a wife and unborn child depending on him. Depending on Elias not to fail them this time, to restore Josiah to health. Needing Elias to make this turn out all right.

Lord, please...

Elias couldn't even articulate his fractured thoughts, but the Lord knew what was in his heart. Knew all the anguish he felt at this moment and what he feared it would do to him if he lost his brother. God would supply the courage and fortitude he'd need to see this through.

The wooden floor creaked beneath Abby's feet as she crossed the room to stand by his side. She placed her hand on his shoulder. "You're not in this alone. Tell me what I can do to assist you."

He drew strength from her support and her gentle touch. Breathing deeply to gain a semblance of calm over the chaos of his emotions, he stepped back into the role he'd forsaken more than a year ago.

"Boil some water to clean the wounds." When she nodded, he turned toward Josiah's wife. "Mattie, do you have any clean linens?"

"Of course." Despite the catch in her voice and the tears on her cheeks, her expression firmed with resolve.

Elias knew that she did better with a task, and it would help distract her from her fear.

With no small show of reluctance, Mattie let go of her hold on Josiah's hand and moved to a bureau to pull open the top drawer. Meanwhile Abby left the room to see to her own task, taking Emma with her.

Mattie returned to the bedside with a stack of folded cotton bedsheets and started tearing them into strips without any prompting from Elias.

He took several of the long sections of fabric and pressed them against the deep furrows on Josiah's back to stanch the flow of blood, eliciting a pained groan from the younger man.

Elias blocked out the sound, as well as thoughts about the added torment he was inflicting on his brother, and focused on what had to be done. "I'm going to need a sterilized needle and a long length of thread to stitch up these wounds," he said, addressing his words to Mattie once again.

"My sewing basket's in the other room." She hurried out of the bedroom to retrieve it.

When Abby arrived carrying a pot of steaming water several minutes later, Elias removed the red-stained pieces of cotton fabric and cut away Josiah's ruined shirt, checking to see that the blood flowing from the wounds had slowed.

A trio of deep gouges striped his bare back, plainly made by the claws of some large wild animal. Elias suspected they were from the mountain lion Josiah had been tracking.

Moving away from the bed, he directed Abby to pour a bit of the hot water into the porcelain basin, which he used to wash his hands. Then he crossed the floor to reach his brother's side once more, seized another strip of clean cloth and set to work gently wiping the gore from Josiah's back.

"I'd better go and see to Emma," Abby broke into the silence that had descended on the small group hovered around Josiah's prone form. "I left her alone in the front room."

Elias spared her barely a glance as she departed. "It doesn't seem that any of his vital organs have been nicked, thank God." Once he'd thoroughly cleansed his brother's wounds with soap, he accepted the sewing needle Mattie had sterilized over a flame and threaded with a length of strong thread.

"This is going to hurt like the blazes," he warned his brother, regretting the fact that all his medical supplies were packed away back in Silver Springs, five miles from here, in an unused clinic, gathering dust. "I'm sorry I don't have any anesthetic to give you first."

"Just get on with it and do what you've gotta do," Josiah gritted out between clenched teeth.

Mattie reached for his hand again and clasped it between both of hers. A glance at her face told Elias that what came next would be almost as excruciating for her to watch as it would be for her husband to endure. But he couldn't dwell on that now.

He pressed the edges of torn flesh together and pushed the needle through muscle and skin…and tried not to think about any of it. He concentrated on placing a neat row of stitches rather than fixating on all the things that could go wrong, such as possible infection, fever or festering of the wounds—or the horrific idea that it might already be too late for his brother.

Elias refused to give even a moment's credence to those kinds of thoughts.

He bent his head to focus solely on the task at hand, shoving all fear and doubts from his mind. They wouldn't help his brother. Or Mattie.

Sweat formed along Elias's hairline and rolled down his temple as he finished sewing up the first laceration. He used his forearm to wipe the trickle of moisture from his brow, then moved on to the next deep gash.

He took heart from the fact that Josiah was still conscious despite the pain and copious blood loss. Though that might have more to do with Josiah's steely determination than as any sort of indicator as to the severity of his condition. Still, if his brother had the will to fight to get well, he stood a much better chance of making a full recovery.

Finally, Elias tied off the last stitch and snipped the thread. He covered the wounds with bandages made from leftover sections of shredded bedsheet and wrapped additional strips of fabric around Josiah's torso to hold the folded cotton pads in place.

As he straightened from his stooped position, the tight muscles across his back protested the movement. He wondered how much time had passed. How long had he spent hunched over the bed while he tended to his brother?

A clock ticked on the mantel in the other room, but it was too far away for him to read its face. He braced his hands against his spine to stretch out the soreness that had settled in his lower back and then glanced toward the west-facing window.

The sun had sunk low on the horizon and would be setting in another few hours.

Mattie hadn't let go of her husband's hand yet. But Elias had done all he physically could for Josiah, for the moment.

He laid his palm on his brother's shoulder above the bandaging. "You still with me, Josiah?"

"Yeah. I'm still here." The reply was softly spoken but unmistakable.

"Good man." Elias squeezed his brother's shoulder gently. "How are you doing?"

"It feels as though my whole back's on fire. But at least I'm not dead. My heart's still beating, and I'm still breathing."

Elias prayed to God that it would stay that way. Prayed that he had done enough to save his brother's life, with the Lord's help. He couldn't—he wouldn't—believe anything else.

I leave the rest in Your hands, Lord.

Elias had to hold on to hope and trust in Him.

That trust came easier than it would have a week or even a day ago. Surely, it was only due to the Almighty that he'd come here when he had, arriving at the ranch at the exact moment Josiah needed him. That it had been *this* day out of all the days he could have chosen to pay a visit to Josiah and Mattie. That he had been placed in a position to help his brother.

Such a precise set of circumstances could only happen through divine providence. *Thank you, Lord.*

Chapter Fourteen

Abby had kept Emma occupied playing with an assortment of items on the floor a safe distance from the wood cookstove. But all the while, she'd stolen glances at the open doorway leading into the bedroom where Elias tended to his brother.

The minutes ticked past, seeming to stretch on forever before Elias walked back into the front room to join Abby and his daughter.

Mattie had stayed with her husband, and when Abby craned her neck to see around the door frame she glimpsed the other woman settled on a chair that had been positioned by the head of the bed. One of Mattie's hands was entwined with Josiah's where it lay atop the quilt while her other hand curved around her distended middle, over the place their child rested. She rubbed circles on the mound of her stomach, though Abby wasn't certain whether the action was meant to soothe the baby or Mattie herself. Perhaps both of them.

When Abby had first set eyes on Josiah's injuries, her stomach had churned sickly, and she'd been forced to look away in a hurry. Dread and horror had filled her over his condition, and those sensations remained with her still. But that was nothing compared to what Mattie and Elias must be experiencing in this moment, witnessing a husband and brother felled.

"Is he going to be all right?" She spoke quietly to Elias so that her voice wouldn't carry to the couple a dozen feet away in the bedroom.

"He's holding strong, but it's too soon to say for sure whether he'll recover," Elias answered in a low tone. "He's not out of danger yet."

"We have to have faith that he'll get better, that he's going to be well again, given enough time." She had no experience with wounds of this sort on which to base her assertion, but it seemed to her that a situation such as this called for a bit of optimism.

Already, there was one bright spot shining through in the darkness. Elias had taken on the task of doctoring once more, displaying no outward hints of uncertainty in his abilities after more than a year's gap in tending patients. Almost as though he'd never walked away from his professional calling.

Despite appearances, she suspected that it had cost him greatly to face down and overcome his inner turmoil when it was his brother's life hanging in the balance. But he hadn't hesitated. Hadn't allowed any personal misgivings to stand in the way of rendering aid to Josiah. He'd placed nothing ahead of healing his brother.

She admired Elias for the will and fortitude that it must have required of him. Surely, his courage would be rewarded with Josiah restored to health soon.

Only time would tell. All any of them could do for now was pray. Abby took a few moments and silently beseeched the Lord to heal Josiah.

Elias bent and picked up Emma, tucking her against his side, weariness and anguish heavy on his features. "I'm worried about infection setting in, and I came ill-equipped for this crisis. We need to return to town as quick as we can so that I can retrieve some medicine from the supply stored at the clinic." He held out a hand to Abby, and once she'd placed her fingers in his, he pulled her to her feet. "I want to get back here before sundown."

"Of course. We'll return to Silver Springs without delay."

Abby guessed that the drive into town and back would take them an hour or two, at least, even if he pushed the rented horse to move as quickly as the plodding animal could bear.

She hated to think of Mattie being left here all alone to watch over her injured husband. "Perhaps I should stay with Mattie—"

"I've already kept you away from town longer than I had intended. Your parents are probably wondering about your whereabouts as it is now. Before long, they'll be growing concerned that something's happened to you." He gave her no opportunity to reply before he started herding her toward the front door.

She glanced over her shoulder in the direction of the bedroom. "Shouldn't we let Mattie and Josiah know that we're going?"

"I've already told Mattie that we'd be departing just as soon as I collected you and Emma," Elias assured

Abby. "The quicker we leave, the quicker I'll be able to return."

Although she felt peculiar about leaving without saying goodbye, she supposed it would be better not to intrude on Mattie and Josiah at this moment. And she certainly didn't want to cause any delay in Josiah receiving the medicine that was vital to his recovery.

She accompanied Elias out to the wagon and clambered onto the bench seat without assistance. Elias handed his daughter up to Abby. She settled Emma on her lap while he circled to the far side of the wagon and joined them, then took up the reins.

"I have a favor to ask of you, Abby," he said without preamble, once they were underway.

"Anything."

His eyes shifted to his daughter. "Could you look after Emma for me when I return to the ranch?"

"Of course."

"Thank you. I appreciate it." He turned his gaze back to the road ahead and adjusted his hat to shield his eyes from the slanting rays of the late-afternoon sun. "Once we arrive in Silver Springs, I'll stop at the clinic to pick up the medicine and pack enough clothing and other necessities for Emma to last several days. Then I'll drop the two of you off at your house on my way out of town."

The "several days" part of his statement brought Abby up short. She'd assumed he meant for her to take charge of Emma for a few hours, or overnight at most—if he decided against making the trip back home in the dark. But clearly, he had something else in mind.

She opened her mouth to question him about it, but he continued before she got a single word out.

"I don't know for certain just how long I'll be gone. With Josiah laid up, Mattie will need someone to tend to the chores around the ranch and see to the horses' training in his stead. She can't handle everything by herself on top of nursing Josiah, especially not in her delicate condition. I intend to stay with Josiah and Mattie for as long as they have need of me, until he's back on his feet."

Though Abby could well understand Elias's desire to aid his brother and sister-in-law during this time, she sensed there was more to his decision than that. More motivating him than what he was willing to admit, perhaps even to himself. She had a strong suspicion that he sought to remain close by his younger brother until he'd assured himself Josiah was truly on the mend and would make a full recovery.

With worries for his brother's state of health weighing utmost in Elias's mind and requiring much of his attention, having a baby underfoot would only serve as an additional burden, pulling Elias away from the person who needed to come first just now. Josiah had to be Elias's priority until he was out of danger.

And Mattie certainly should not have to concern herself with tending a small child on top of caring for her injured husband, taking her single-minded focus away from him.

"I'm happy to help in any way I can. But Mother might get the wrong idea when she discovers Emma's staying with us for an indeterminate length of time," Abby cautioned him.

The older woman hadn't given up her aim to see Emma placed in the Warners' care permanently.

"I'll be sure to set her straight on that point if she should mistake my intent, have no fear," Elias said, dismissing the warning.

He set a fast pace back to town, and they reached the outskirts in under half an hour. A short time later, they had collected the necessary items from Elias's place and were pulling up in front of the Warners' house.

He didn't linger after he'd carried Emma's things inside. Leaning in close to Abby, he gave his daughter a kiss goodbye. "I'll be back for her just as soon as I'm able. Take good care of my baby girl for me while I'm gone," he requested, as he moved toward the wagon and hoisted himself onto the bench seat.

"I will. You don't have to worry about Emma. I'll watch over her. She'll be fine with me until you return." Abby hitched the baby up on her hip and patted her back. "Go to your brother and Mattie. Focus on them and their ranch. They need you now."

He nodded. "I'll be seeing you again soon. Until then." He touched the brim of his hat in farewell and clucked to the horse, setting the buckboard in motion.

Abby watched as he drove toward the edge of town. She headed into the house with Emma only after Elias had disappeared from sight.

Elias stood motionless at his brother's bedside, his gaze centered on the steady rise and fall of Josiah's back, even after the younger man had dropped off into a fitful sleep.

"How long must we wait for the medicine to take

effect? When will we know whether it has done its job and the danger of infection is past?" Mattie asked from her place at Josiah's side, her hand clenching her husband's, though his fingers now laid limp within her grasp.

"Not for some hours yet," Elias answered, giving her the plain truth. "For the time being, we should leave him to rest."

She nodded her head in response but didn't release Josiah's hand or shift from her spot.

Elias gently disengaged her hold and steered her from the bedroom. "Why don't you sit down at the table while I rustle up something to eat?"

He suspected that she'd gone the whole of the afternoon and evening without putting any food in her stomach, due to her anxious state. As for himself, it had been hours since the meal he'd consumed around noon and was well past suppertime now. Hunger gnawed at his insides.

"I don't think I could swallow a bite," Mattie protested. "My throat's closed up and my stomach's a mass of knots."

Pulling out a chair, he applied gentle pressure to her shoulder. She dropped onto the seat like a rag doll.

He didn't bother to argue with her as he prepared a simple meal. But when she tried to push away the full plate of food he set down in front of her, he stayed her with a hand on her arm.

"You need to eat in order to keep up your strength." When it looked as though she intended to debate the point, he settled the matter in a way she wouldn't be able to refute. "If not for Josiah's sake, then think of the baby," he urged, hitting her with both shotgun barrels at once.

Mattie scowled, undoubtedly vexed by his high-handedness, but she took up her fork without further objections.

Though he wasn't a great cook, he'd learned the basics necessary to get by during his childhood. There had been little choice once his father had taken him away from his mother.

Mattie ate in silence, managing to force down a half dozen bites of food before she laid down her fork. She returned to the bedroom to take up her position at Josiah's side once more while Elias finished his own supper, then saw to washing up the dishes and cleaning the kitchen. Once those tasks were complete, he followed in Mattie's wake and entered the bedroom.

He cleared his throat to gain her attention, waiting to speak until she turned her head in his direction. "I'm going out to the barn to see to the horses. If you need me, just holler and I'll come right back. I don't expect to be gone long, but it should give you sufficient time to change into your nightclothes and prepare for bed."

She nodded once before shifting her gaze back to her husband's still form.

Elias headed outside and caught the reins of the rented horse from Mr. Rothmeier's livery stable. He had left the animal harnessed to the buckboard after his return to the ranch, when more urgent matters had taken precedence.

He led the horse toward the barn, where he unhitched it from the wagon traces and settled it in a vacant stall with a heaping helping of oats. Making quick work of the remaining chores, he crossed the short distance back to the cabin and found that Mattie had heeded his suggestion to complete her nightly routine while his absence had afforded her a bit of privacy.

He joined her at Josiah's bedside, standing next to the wooden ladder-back chair she occupied. It didn't look to be a comfortable seat for a nightlong vigil. Not that he intended to allow an expectant mother to stay up until dawn.

"You should try to get some rest, Mattie."

She shook her head. "I doubt I'd be able to fall asleep. Besides, I don't want to jostle Josiah by climbing into bed next to him."

"Go and lie down on the pallet in the other room," he pressed her.

She had set up the makeshift bed for Elias after learning he would be staying with them for a time.

However, he had no plans to make use of it tonight. "I'll sit up with Josiah and keep an eye on him during the night."

"I suppose it's much more sensible for him to have a doctor tending to him rather than a fretful wife hovering uselessly about at his side."

"You're far from useless. I'm sure he'd much prefer waking up to your face than mine. Unfortunately for him, he doesn't get a vote. He's got no choice but to make do with me instead."

Her mouth turned up slightly at the corners in response to his words, but the tiny smile soon faded and anxiety darkened her expression.

"Try not to let worry keep you from sleep," he admonished. "You and the little one need your rest."

The last of her resistance dissolved at the mention of her unborn child. "Yes, Doctor," she replied meekly.

Surprisingly, her use of his professional title didn't make him uncomfortable. Though he had long denied the truth to himself and turned his back on his calling for over a year, his avoidance hadn't changed who he was, who he would always be, no matter that he'd tried to ignore it and done his best to forget. He was Dr. Elias Dawson.

Mattie reached out a hand to stroke Josiah's hair off his forehead, then leaned forward and placed a kiss on his temple. With a weary sigh, she stood up. For a moment, she paused motionless, looking down at her husband.

Finally, she turned to face Elias. "Thank you for being here."

"There's no need to thank me. He's my brother." And every bit as important to Elias as he was to Mattie. "I couldn't have done anything less."

"I'm grateful, nonetheless." She rose up on tiptoe and kissed his cheek. "Good night, Elias," she murmured as she left the bedroom on quiet, slippered feet.

He sat down in the chair Mattie had vacated at Josiah's bedside.

She hadn't closed the door between the two rooms, and the sounds of her moving around as she settled in for the night carried to him easily. The view through the open doorway was thrown into shadow when she extinguished the oil lamp on the kitchen table. A few minutes later, silence descended inside the cabin.

He turned down the wick on the lantern positioned at the side of the bed until only a tiny flame still flickered, allowing him just enough dim light to see by. Hopefully, it wouldn't disturb Josiah or Mattie's sleep.

Elias had no difficultly staying awake. His head was filled with too many thoughts for him to find any rest. So much had happened in such a short span of time. It seemed an eternity since he'd discovered Josiah wounded and bleeding, barely able to stand, when in fact it had been a matter of mere hours.

There was no point in dwelling on his brother's injury, however. Doing so only served to unsettle Elias further. With a conscious effort, he turned his mind to other things. Such as wondering how his daughter and Abby were faring without him.

He reckoned that it must be nearing midnight by now. Emma would be fast asleep, lost in peaceful slumber. But how had she reacted to his departure earlier that evening? Entrusting her to Abby was what he'd deemed the best possible option open to him under the circumstances, since he needed to devote his full attention and energy toward treating Josiah. Still, it'd been a wrench for Elias to drive away from his daughter and leave her behind in town. It had felt as though he'd left a piece of his heart back in Silver Springs.

He prayed that their separation had been easier on his baby girl, that it hadn't upset her unduly, as Mattie and Josiah's parting had all those weeks ago. He hated to think of Emma distressed. He imagined Abby rocking his daughter as she cried herself to sleep. The thought of Emma's tears felt like a knife stabbing in to his heart.

Several hours later, Josiah shifted restlessly on the bed. Elias turned up the lantern wick once more, flooding the bedroom with bright light. He laid his hand on his brother's back and found Josiah's skin burning with fever.

"Josiah, can you hear me?"

The younger man mumbled something, but the words were unintelligible.

Retrieving the pitcher of water and the bowl from the bureau top, Elias wet a cloth and began bathing Josiah's heated skin in an effort to bring down his high temperature.

As he toiled alone, tending to his brother, he wished for Abby's presence by his side, yearned to have her support and encouragement during this difficult time. She was always a voice of optimism against the dark thoughts preying on his mind. Her knack for refusing to allow him to give in to despair never ceased to amaze him.

That her presence, or lack thereof, had such a profound effect on him caused a twinge of disquiet, but he reasoned that he was making too much of nothing. There was no call to let it trouble him. He had grown used to Abby's positive outlook lightening even the grimmest situations and felt its absence now. But that didn't signify anything else, wasn't an indication that he had more than friendly feelings for her.

Though he admired Abby and felt a measure of affection toward her, that didn't mean she had gained access to his heart. Or ever would.

And even if by some small, unlikely chance she found a way to breach his defenses, it would lead nowhere.

He couldn't allow whatever fondness he felt for Abby

grow into something more, no matter how highly he'd come to regard her. He wouldn't willingly lay himself open to further misery and pain, wouldn't risk his heart a second time. He never again wanted to love a woman so deeply that he would be devastated by her loss.

Forcing those unwanted thoughts from his mind, he focused on his brother.

Throughout the course of the dark early-morning hours before daybreak, Elias continued to apply the wet cloth to Josiah's fevered skin, repeating the process again and again. By the time dawn had arrived and pale light spilled through the window, his muscles ached from the constant movement of administering to his brother. But Josiah's fever had broken at last. *Praise God.*

Elias's efforts seemed to have made a difference. He bowed his head and gave thanks to the Lord for his brother's improved health.

Chapter Fifteen

Elias shifted from one foot to the other as he stood on the Warners' front porch, waiting for somebody inside to answer his knock. Hoping he'd be greeted by Abby rather than her mother.

When the door opened, a huge grin split his face at the sight of his daughter snuggled in Abby's arms. Emma squealed with delight the moment she spotted him and launched herself toward him.

"Whoa there, baby girl." He grabbed ahold of her before she ended up taking a tumble. "Careful now."

"Papa!" She wrapped her arms around his neck and burrowed her head under his chin.

Abby laughed at Emma's exuberant display. "She's missed her papa, in case you haven't already guessed."

"I've missed her, too." Every day he was away, he'd yearned to cuddle his daughter close and feel her warm weight tucked against him, as she was now.

He placed a kiss on the top of her head and then raised his gaze to Abby.

She was dressed in a simple cotton gown of spring

green, with a smudged apron tied around her slim waist. Wisps of hair escaped from the knot secured at the back of her head, and a streak of what appeared to be flour decorated her cheek. Obviously, he'd interrupted her while she was in the middle of some baking.

"I'm sorry if I've come at an inconvenient time."

"You haven't," Abby denied. "Emma and I are glad to see you. You're always welcome."

"At least when your mother's not home." He glanced past Abby, fearing he might see his former mother-in-law bearing down on him. "She isn't here, is she?"

"No. You're safe for now. She's not due back for another hour or so. Come on in."

Accepting the invitation, he stepped over the threshold. The sweet scent of warm spices and sugar filled the air. He followed Abby through the house and into the kitchen.

Unsurprisingly, he found that everything had been abandoned in the midst of a task. Items were strewn across the table in haphazard disarray.

Abby moved to the far side of the table to pick up where she'd left off. "Please pardon the mess and pull up a chair. I'll be done in no time if you keep Emma occupied while I work."

He sat down on the opposite side of the table from Abby so he wouldn't be in her way and settled his daughter on his lap. "What are you making?"

"A pair of pies." She sprinkled a bit of flour on the wooden tabletop before applying her rolling pin to a lump of dough.

"Peach pies?" he questioned, a hopeful note ringing clearly in his voice.

Her expression turned rueful as her gaze met his. "Sorry, no. They're apple pies with a crumble topping. Or they will be when I'm finished with them. I didn't know you would be coming today. Once I get the pies in the oven, it will take me only a few minutes to pack up Emma's things."

"Actually, I'm not ready to take Emma back home just yet. I merely came by to check and see how you two were doing. I'll need to return to the ranch shortly." He smoothed Emma's cap of silky red curls. "If it's not too much trouble, I'd appreciate it if you could keep her here with you for a bit longer."

Abby's eyebrows knit together above pale blue eyes clouded with worry. "I assumed that this trip into town meant your brother was doing well. Is that not the case?"

"He's on the mend," Elias rushed to assure her. "You weren't wrong about that. But it'll be another week or more before the stitches can be removed. Until then, he's liable to rip open the wounds if he attempts to do his usual chores around the ranch—which he absolutely will if I'm not there to stop him. Mattie would not be pleased with him, or me, for allowing that to happen."

Abby nodded in agreement. "I see your point. She's been through more than enough already. I'm happy to continue taking care of Emma for however long you're needed elsewhere."

"Thank you. That's a weight off my mind."

Her cheeks flushed light pink, and a smile curved her lips as she returned her focus to rolling out the dough for the piecrusts.

Emma stretched out her arms toward the rolling pin.

Elias resituated the baby on his lap, keeping her little fingers out of mischief. "Once the stitches come out and Josiah's able to resume his duties, things should get back to normal fairly quick. As long as he doesn't try to tangle with any more mountain lions from now on, he should do fine. I went out and tracked down the one he had the run-in with—"

"You did *what*? Have you lost your wits?!" she demanded, taking him aback with her vehement reaction.

She seemed mad as a hornet, though he wasn't even sure what offense he could have committed to set her off like that.

Abby's heart pounded, and she had trouble catching her breath as she envisioned what could have happened to Elias. "You saw what that animal did to your brother. You spent the better part of an hour repairing the damage it inflicted. How could you—?" She couldn't even finish the sentence as her throat closed up with horror.

The thought that he had willfully risked his life felt like a fist squeezing around her lungs and cutting off her air. She blinked rapidly as tears filled her eyes.

Elias leaned toward her, his expression earnest. "I had to protect my family and make sure that cat wouldn't pose a problem to Josiah and Mattie or their livelihood any longer."

"And what of Emma? What would have become of her? Did you give a thought to that?"

His eyebrows knit in confusion. "The mountain lion was a potential threat to her, as well," he replied, seeming to miss Abby's point.

She waved his words aside. "That's not what I meant.

Did you even once give a thought for what would become of your daughter if something had happened to you—if the mountain lion had harmed you? Killed you?" Had he considered what his death would have done to Abby? But why did she imagine that she should have factored into his decision-making anywhere? She pushed those questions from her mind and returned to her original one. "How could you be so careless of your own welfare when you have a child who depends on you?"

"I was never in any danger. Josiah told me he got off a shot and hit the mountain lion when it attacked him. I came across a blood trail running alongside the animal's tracks a few miles from the cabin and followed them. When I found the cat, it was already dead. Josiah's shot had found its mark, and though it took some time, the wound proved fatal in the end." He placed his hand on her arm in what he'd doubtlessly intended as a soothing gesture.

She wasn't in the mood to be soothed and jerked away from his touch. "But you didn't know that at the time when you set out! You went after a wounded wild animal alone, knowing how dangerous it could be, how hazardous it had already proven to be for your brother. Have you no regard for your own safety?"

"I promise I was careful, and I didn't take any unnecessary risks. As you can see, I'm perfectly well." He made a sweeping gesture in front of him with his hand, indicating that he was whole and unharmed. "You're making too much of this and fretting needlessly."

His assurances didn't calm her at all. She couldn't stop imagining the possibility that he might have been seriously injured—or worse. The nightmare images crowding her head left her feeling gutted, as though she was in real danger of losing something vital. It was almost more than she could bear.

Elias's well-being was of utmost importance to her. Having him in her life—even as nothing more than a brother-in-law and friend—was essential to her. If he'd been killed due to his foolhardy actions, his death would have left a void in her heart that she suspected no one and nothing else could ever hope to fill.

At that moment, she realized why just the thought of him hurt, his body lying lifeless, had made her feel as though her heart had been ripped wide open. She loved him.

But she shied away from revealing her vulnerability to him. She couldn't bear to endure the hurt she'd suffer if he took away all hope that her love might be returned.

"I'm sorry if it seemed as though I overreacted. I was merely concerned about the effect it would've had on Emma if things had gone wrong," she said, unwilling to let him know the depth of her own newly discovered feelings for him.

She wasn't foolish enough to expect that his feelings for her had become something more, just because hers had undergone a profound change. He loved Rebecca still, and that love might always stand between him and Abby.

Though she prayed that his heart would heal, that he'd open himself to love again one day, Abby had to face the possibility that he might never feel any deep emotion for her.

But she couldn't imagine herself married to any man

besides him. Nor could she envision starting a family with someone who wasn't Elias, though she desired children of her own.

Perhaps it was a part of God's plan that Abby would only ever be an aunt—never a mother. She'd have to resign herself to helping care for Emma and stepping in on the occasions when a feminine influence was needed in her niece's life, rather than raising her own brood. She'd pour all her love into her sister's daughter while quietly loving Rebecca's husband.

It was a disheartening prospect to think she might never have more than that. Of course, loving Emma was no small thing. But as to the rest, she prayed her life would go a different way.

Now wasn't the time to contemplate that, however, with Elias looking on and perhaps noticing something she would much rather he did not. She preferred for him to remain unaware of her innermost feelings while she came to grips with this life-altering realization.

Busying herself with the pie dough once more, she rolled it around the wooden rolling pin and transferred it to a pie tin. She pressed the dough into the bottom of the tin and cut off the excess, then pinched the edges along the rim.

She repeated the same process a second time, readying the other piecrust, and carried both tins to the counter that butted up against the cook stove. The move put her back to Elias, which meant she didn't have to worry about guarding her expression to make sure she gave nothing away.

Nonetheless, she tried to keep her attention focused strictly on the task in front of her.

She checked the apples cooking in a pot on the cast-iron stovetop and found them tender. Using potholders to protect her hands, she poured half the filling into each pie tin before sprinkling the sugared crumble over the top.

After she'd placed the pies in the oven, she stood facing the open window for a moment more. A slight breeze fluttered the curtains and lifted a strand of hair off her damp forehead.

Breathing in a fortifying breath of fresh air, she turned back to face Elias. "I'll take Emma now so you can get back to your brother's ranch."

"I suppose I should be heading out. I don't want to leave Mattie to cope on her own for too long." He shifted his hold on Emma and stood up.

Abby walked with them to the front door and stepped out onto the porch. Elias placed a kiss on his daughter's head and then passed her to Abby.

His gaze settled on Abby's face. Reaching up, he brushed his thumb across her cheek.

She was struck mute by the gentle touch. Had he read something in her expression?

Elias's hand fell away, and he cleared his throat. "You had a bit of flour there."

Her hopes deflated as he moved toward his mount.

He climbed into the saddle, glancing toward Abby and Emma one last time. "Take care until my return."

"Have a safe journey," Abby replied.

Once he had gone, she returned inside with Emma. But as she waited for the pies to bake, she gave her thoughts free rein at last.

While Elias stayed out at the ranch, Abby couldn't

help missing him. He had told his daughter that he'd missed her. But had he missed Abby, too? Had he left that particular sentiment unsaid in order to protect his heart, as she had done when she'd concealed the depth of her emotions from him? Or did his silence mean that his heart was closed to her?

What were his feelings toward her? Could they ever grow into love? Was there hope for her and Elias yet?

That they might be together one day was her most heartfelt prayer.

The following week, Elias sat in church with Emma on his lap and his brother and sister-in-law by his side. Josiah had recovered sufficiently to make the trip into town to attend Sunday service. His improved health had also allowed Elias's return home the day before yesterday, when he'd retrieved his daughter from the Warners.

Since then, he'd done a lot of thinking and had come to a decision about some long-overdue changes he needed to make in his life.

The preacher drew the sermon to a close and folded his hands atop his Bible. "Our new town doctor will be arriving in a few weeks," he said, before relaying the message Elias had asked him to deliver. "In the interim, Dr. Elias Dawson has kindly offered his services. He invites all those who have a medical need to visit him at the clinic for treatment of your ailments and injuries, starting tomorrow morning."

There was murmuring among the gathered parishioners at the surprise announcement, followed by much shifting and craning of necks as the people around Elias angled themselves to look in his direction. He felt the weight of countless curious eyes focused on him.

Abby turned in her seat in the pew directly ahead of the Dawsons and graced Elias with a radiant smile. It warmed him deep down inside, in the place that had been numbed for so long. The sweet glow of it thawed the last traces of ice from his heart.

Everyone else around him seemed to fade into the background in that moment of perfect accord with Abby. He cared about her good opinion, wanted her to think well of him, to respect and admire him—was resolved to earn her respect and admiration.

He intended to do whatever was within his power to restore the health of any who sought his aid while finding the strength to accept that the final determination between life and death was in the Lord's hands. It would mean reaching deep inside himself for the necessary courage to keep on moving forward, no matter the ultimate outcome. He was under no illusion that it would always be easy, but finally, he was in a place where he believed it possible for him to do that. Able to face what was ahead at long last.

He had let go of the guilt he'd felt for what he viewed as his failure and come to terms with the fact that some things were simply out of his control. And he had Abby to thank for that. She'd helped him see his way through to the truth.

The preacher regained the parishioners' attention and led them in a final prayer before sending his congregation on their way.

A few townspeople paused in the churchyard to exchange a handful of words with Elias, but then he found himself standing alone as Josiah and Mattie moved off to greet acquaintances they hadn't seen in a couple of weeks while Josiah had been recovering.

Elias scanned the small clusters of people surrounding him. His eyes alighted on Abby, standing a dozen yards from him. As though she'd sensed his gaze on her, she turned in his direction. He watched her break away from her mother's group and head toward him.

Emma reached out for her aunt when she drew near, and Elias transferred his daughter into Abby's outstretched arms.

Abby's pale blue eyes lit up like sunshine sparkling on the surface of a clear mountain lake as she greeted her niece.

She settled Emma on her hip and kissed the baby's head, then shifted her gaze to Elias. "I'm glad to hear that you'll be seeing patients again."

He didn't know quite what to do with his hands now that Emma was no longer in his arms. His fingers tapped out a restless tattoo against the leg of his trousers. "It was past time I made a change." And better belatedly than never.

"What brought about this decision? Was it aiding your brother in his time of need that made you realize there's so much more good you can do for others, as well?"

Somehow, it didn't come as much of a surprise to learn Abby knew him well enough that she could easily surmise the reasons behind his actions. It seemed as though she could see inside his heart. Perhaps that was why she'd never lost her faith in him, although he had harbored doubts within himself for much too long.

"Even though there's a new doctor set to arrive soon, he isn't here yet," he pointed out. "And it's a long trip to Bear Butte from here to see the doctor there. I hope to spare a few folks from having to make that journey. If someone else should suffer a serious injury like Josiah's, then bouncing along miles and miles of rutted wagon trails would be brutal agony for the wounded person—and sending a rider to fetch the doctor might take too much time.

"I want to be a help to some of these good people." He tipped his head to indicate the scattering of church-goers around him and Abby.

He counted himself fortunate that no casualties had occurred in the area during the past year while he'd allowed his personal tragedy to keep him from opening the clinic and putting his doctoring skills to good use. If the worst had happened, that would have been on him. And once the numbness of his grief had passed, it would've been nearly impossible for him to live with that.

Surely, it was due only to the grace of God that Elias didn't have another death on his conscience.

But would any of the townspeople be willing to give him a chance at this late date? He'd let so much time pass with no thought for the welfare of their community. Had he squandered the chance to earn their trust? With the new doctor scheduled to arrive soon, they might decide that there was a better choice in the offing and they'd prefer to wait for the other man to tend them.

As much as Elias desired to be of help to the local population, he could do so only if others allowed it.

"Will anyone turn up at the clinic tomorrow?" he asked, voicing his doubt aloud.

"They will," Abby assured him. She turned a considering look toward his daughter. "And you'll need someone to keep an eye on Emma while you're busy attending patients. I'm happy to come by tomorrow to take care of her for you."

"Aren't you needed at the mercantile? Doesn't your father expect you there in the morning?"

"Papa can get by without me." She shifted her hold on Emma and patted the baby's back. "I'm sure he won't mind once he hears the reason for my absence."

Elias thought about declining Abby's offer but realized that he wanted her there with him tomorrow, whether Emma needed watching or not. Though his daughter provided a very handy excuse. "Well, you can keep me company, at least. And take my mind off the lack of patients, if it comes to that." Which it very well might.

"It won't," she refuted. "I predict that you'll be inundated with people who have put off seeing a doctor because they didn't want to go all the way to Bear Butte."

He admired her certainty and wished he felt even a smidgen of it himself. He prayed she was correct in this, as she had been about so many other things in the past.

Chapter Sixteen

Long shadows stretched across the hardwood floorboards in Emma's bedroom above the clinic late the
next day as Abby lifted the baby from her cradle following her afternoon nap. Returning downstairs with
Emma, Abby settled her niece on the rag rug in the
kitchen with an upturned pot and a wooden spoon and
then resumed her preparations for supper.

Emma set to banging her spoon against the cast-
iron pot, making loud clanging sounds, which assured
Abby that the little one wasn't getting up to any mischief while her back was turned.

Checking that the roast with carrots and pearl on-
ions was done, she pulled it from the oven and left it to
rest on the back of the stovetop away from the hottest
part, then slid a baking sheet of biscuits into the oven.
After that, she spooned out the beef drippings from
the roast in to another pan to make into gravy for the
mashed potatoes.

A short time later, she heard the sound of boot heels

moving down the hall toward the kitchen. Glancing over her shoulder, she saw Elias appear in the doorway.

Throughout the hours he'd spent seeing to patients, Abby had felt a wellspring of gladness bubbling up inside her at this proof that he was taking purposeful steps to move beyond the tragedies in his past at last.

Even as she knew he would've done anything to spare his brother the recent pain he'd suffered from his near-fatal injury, Abby recognized that some good had come out of it. It had awakened the doctor inside of Elias.

She was heartened by the signs of Elias's healing and wished for nothing so much as to see him happy and contented once more. She wanted him to be the best possible father he could be for his child.

When Emma reached up toward him, he moved forward and hoisted her into his arms. He sat down at the kitchen table with his daughter tucked against his shirtfront. "I believe I'm done for the day. No one was left in the waiting area after I finished bandaging up a cut on Isaiah Greene's hand and sent him on his way."

It was a source of true joy for Abby to witness Elias's willingness to offer of himself and use his skills for the good of the citizens of Silver Springs. And as she'd guessed, a lack of patients hadn't proven to be a concern. There had been a steady stream of people turning up at the clinic since early that morning when the first arrivals had appeared shortly after breakfast time.

Elias leaned back in the chair with a sigh, seeming weary but pleased, as well. "Most likely, tomorrow won't be quite as busy. I reckon that a fair number of folks who had put off seeing a doctor previously have come and gone today."

"It could be that there's a greater number who waited to hear how things went for the others. You might have even more people coming to see you tomorrow," she pointed out.

"You could be right on both counts. Time will tell, I suppose," he replied noncommittally as Emma latched on to his hand and brought it to her mouth. "I noticed that this little one seemed to be a favorite topic of conversation amongst those in the waiting area earlier today. Several folks asked after her, including Mrs. Wheeler, who accompanied her youngest daughter, Helen. Apparently, Miss Wheeler's wedding day was in danger of being ruined by a summer cold."

"How so?"

"She was concerned that a dripping nose might send her groom fleeing from the altar before he spoke his vows. I assured her and her mother that Helen should be fully recovered in time for the ceremony on Saturday."

Elias jumped as Emma gnawed on his thumb and sharp baby teeth bit into tender skin. "Hey, take it easy on your papa, baby girl." Despite the admonishment, he didn't pull his hand away from her. "If today's events are anything to judge by, then I suspect that there'll be no shortage of women willing to look after Emma for me on the days when you're unavailable."

Abby tried to offer Emma her rag doll in place of her papa's bite-marked thumb, but the little girl refused to be diverted from her current teething remedy of choice. "Babies seem to have a special knack for breaking down walls and drawing people together."

Emma had certainly brought Abby and Elias closer over the course of the past two months.

And his neighbors had started to warm up to him, too, since he'd made the effort to meet them halfway. The first steps had been taken when he'd returned to church. Now that he'd embraced his profession again, the town was ready to welcome him with open arms.

The results had been just as restorative to Elias, himself. Already, Abby could see the positive effect his return to doctoring had had on him and those around him. It seemed to her that he found true contentment in helping others.

"I think it's wonderful that you've decided to open the clinic and start attending patients again. But what will you do after Dr. Michner arrives and takes over here?"

Though she didn't wish to think about it, she had to face the fact that Elias would be compelled to vacate this house in a matter of weeks in order to make way for the newcomer. Silver Springs wasn't a big enough town to require two doctors, and the clinic and residence had already been promised to the other man.

Elias's mouth turned down at the corners, indicating he hadn't figured things out that far ahead yet. He didn't respond to her query immediately, but to her mind, only one logical solution presented itself.

She took a deep breath and said the words that would leave her heart bleeding. "I suppose you'll have to find a post elsewhere." There were plenty of other places in Oregon Country that could use a doctor.

"I don't… I hadn't considered pulling up stakes and relocating…" He floundered to a halt, as though her words had placed him unexpectedly at a crossroads, and he was now uncertain which direction he should take.

But Abby had no such doubts.

Elias possessed knowledge and experience that was sorely needed in this rugged land. Surely it would be a sin for him not to use his God-given abilities in aid of his fellow man. The Lord was leading him down this path, back to his calling, and she had no doubt that he would ultimately follow the Lord's way. Aiding others however he was able, doing all the good he could.

Which would mean he'd move away from Silver Springs. And Emma would go along with him.

His brows pulled together in consternation, and he raked his hair away from his forehead with one hand. "I don't like the thought of taking Emma far away from her family. Away from Josiah and Mattie, and you. Especially you. I know how much she means to you."

Seeing him struggling with the opposing dictates of his heart and head, plainly troubled by this new realization of how his actions might affect her, she tried to make it easier on him. "You need to earn a living in order to provide for your daughter. I understand that. I would never expect you to put my wishes and wants ahead of what's best for you and Emma." No matter the pain their separation would cause her personally.

Unless…she went with them instead. She'd follow Elias to the ends of the earth if he asked it, and never once regret it.

It would be too presumptuous, however, for Abby to make the suggestion herself. Wouldn't it?

Still, he would need someone to take care of Emma while he saw to patients. And who better to act as his daughter's caregiver than Abby? Would he offer her that option? She'd latch on to it in an instant, if given half a chance.

"If I were to leave Silver Springs and settle in another town you'd be welcome to come and visit us any time you please," he assured her.

His words crushed her fledgling hopes once more. He saw her as a future guest—he wasn't inviting her to stay with them always. Clearly, it hadn't even crossed his mind that she might wish to join them on a more permanent basis.

Abby turned back to the stove to hide her reaction from him. Her thoughts weren't on the task in front of her, though the gravy was surely a mass of lumps after being left unattended for so long. She couldn't work up the effort to care that supper might be ruined.

She wanted to beg Elias to stay here in Silver Springs after all, but it would be for her own selfish reasons— to keep him and Emma close to her.

She had to let them go.

It seemed that he'd made significant strides toward getting beyond the loss of his wife these last several weeks, and Abby wouldn't stand in the way of him moving on with his life and embracing his true purpose merely because the divergent path ahead must lead to their parting.

Only now, when all hope was gone, did she recognize that she'd allowed herself to wish for the impossible. Though her logical mind had tried to rein in unrealistic dreams, in her heart, she'd entertained thoughts of so much more.

But she had to acknowledge the hard truth at last.

That Elias would never love her as she yearned for him to. He'd never want a life with her as his wife.

Lord, please, give me the grace to accept this.

Watching Abby as she tended to the pan on the stovetop, Elias was surprised to discover that the thought of leaving her behind created a curiously hollow sensation in his chest.

She, on the other hand, seemed to accept it without any overt expression of distress, as though none of this bothered her a bit. That couldn't be true…could it?

Though he had no doubt that she'd miss Emma something fierce, he couldn't help but wonder—would Abby feel the slightest twinge over *his* absence in her life?

He didn't care to examine too closely why that question should cause a sharp pang in his heart, so he changed the subject.

"Supper smells delicious. The aroma has been wafting through the front hall for the past hour, making my mouth water and my stomach rumble loud enough for the patients to hear. I'm starving. I've worked up quite an appetite in my first day back to doctoring, I don't mind saying."

She stirred the steaming liquid in the pan, her movements brisk. "Well, everything should be ready in just a few more minutes."

"I appreciate you cooking this wonderful meal for me." He got up from the chair and crossed the room to stand beside her. "How can I thank you after all the trouble I've put you to today?"

She didn't shift her gaze from her task. "No thanks

are necessary. It wasn't any bother to cook supper for you. Besides, it gave me something productive to do while Emma napped this afternoon."

"Well, the least I can do to show my gratitude is to set the table." Shifting Emma to one arm, he moved to collect utensils and two plates from a shelf beside the stove. But he paused with his hand on the second plate and glanced in Abby's direction. "Will you be joining us tonight for supper? It looks like you've made plenty, more than enough to share."

She shook her head. "No. I can't stay. My parents are expecting me home for supper. And this way, you'll have enough leftovers for a day or two."

After he finished setting the table, he turned to face Abby again. His gaze landed on her back, and he admired the elegant curve of her neck, revealed by her pinned-up hair—with the usual wayward strands curling around her face.

With an effort, he dragged his focus away from the intriguing bit of exposed skin at her nape. "Is there anything else I can do to help?"

"You could carry the pot of roasted beef and vegetables and the bowl of mashed potatoes to the table."

While he completed that duty, she gave the gravy a final stir, then poured the rich brown liquid into a serving dish and deposited it on the table. She pulled fluffy biscuits from the oven, using a towel to protect her hand as she transferred them to a cloth-lined basket positioned within easy reach of his plate.

After removing the apron tied around her waist, she hung it on the hook attached to the wall by the back door. "I think that's it. If you don't need me for anything else, I should get going now."

"You've done more than enough," he assured her.

She bent down to kiss Emma goodbye. "Be good for your papa. He's had a long day."

When Elias made a move to walk with her to the front door, she stayed him with a gesture of her hand. "There's no need to see me out. Sit down and enjoy your meal while it's hot."

The food wouldn't grow cold in the warm kitchen during the few minutes it would've taken him to see her to the door, but he didn't argue. "Will you be coming by again tomorrow?"

"Probably not. My father's expecting me to work in the mercantile in the morning, and I don't think he'll be able to spare me for a second day away. And since you've had so many volunteers, I won't have to worry about you being without someone to watch Emma. But if it turns out that you find yourself lacking in childminders, I can look after Emma at Papa's store. You can bring her by, if need be. I'm sure I could hunt up something to keep her entertained in the back room."

"I don't wish to overtax your father's good will toward me. I'll figure out another solution."

"I hope that things will go well for you and Emma tomorrow. However, my offer's open, just in case."

Elias watched Abby disappear through the doorway leading into the hall and listened to the sounds of her footfalls on the wooden floor growing fainter as she headed toward the front of the house.

The kitchen seemed somehow dimmer and devoid of warmth without Abby's presence, though that made no rational sense. He heard the front door open and close, then silence descended, leaving him alone with only Emma and his thoughts for company.

For the most part, those thoughts were positive. There was no denying that after treating at least a dozen patients over the course of several hours, he felt that he had done some good. It hadn't taken long to be reminded that doctoring was his true calling. Improving the quality of life for others elsewhere in Oregon Country would be a worthy undertaking, as well, even if it meant moving away from Silver Springs.

So, why was he suddenly experiencing an overwhelming urge to turn his back on that conviction in favor of remaining here near Abby?

Abby knew she couldn't have sat through a meal with Elias, pretending everything was fine. Not at this moment. Although she wanted to cherish every precious second she had left with both Emma and Elias while they were still close by, she needed a bit of time to strengthen her heart in order to conceal her pain so he couldn't see it.

It wouldn't be fair to make him feel guilty just because it seemed as though she couldn't bear the thought of being parted from him and Emma. Even if that wasn't too far off from the truth.

After her hasty retreat from Elias's house, Abby was in no rush to get home. Instead, she headed for her father's mercantile to help him close up for the night.

The bell on the door jingled as she pushed it open and entered the store, breathing in the familiar scents of spices and tanned leather.

Surprise lit her father's eyes when he caught sight of her. "I wasn't expecting you to come by this evening. What brings you here to see your old pa?"

"Can't a daughter pay a visit to her father for no special reason?"

"Well, course she can." But the bemused expression on his face spoke volumes, seeming to say that it wasn't her habit to do so, and that, in fact, she'd never done it before.

She wandered down the length of the counter, her hand trailing along the glass top. Her eyes focused downward, as though inspecting the merchandise on display. But her mind wasn't on the items on the other side of the well-polished glass.

Her father cleared his throat. "Is there something the matter?" When she hesitated in answering, he continued, "I hope you know, you can talk to me about it."

She wished she could unburden herself to him, but if she told her father about Elias's future plans to relocate with his daughter, there'd be no keeping it from her mother. And Abby could well imagine how the older woman would react to the unwelcome news that Elias might be taking her granddaughter away.

Emmaline Warner hadn't wanted Emma living with Elias just down the street from them. She'd gone so far as to try to keep the baby from him when he had come to their house to pick up his daughter upon his return to town the week before. It stood to reason that she'd loathe even the suggestion of her grandchild moving miles and miles away from her to an as-yet-undetermined destination.

She would fight against it tooth and nail, kicking up

an almighty fuss, Abby had no doubt. The lengths the older woman might go to in her bid to keep her grand-daughter close didn't bear thinking about.

Not for a single moment did Abby consider setting her mother loose on Elias to further her own selfish longings. It didn't matter how deeply the pain of his departure—and Emma's—would cut her. She loved him and Emma enough to put their needs ahead of her own. She would wish him well as he left—even though it would likely break her heart to say goodbye.

She'd always known doctoring was Elias's true call-ing, and now that he seemed to have finally recognized that truth for himself after so long, she wouldn't ever place herself in the way of that or set herself against him with deliberate intent. She only wished he could treat patients *and* remain here in Silver Springs, as well.

Even accepting that he'd never feel anything more for her than brotherly affection, she could have taken joy in seeing him often—and most especially, in seeing him as he'd been today, filled with purpose and faith in himself. Now she wouldn't be granted even that small comfort, however.

In all likelihood, he'd end up more than a day's ride from here. Opportunities for visits would be limited to a few times a year at the most, due to her family's re-sponsibilities at the mercantile, and further restricted by the effects of weather on poorly maintained roads during the winter and early spring.

Her heart ached at the inevitable parting, knowing that he and Emma would take a large chunk of her heart with them when they left. She wouldn't be the same once they were gone.

And Abby's mother had unwittingly helped to orchestrate the very situation that would send her granddaughter away. She'd been shortsighted to not anticipate the potential pitfalls in the course of action that had been determined by the town council's decisions. In all her managing, she'd failed to account for Elias finding the strength to carry on with his life after Rebecca.

She wouldn't be pleased to learn she'd miscalculated. Abby didn't expect that her mother would take any responsibly for her part in this, however.

It was too much to hope she'd show a calm and reasoned response—or even a smidgen of restraint. On the contrary, she'd loudly voice her objections once she learned of Elias's plans.

She would have to be told eventually, of course. But for the time being, Abby intended to put off the confrontation for as long as she could.

She had enough to cope with sorting out her own roiling emotions without the added burden of her mother's vitriol piled on top of that, too.

Her father's gray eyebrows beetled above his concerned gaze. "I'd like to help you, if I'm able."

Abby rose up on tiptoe to kiss his leathery cheek. "Thank you, Papa, but I'm okay. I promise." Or she would be, given enough time.

She had to be.

Chapter Seventeen

❧

"I appreciate you keeping an eye on Emma for me while I was busy with patients this afternoon, Tessa," Elias thanked the preacher's wife a few days later, holding his daughter close after several hours spent apart from her. "I hope it wasn't too much trouble for you to take care of her along with your own two children."

"Emma was no trouble at all. Unlike someone else who shall remain nameless." She eyed her dark-haired, six-year-old son, Henry, who wore an expression of feigned innocence that didn't fool the adults for an instant. "He's been cooped up inside for too long, I suppose. I'd best get him and his sister home."

"Thank you again for everything."

"I'm happy to help again any time." After collecting three-year-old Lizzie from the spot on the sitting room floor where she'd been playing quietly, Tessa shepherded her children down the stairs.

Elias followed behind them with Emma perched on his arm. When they reached the front hall, he held the door open for the Lintons as they prepared to leave.

The boy immediately went tearing across the wooden boardwalk that fronted the clinic.

"Henry David, stop right there and wait!" Tessa called, as he hopped down the two steps leading to the street.

He skidded to a halt and pivoted to look at his mother.

"Wait for me and your sister, please," she admonished, before turning back to Elias. "Hopefully, he'll run off some of that excess energy on the walk through town without sustaining any bodily injuries that would require our immediate return here. Barring any such unfortunate incidents in the next quarter hour, we'll see you at church on Sunday." She stepped across the threshold, leading Lizzie by the hand.

"I'm looking forward to that." He waved goodbye to them, then closed the front door behind Tessa and her children. Shifting his gaze to his daughter, he started down the hall toward the kitchen. "Did you have fun playing with Lizzie this afternoon?"

He'd picked up the recent habit from Abby of carrying on one-sided conversations with Emma. Just one of the many ways Abby had affected his life. All of them were for the better. He liked the person he had become because of her. She made him want to strive to be a more selfless man, a better father to Emma than he'd been before.

His daughter babbled an answer in response to his question, which he took as agreement.

"Now, let's see about rustling up some supper, shall we?"

When he entered the kitchen, there were no simmering pots on the stove or mouthwatering smells of food cooking in the oven as there'd been when Abby was here taking care of Emma—and Elias, besides. But Abby hadn't been tasked with the responsibility of keeping three small children safe and contented, unlike the preacher's wife.

Tessa had offered to prepare his supper, but he'd insisted that she not trouble herself on his account while riding herd on the trio of little ones, including one small, rambunctious boy with a knack for getting up to all manner of mischief when he wasn't closely supervised.

Elias certainly wouldn't want to have charge of three young children and, at the same time, be expected to get much of anything accomplished. It wasn't that long ago that it had been almost more than he could handle to care for a single child, and even then, he'd needed help from others—most especially from Abby.

And now he had patients to attend, too. Which didn't bode well for a move away from the support he'd found in Abby and several other women in Silver Springs.

True, the people in another town would likely be every bit as welcoming and helpful toward the new doctor in their midst as the folks were here, but there was one person in his current location who nobody else could hope to replace in his life. Abby. She wouldn't be there with him—wherever *there* turned out to be.

That fact was impossible to escape, though he tried not to think about it. Likewise, he refused to dwell on what it might signify about his feelings for her.

He prepared a simple meal, then sat down at the table with Emma. Once she was fed, he set her on the multicolored rag rug, freeing up his hands to tuck into his own plate of food.

Emma used the table leg to pull herself into a standing position and tottered a few steps on unsteady legs. No sooner had she released her hold on the wooden support than she plopped down on to her rear on the floor. She looked up at him as though to ask what had gone wrong.

"Don't worry, baby girl. With a little more practice, you'll get the hang of this walking thing. Then you'll really keep me on my toes, won't you?"

Almost as if she'd understood him, she graced him with an adorable smile, revealing two baby teeth.

A moment later, his brief feeling of levity drained away as he contemplated all the milestones Emma would celebrate in the years to come without Abby there close by them to share in the achievements with him and his daughter. His heart sat heavy in his chest.

His mind circled back to his previous thoughts.

How would he cope without Abby, in some strange new town as his daughter grew older? Could he be the father Emma needed day in and day out if Abby wasn't standing by his side? There would be occasions when he felt bone weary and frustrated. Times when he would have to come to grips with the loss of a patient, though he hoped those would be few and far between. Could he give of himself fully to his precious baby girl no matter the outside forces that might seek to weaken his emotional fortitude?

He recalled all the instances that Abby had stepped in to lend a hand or offered him support and encouragement when he'd been plagued by doubts.

He wouldn't allow those same, pervasive doubts to regain a foothold now.

It had taken a long while, but he believed that he had the necessary strength of will to overcome whatever obstacles might lie ahead of him. He didn't require Abby to hold his hand through the rough patches. But his preference? It wasn't to go it alone.

Despite several days passing and time running short, he'd made no effort to search out another town in need of a doctor. He could make excuses, say that he was busy with Emma along with patients who needed his full attention. But if he was honest with himself, Abby was the reason for his stalling.

How had she become such an essential part of his happiness? And how had it happened without him realizing it? When had she begun to mean so much to him? When had he come to…love her? As soon as the thought formed in his head, he recognized it was true. From friendship and caring had grown an abiding love.

He loved Abby with every bit of his damaged heart. Only it no longer felt quite so wounded now that she filled it.

How long would his heart feel whole, though, if that love was not returned? He feared that his newfound emotions for Abby might not make a speck of difference to her.

Would she even want to know about those feelings? Or would learning of his love for her only make her feel awkward and uncomfortable in his presence?

It didn't automatically follow that because he loved her she would ever come to care as deeply for him in return. And if the Lord never saw fit to grant Elias that blessing, then his heart would surely shatter, perhaps irreparably.

He didn't know if Abby felt any deeper emotions for him. Would she want to share her life with him? Or would she always view him as Emma's father and Rebecca's bereaved husband and nothing more?

The only thing he knew for certain was that he didn't want to be apart from her. He'd missed her, had felt her absence sharply while he was staying out at the ranch, and that had been for just a short time. How much worse would it be over longer stretches when he moved away to a distant town, with no hope for more than an infrequent visit every now and then? An arrow of pain embedded in his heart at the thought.

If tragedy should strike, Elias would feel Abby's loss every bit as deeply regardless of whether she lived nearby or miles distant from him. He would know grief either way. And until then, he didn't want to regret giving up the time they could have had together.

But he had to earn a living. He couldn't do that in Silver Springs. At least, not as a doctor. So, where did that leave him?

Supposing he turned his back on his plans to continue doctoring in order to stay here near Abby instead? Would it even matter to her beyond her joy in keeping her niece close by? And that aside, should he even be contemplating the notion of forsaking such a significant part of his life when he'd only just found his way back to it?

The alternative would be to implore Abby to come with him. But he couldn't do that. He wouldn't ask her to leave behind the place where she'd set down roots and was surrounded by everything familiar—her home, friends and neighbors—on his account. Wouldn't ask her to choose between him and her parents. He loved her too much to force her to make that kind of choice. He'd learned that lesson with Rebecca.

Or maybe it was that he feared what Abby's choice would be.

Emma toddled over to him and latched on to his knee. He lifted her onto his lap. "Is your papa acting like a coward?" By not grasping the chance—however slim—for true happiness through a deep and meaningful relationship with Abby.

Was he brave enough to speak aloud his feelings, to offer his heart to her, leaving himself defenseless against the pain if she rejected his love?

He thought back on her unwavering faith in him over the last few months. Could it be a sign that she felt deeply for him? Perhaps had felt something more for him all along, even when he'd been at his lowest?

Or was he hoping for too much? Wishing for the impossible?

Should he content himself with friendly affection from Abby rather than looking for anything more?

His mind was a tangled mass of conflicted thoughts and feelings, and he struggled to find his way through them.

He didn't know what to do. Which decision was the right one? For himself, for Abby? And for Emma?

"Ba, ba, ba, da," Emma babbled.

Though she couldn't offer an intelligible reply, somehow simply saying the words out loud had brought the truth home to him. "You're right, Emma, keeping silent is the coward's way. Papa has a lot to answer for."

He refused to let cowardice dictate the course of his life. No matter that he'd never thought he would be willing to risk his heart again.

Abby had captured his heart before he'd even realized it. He had to take a chance, or it was for certain that he'd lose her.

Of course, even if she returned his feelings and consented to be his wife, there would still remain an obstacle standing in the way of a truly happy life together.

Abby had never made any secret of her longing for a family of her own. Though he already had one child, he knew Abby would want more. But how could Elias give her that? How could he willingly seek to bring another child into the world when it meant he'd risk losing Abby in childbirth? How could he bear to put her life in danger that way? Even the mere thought of losing her was almost more than he could endure.

How could he accept the possibility of living in a world where Abby was gone completely? How could he face the prospect of raising more than one motherless child alone?

But neither did he want to deprive Abby of her heart's desire to have a house full of children. Could she love him enough to accept his limitations? Or would trying to place bounds on their family turn her heart against him?

He'd do everything he could to make her happy, grant her anything else that she wished, but what if it wasn't enough?

What if *he* wasn't enough?

Did it make him unworthy of Abby to even contemplate asking such a sacrifice of her, for her to consider marriage to him when he couldn't give her the promise of more children?

He couldn't ask that of her. *Wouldn't* ask it of her.

Yet, he didn't know if he could do what was necessary to ensure Abby's happiness. Didn't know if he could ever welcome more children into his life. And until he figured out the answer, he couldn't ask her to marry him.

He appealed to the Lord for guidance as he wrestled with that for several days, struggling to determine which path to take. But time continued to slip past, and still he was no closer to conquering the fear that was keeping him paralyzed.

It was driven home to Elias just how uncertain the future was only a few weeks later. When he received word from Benjamin McClain, one of his brother's neighbors, that Mattie and Josiah's baby was coming almost a month and a half early, Elias was called on to deliver the child.

As he urged the horse to greater speed, it felt like history was repeating itself. Emma had come early, too. And Rebecca had not survived the birth.

He'd never wanted his brother to have to go through the same sort of gut-wrenching turmoil. It seemed too cruel that another Dawson was facing the very real possibility of losing his wife and child. And was dependent on Elias to find a way to save them somehow, even though he had failed to save his own wife in all-too-similar circumstances.

Abby sat on the wagon seat next to him with Emma perched on her lap, silently offering him support and encouragement. Before leaving town, he had stopped at the Warners' house with the intention of dropping off Emma so that his attention wouldn't be divided between tending to Mattie and worrying over his daughter's care. But Abby had insisted on accompanying him instead.

As much as her presence at his side helped to soothe him, it could not quiet the doubts filling his mind.

The new doctor should've been here by now—should be here in Elias's place at this very moment—but his arrival in town must have been delayed somehow. The specifics weren't known since Dr. Michner hadn't managed to send word with any updates. Not that the reason made any difference right now. The only thing that mattered was that he wasn't here.

Which placed the burden of responsibility squarely on Elias's shoulders.

Would he be strong enough to bear up under the heavy weight?

When he'd taken up doctoring again, he hadn't figured on having to assist Mattie through this difficult and precarious time. But nothing had worked out as he'd imagined.

It wasn't supposed to happen this way. He wasn't supposed to be the one to deliver his brother's child. Yet there was no other choice.

He couldn't let Josiah down. Because he couldn't bear for his brother to know the same pain as Elias had.

Especially if Elias was the cause.

* * *

The late October weather turned gray and cold as Mattie labored through the morning and into the afternoon. Abby spent most of the day in the bedroom with her, splitting her attention between caring for Emma and assisting Elias by holding Mattie's hand and wiping her brow with a damp cloth.

But a short time ago, Abby had been forced to leave the room when Mattie's cries started to distress Emma. Given how upsetting they'd been to Mattie's husband, as well, Josiah was not in any condition to watch over the little girl.

A baby's cry suddenly broke out, but a moment later all was quiet in the bedroom once more. Yet the door did not open and Elias didn't appear.

Abby felt her heart sink with looming dread.

Josiah stood up and took a step toward the bedroom, then hesitated. Turning back around, he sank down on the chair opposite Abby in front of the hearth, and bowed his head, his hands clasped in silent prayer.

His head came up at the sound of the bedroom door opening a few minutes later.

Elias moved into the living room, and Josiah stood to rush to his older brother's side. But he couldn't seem to find his voice to ask the questions that must be utmost in his mind at the moment, doubtlessly fearing what answers he might receive.

Lines of fatigue were cut deep into Elias's face, but his expression didn't look like that of a man about to deliver devastating news.

Abby held her breath as she waited for him to speak.

"You have a son, Josiah. And a daughter."

Josiah's eyebrows pulled together and he shook his head in incomprehension. "What?"

"A boy and a girl," Elias said, as the corners of his lips started to edge up into a smile.

Josiah's mouth dropped open. "Twins?"

"Yep. Congratulations, Josiah." Elias clapped his younger brother on the shoulder.

Josiah seemed dazed but for only a few seconds, then his gaze sharpened. "How's Mattie? Is she all right?"

"Yes. And the babies are fine, too, even though they came early." A wide grin now lit up Elias's features.

"Thank the Lord." Josiah closed his eyes and breathed deeply for the span of half a dozen heartbeats. When he opened his eyes again, his gaze met his brother's. "Thank you, Elias."

Elation that his wife had safely delivered two healthy children was quickly replacing the look of fear that had been clouding his expression since their arrival.

Josiah wrapped his brother in a tight hug, holding on for several long moments.

"Go on in and meet the newest members of our family," Elias invited when Josiah finally released him and stepped back.

Once the younger man entered the bedroom, Elias closed the door behind him, giving Josiah and Mattie the opportunity to share a private moment getting to know their new son and daughter. The quiet murmur of voices filtered through the wooden door, too low for Abby to make out the words.

Elias crossed the floor to sit down beside her on the horsehair sofa. She shifted Emma to a more comfortable position on her lap as rain pounded on the roof overhead.

Elias's mood had seemed just as grim as the dark sky outside during the journey to Mattie and Josiah's log cabin. The fact that his brother's wife was the first woman he'd attended in childbirth since Rebecca's passing must have made the situation even more nerve-racking for Elias. For those hours, he'd held Josiah's whole world in his hands.

The weight of that responsibility had to be crippling, especially knowing the devastating heartbreak wrought by that sort of loss. There would have been no ignoring the possibility that more tragedy could befall the Dawson family.

Yet, Elias had shown no outward signs of turmoil in front of Mattie or Josiah. He'd been so wonderful—Abby was glad she'd been there to see it and to do everything she could to lend him her silent support.

Only now, when the threat of danger was passed and he was alone save for Abby and Emma, had he relaxed his guard enough to reveal that he wasn't unaffected by the ordeal.

Fortunately, they had come through the birth with a healthy mother and babies to show for his efforts.

Abby lifted Emma onto his lap, and he hugged his daughter against his chest. The little girl laid her head down on her papa's shoulder.

Placing one hand against Emma's back, Abby rested her other hand on Elias's arm. "You've done well."

"With your help and the Good Lord guiding my hands," he avowed.

She agreed wholeheartedly that it was a blessing

from above that everything had turned out well. But Elias had much to do with it, too. The Lord had truly given him a gift for healing.

He wrapped his arm around Abby and pulled her close. "Thank you for staying by my side through this and everything else I've struggled with over the past several months. You'll never know how much that meant to me."

"I do know." Because there was nowhere she'd rather be than with him, whether through the happy times or the ones that tried her.

But she forced herself to pull away from his embrace after only a moment.

Although the town's new doctor was late in arriving in Silver Springs, he would be here any day now. And then Elias would be gone.

Abby's heart broke at the thought.

Chapter Eighteen

Elias had done a lot of praying over the last few weeks, first searching for a means to move beyond his fear and then praying that he wouldn't lose Josiah's wife in childbirth.

Thankfully, Mattie had come through it fine. And now had two beautiful babies to show for it.

Yet, Abby had appeared sad on the way back to Silver Springs. Though he had tried to talk to her, she hadn't seemed to want to say much. After he'd dropped her off at her parents' house and returned to his own home above the clinic, he couldn't help but wonder once again if she would be sorry to see him leave town.

He had no doubt she'd miss Emma. But would she miss *him* at all?

That question had kept him from sleep all last night and refused to leave his mind this morning.

Although the thought of the risk Abby would face going through childbirth still caused him to break out in a cold sweat, for the first time it felt as if he would risk losing more by letting his fear control him.

He'd found the strength to see Mattie through her recent trial, despite his fear. So how could he allow it to keep him from trying to gain what he wanted most—having Abby in his life always.

Suddenly, he realized that the Lord had been listening all along and had answered his prayers. By going through the test of helping Mattie during the delivery of her twins, Elias had gained the courage necessary to open his heart to the possibility of more children of his own. Children with Abby as their mother.

But would Abby want that, too? Would she want *him*?

Again, he looked to God for guidance.

Lord, please give me the courage to speak the words that are in my heart.

He needed to talk to Abby. And he didn't intend to hold anything back.

Because his heart wouldn't be whole without her. He yearned to spend every day with her, sharing their joys and whatever heartache may come. To have her by his side to celebrate his successes, always, and to offer a shoulder to lean on during hard times. He prayed for all of that with Abby. Longed to build a life with her, if she'd have him.

He wasn't satisfied to have her merely on the periphery of his life.

But whether she would want her role to continue as Emma's aunt only or something more… That remained to be seen—and couldn't be determined until he gathered the courage to act.

Pushing away the plate of breakfast he'd hardly touched, he stood up from the table and lifted Emma into his arms. "We're going to pay a visit to your Aunt Abby."

After bundling Emma up in a coat to guard against the cool autumn weather, Elias stepped outside and paused on the wooden boardwalk. The most sensible place to start looking for Abby was at her home. Of course, if he went there, he'd likely run the risk of encountering Mrs. Warner, as well. But he would willingly brave his former mother-in-law in order to talk to Abby.

However, when nobody answered his knock at the Warners' front door, a feeling in his gut he couldn't explain prodded him to check her favorite sketching spot before toting Emma all the way to the mercantile.

There was a chill in the air, but it was still a bit too early in the year for snow, and the sun shone brightly as it climbed higher in the sky to the east.

Reaching the meadow at the edge of town, Elias sighted Abby beneath the branches of the oak tree she favored. Its leaves were turning brilliant shades of yellow and orange and red, and several had fallen to the ground, where they lay scattered around Abby.

She sat with her head bent over the open sketchbook balanced on her lap. Seeming lost in deep thoughts, she didn't react to his approach. Her face remained turned away from him.

As he drew closer to her, he caught a glimpse of what she was focused on so intently.

It was a drawing of him.

In it, he appeared happy and untroubled. Was that truly how she viewed him? But then, she always seemed to see the best in him.

And perhaps she wasn't too far off in her depiction of him, at that. He realized he'd felt more content and much less unsettled these past several months.

He had Abby to thank for the change in him. She had made the difference. She and Emma had saved him.

After he lost Rebecca, he had thought he could never love another woman, but he'd been wrong. Abby had snuck past his guard and into his heart without his awareness. When he'd opened his heart enough to let his daughter in, Abby had somehow found a way through the Emma-size gap, as well.

Elias was a better man for it and was grateful for that, whether she returned his love now or ever.

He watched Abby as she traced her finger along the outline of his jaw in the picture, her expression melancholy.

Was she rubbing the charcoal lines to smudge them, to create depth and shading? Or were her actions motivated by something else completely?

Did she feel anything beyond friendly affection for him? Could she return some small measure of the deep emotion he felt toward her? Seeing her sketch of him gave Elias a bit of hope that she might. He prayed it was so.

Even in profile, he could see that sadness blanketed her features, and he considered the reasons behind it.

Was she distressed at the thought of saying goodbye to *him* and not just to Emma?

There was only one way to know for sure.

He took a deep breath to calm his nerves and gathered his courage. "May I join you, Abby?"

* * *

Abby started at the sound of Elias's voice and tilted her head up to meet his gaze. "Of course," she replied after a tiny hesitation.

As he sat down beside her, placing Emma on the grass that had turned brown with the advent of colder weather, Abby couldn't help but wonder why he was here. Not that she'd send him away, regardless of his reasons, but what cause could he have to seek her out? Because surely, he *had* sought her out. He had no reason to come to this spot unless he was specifically looking for her.

Despite the fact that he'd asked her to watch Emma yesterday, he didn't really need her help anymore, didn't need *her* anymore. Even as she took joy in Elias finding a measure of contentment and stability, at last, caring for his daughter and choosing to live with hope for the future instead of grief and self-recrimination about the past, that didn't lessen the pinprick of hurt at feeling suddenly without purpose.

"I wasn't aware that you had a talent for portraits along with landscapes," Elias remarked, breaking into her thoughts.

She'd allowed him to see only the drawings of outdoor scenes previously. It had been a deliberate action on her part. She'd never shown anyone her sketches of people because the pictures revealed too much of herself. When she sketched a person, she put her emotions into it. Whatever she felt for the individual ended up on the page for all to see. Now her innermost feelings for Elias had been exposed to him. Would he comprehend that and recognize the depth of her love for him?

Her cheeks heated, imagining what conclusions he would likely reach after catching her mooning over his likeness. She shoved the sketchbook into her canvas bag and prayed that once the drawing was out of sight, Elias would forget about it.

But just in case he didn't let it go at that, she hopped to her feet and made a show of looking at the sun's position in the sky. "I didn't realize it was getting so late."

"Abby, wait." He picked up Emma and then stood, reaching out a hand toward Abby to stop her from leaving. "There's something I need to say."

If it was what she suspected, that he could never love her in return, then she didn't want to hear it. "I have to get home," she replied as she edged toward the houses on the outskirts of town, hoping to forestall further conversation.

Elias fell into step beside her. "I'll walk with you."

She tensed up, braced to listen to his well-meaning but unwelcome explanations. However, he surprised her by remaining silent for several long moments as they crossed the meadow of tall, dry grass.

Glancing at him out of the corner of her eye, she saw his mouth turned down in a frown, his gaze focused on the ground in front of him.

Doubtlessly, he was searching for a way to let her down gently. She turned her head away, biting into her bottom lip.

Though it was a childish impulse—and useless besides—she wanted to put her hands over her ears when he began to speak.

"I've been doing a lot of thinking about what it will

mean if I find a doctoring post in another town and whether or not leaving would be the right choice."

It wasn't the speech Abby had expected. She missed a step and stumbled. His free hand came up to steady her, then fell away as she started forward again.

Her mind raced, trying to figure out where he could be heading with this conversation, but she was at a loss. Was he rethinking his plans? It didn't make sense to her. She couldn't see any reason for him to go back over a decision he'd already reached.

Except for one.

"If this is my mother's doing, you can't let her—"

"What does your mother have to do with this?"

Abby snapped her mouth closed. If her mother hadn't discovered Elias's intentions and persuaded him to re-think moving away with Emma... "Then, why are you reconsidering?"

"Because it doesn't affect only me and Emma. I don't want to cause you any pain." Before she could get too elated at that admission, he continued. "And then there's Josiah and Mattie as well as your parents to take into account."

That last bit deflated her spirits entirely. It seemed that she wasn't anyone special to him, just another relation. Ranking somewhere below his brother and sister-in-law but hopefully above her parents—and her mother in particular.

Abby had known as much, of course, though she'd fooled herself for a time.

"You have to go," she insisted.

"Don't you want me—us—to stay?" His eyebrows bunched together as hurt shone in his dark gaze.

"Of course I'd like for you to stay here." How could he think otherwise?

"But only to keep Emma close by," he said before she could finish her explanation. He didn't phrase it as a question.

Was it possible that Elias hadn't guessed the truth when he'd seen her sketch? That he didn't realize she would miss him every bit as much as she'd miss Emma, feel his absence just as intensely?

Abby couldn't let his misconception stand, despite a little voice in the back of her head cautioning her to protect her heart. "That's not true. You've got it wrong."

His fingers absently stroked his daughter's curls. "If not because of Emma, then why does it matter to you one way or the other?"

She searched her mind for a reply, discarding a handful of responses, and ended up saying nothing.

They had passed the first few houses on the edge of town. She picked up her pace, hoping to get home and make her escape before she revealed more than she considered wise.

Elias lengthened his stride to keep up with her. "Why, Abby?"

Why did he keep pushing her for an answer? Why couldn't he simply leave it be?

"Just tell me, why?" he pressed her once more.

"Because I love you!" She clapped her hand over her mouth and groaned, wishing for nothing so much as to hide in her bedroom at this moment and not come out again until after Elias had left town. She lowered her arm, her fingers curling into a fist at her side, nails digging into her palm. "I didn't mean to say that."

"You didn't mean what you said?" Elias challenged, shifting his hold on Emma and hitching her higher up against his chest.

"I *did* mean it. I love you." She didn't give him the opportunity to form a reply—if any had been forthcoming—before she rushed on. "But I know you don't hold me in the same kind of regard. There's no need to concern yourself with trying to spare my feelings. You don't have to say anything—"

"Yes, I do."

"No! Please, don't. I can't bear to hear you say you'll never love any woman but Rebecca." She moved away from him, trying to outdistance the pain.

"Abby, stop." When she didn't immediately halt her steps, he reached out and wrapped his fingers around her wrist, pulling her to a standstill in the middle of the street. "Look at me. Please." He waited for her to meet his gaze and then continued. "Rebecca will always have a piece of my heart. That won't ever change."

Abby turned her face to the side, agony like a hot iron poker stabbing into her unmercifully. Elias released his hold on her wrist and laid his palm against her cheek, bringing her focus back to him, refusing to allow her to look away again.

But she could barely make out his features as she stared at him through the wash of tears in her eyes. One slipped past her lashes.

He brushed away the teardrop, stroking the pad of his thumb across her skin. "Don't cry. You didn't let me finish."

His gentle tone caused more tears to well up in her eyes, but she nodded for him to continue.

"I believed that I could never feel for another woman what I had felt for Rebecca, and in a way, that's true. But it doesn't mean I can't love anyone else. Though I thought my heart would remain buried with Rebecca always, you brought me back to life, Abby. Through your love for my daughter, and your unfailing faith in me, you showed me that I had something—someone— worth fighting for. I love you, Abby."

Was her mind playing a cruel trick on her, imagining that he'd said what she so desperately wanted to hear? Could it possibly be true that he loved *her*?

She blinked her eyes to clear her vision and saw the sincerity in his gaze, rejoiced at the genuine emotion shining brightly in his dark eyes. Her tears of pain and sorrow turned into tears of happiness. Laughing as they spilled over, she wiped them away.

When he leaned down toward her, she tipped her face upward, taking care not to squish Emma between them.

Elias pressed his lips to hers in a tender kiss right there on Maple Street, in front of God and anyone who happened to walk past.

Joy swelled inside Elias's heart, his love for Abby brimming over.

He drew back and reached for her hand, determined to get this right. "I fear I don't deserve you, but I'll gladly spend my days trying to prove myself worthy of you. If you'll have me." He considered dropping down to his knee right there in the middle of the dusty road but decided that probably wouldn't be a wise decision while he was holding Emma. "I'd like nothing more than to have you as my wife, Abby. Will you marry me?"

Her smile rivaled the brilliant rays of sunlight shining down on them, warming the cool autumn air. "Yes, I will marry you. But you're wrong, you know. You don't have to work at earning my affection, Elias. You're worthy of my love just as you are, because of the man you've become. The Lord has answered my prayers, and I can't wait to begin a life with you and Emma. Moving to a new town together will be an adventure."

Though she put a brave face on it, Elias imagined that it wouldn't be easy for her to leave behind the settled life she had here in Silver Springs. Impossible that she wouldn't feel apprehensive about the upheaval and uncertainty of relocating. Especially when winter snow would soon blanket the countryside and cut them off from her family.

Abby had done much to lighten the burden Elias carried. He didn't want it to all be one-sided, with him taking from her and giving nothing in return. It wasn't right that she should be the one to make this sacrifice—even if she didn't acknowledge it as a sacrifice.

He wouldn't force her to compromise after she'd offered so much of herself to him and his daughter already.

"I've decided against dragging you and Emma to goodness-only-knows where," he revealed. "We'll stay here in Silver Springs instead."

"But the new doctor will be arriving any day. Maybe even today." Her eyebrows pleated together above her pale blue gaze. "Unless Mother has neglected to inform me otherwise."

"No, nothing's changed in that respect—at least, as far as I know. Once Dr. Michner takes over, I figured on living out at my brother's ranch. I'll have to talk with him first, of course, but I don't foresee any impediments to becoming a partner in Josiah's horse ranch. I'll build a cabin on the property for you, me and Emma."

"There's most definitely a problem with that," she disputed.

"What? You don't wish to live outside of town?"

"No, that's not it at all. You aren't meant to be a rancher, Elias." She laid her hand against his cheek. "You're a doctor. It's not merely a profession for you— it's who you are. You can't give up tending to patients."

He knew full well what he would be surrendering in order to remain in this area and near her family, but Abby meant more to him than anything else apart from his daughter. As long as he had them, nothing else mattered.

He reached up and shifted her hand away from his face, interlocking his fingers with hers. "I can't ask you to leave your parents."

"You aren't asking. I'm offering—no, I'm insisting. It's my choice to go with you. I won't be the reason you forsake your calling. The Lord blessed you with skills few others have. You can do so much good for so many people in another town. You can't turn your back on them."

He shook his head. "I won't put you in the same position as I did Rebecca. Once I let go of my anger and resentment toward her and stopped placing blame on her, I took a good, hard look at what had driven her and acknowledged how difficult she found the prolonged separation from her family. We stayed in Nashville when the rest of you came out here because I didn't want to leave behind my established clinic. If I hadn't put that first, who knows what it would have changed? I can't go back and do things over again with her, but I'll make different choices this time around."

"Don't compare me to Rebecca."

"I wasn't—"

"I'm not her."

"I know that, Abby." He squeezed her fingers. "I'm not expecting you to be. Never doubt it. I just don't want to repeat the mistakes *I* made in the past."

"The only mistake you're in danger of repeating is abandoning your calling. Besides, this isn't the same situation as you faced before with Rebecca. I'm not close with Mother, the way my sister was."

That fact hadn't escaped Elias's notice, and to his mind, the distance between Abby and her mother wasn't necessarily a bad thing. He recalled how he'd often thought Rebecca was just a bit *too* close to the older woman.

"I suppose a day or two's ride isn't terribly far to travel for a visit." Not when compared to the two thousand miles between Tennessee and Oregon Country that had separated Rebecca from her parents and sister.

Granted, Thomas and Emmaline Warner couldn't drop in to visit Abby on a whim—but that was almost certain to make for better relations between Elias and his in-laws. And anyway, she would be able to see her father and mother several times a year, just as Mattie was able to see her sister, aunt and uncle.

"Are you sure this is what you want?" he questioned.

"Yes. There's nothing I'd like more than to see you continuing to do good works as a doctor and to know I helped you achieve that end."

Elias was heartened by this further proof of her enduring support for him. Hearing her encouragement and knowing he had her wholehearted approval lifted a weight off him. One that he hadn't even realized he'd been carrying.

Abby was right about this, and so much more. Doctoring was more than a mere job to him. It served a higher purpose.

And he should have recognized that she would urge him toward this path. The Lord had placed her in Elias's life because He knew she was exactly what Elias needed most. Though it had taken him much too long to grasp His wisdom.

Thank you, Lord, for Abby.

She was a blessing beyond compare. Never had she put herself ahead of him or failed to give his feelings and wants equal, if not greater, consideration than her own.

Elias could do no less for her.

For a long time—too long—he had doubted himself. But he knew now that he was strong enough to endure whatever might come. With the Lord's help.

Anyone he loved could be taken from him at any moment, and that's why he needed to cherish every second he was granted with them. He would pray every day for God to keep Abby and their family safe from harm—and thank Him for the blessings He'd given to Elias.

He enclosed Abby and his daughter in the circle of his arms and hugged them both close, his chin resting against Abby's temple. He broke the silence by clearing his throat. "I think that Emma might like to have a baby brother or sister before too long."

Abby pulled back slightly in order to see Elias's face. Did he truly want that? Or was he merely saying it because he knew how much she wanted it?

"I won't deny that I'd love to have a house full of babies, but more children aren't necessary for my happiness. I only need you and Emma to make my life complete." She held out her arms toward Emma, and he willingly relinquished his daughter into Abby's keeping. "I love her as though she's my own, and I'll be content to be a mother to her."

Abby's feelings for Emma ran deep. She would give her sister's daughter all the love Rebecca wasn't able to offer. She'd always regret that her sister wasn't here for Emma, but Abby would take joy in nurturing and guiding the little girl as she grew older.

"You'll be a wonderful mother to Emma, but I know how much you yearn for more children to love. I want to give you that. And I want it for Emma, too. I spent most of my growing up years without my brother, and I felt the lack sharply. It's lonely in a household without brothers or sisters. Even though Emma will have cousins to play with, there's no other bond quite like that between siblings."

"I don't have to give birth to a child in order for us to add to our family." She knew the wounds Elias carried and she loved him enough not to put him through the anxiety he'd feel if she was with child. That was too much to ask, if it wasn't something he truly wanted for

himself. If he was agreeing to this for her sake alone...
they could take in an orphaned child instead. "I would
never want to cause you a moment of added worry or
strain."

Elias laid his palm against Abby's cheek and looked
deeply into her eyes. "You have so much love to offer.
Any child would be fortunate to have you as a mother.
But I'm not merely doing this for you. Or for Emma.
I'm doing this for me, too." He took a deep breath before
continuing. "It's time I stop allowing fear and memories of the past to overshadow my faith in the Lord. I'll
put my trust in Him and open my heart to accept the
family He, in His infinite wisdom, sees fit to bless us
with—however many children that may be."

"Are you certain about this?"

"Yes. As certain as I am that I love you. I never
thought I'd be able to take that kind of risk again to welcome more children into my life, never thought I'd want
to, but you give me strength and courage, Abby. I'm
ready to face whatever's ahead, with you by my side."

The thought of giving Elias a child born of their
love filled Abby with joy. A child of their own, nur-
tured under her heart until the day they welcomed the
precious new life into the world.

His thumb stroked along her cheek. "I pray you don't
have your heart set on a long engagement or a spring
wedding. I want you as my wife before I take a post in
another town, and I'll be looking for one just as soon
as the new doctor arrives."

"I've always dreamed of an autumn wedding, when
the air's crisp and fresh and families are coming together for Thanksgiving. And then, perhaps, you and I

and Emma can get settled into our new home, together as a family, before the first snowfall."

"There's nothing I would like more than that," he echoed her earlier words.

Encircling both Abby and Emma in his embrace once more, Elias bent his head to place a kiss on Abby's lips, with their daughter snuggled securely between them.

Her heart filled with love and thankfulness for the Lord's many blessings in her life.

Epilogue

Silver Springs, Willamette Valley, Oregon Country
Early December, 1847

Abby Warner Dawson settled back against the pillows, a sleeping infant cradled in her arms. Her husband sat in a chair at her bedside, and their two-year-old daughter, Emma, was curled up asleep next to Abby.

She turned to gaze out the window of the bedroom located above the doctor's clinic. Fat flakes of snow drifted to the ground, carpeting the town of Silver Springs in glittering white, while inside, Elias and Abby's home was filled with love and warmth.

A short time ago, Elias had delivered their healthy baby boy after assisting Abby through a long but thankfully trouble-free labor. She strongly suspected that Elias was the one who had suffered the most during the birthing, though his pain hadn't been physical.

Now his head was bowed and his forearms propped against his upper legs, his hands clasped between his knees. But it wasn't a dejected pose. His demeanor was one of reverence. Abby imagined that he was saying a silent prayer of thanks to the Lord.

They had named their son Nathaniel, which meant "gift of God." And that was just what he was. The perfect early Christmas present for the entire Dawson family during this season of giving and celebration for the wonder of their Savior.

Abby reached out and placed her hand over Elias's interlocked fingers. Though his eyes remained closed, he turned his palm up to lace his fingers with hers. A few silent minutes passed before he opened his eyes and raised his head to meet her gaze.

"How are you feeling?" he asked, tenderness for her lighting his expression.

"Tired. But happy." She offered him a smile that felt as though it sprang from the very depths of her heart.

He lifted his hand to gently caress her cheek. "Do you want me to take little Nathaniel so you can get some rest?"

"Not just yet." She wasn't ready to give up this precious moment surrounded by her family.

Dr. Hiram Michner had never made it to Oregon Country. Only a few days before Elias and Abby's wedding, the sad news had reached Silver Springs that the doctor had succumbed to an outbreak of sickness along the trail that had taken the lives of roughly half his wagon train. When the town council approached Elias about filling the vacancy left by the other man's untimely demise, he'd readily agreed to step into the void, turning his short-term stint of tending patients at the clinic into a permanent arrangement.

Over the past year, Abby's mother had become less

vocal in her censure of Elias as he had settled in as the town's doctor and worked hard to gain the townspeople's respect. Though the shift was more likely due to the fact that recent events had pleased the older woman rather than any softening in her critical nature, Abby nonetheless looked upon the improved relations between Elias and her mother as cause for rejoicing.

And since Abby had married Elias and moved out of her parents' house, she'd found that her mother seemed to have tempered her criticisms of Abby's appearance and behavior, as well. Even when the older woman did voice a complaint, it no longer bothered Abby the way it once had. Elias loved her just as she was, and she'd come to realize that his good opinion was the only one that truly mattered to her. Holding that thought close to her, she could let her mother's occasional barbed comments pass by without taking them too much to heart—especially when Elias deftly parried any that were uttered in his hearing.

Abby felt a pang for her husband every now and then, that the poor man was once again saddled with Emmaline Warner for a mother-in-law. He bore up under it admirably, but Abby couldn't deny she'd harbored a kernel of fear deep down in her heart during their short engagement that he might decide against going through with the wedding when it dawned on him what he'd be opening himself up to once their vows were spoken.

That he had stood proudly by her side at the front of the church on their wedding day was a testament to his strength of character and the depth of his love for her.

Abby thanked the Lord daily for all He had given

her. His blessings enriched her life and brought her joy beyond anything she'd ever imagined possible.

She had a daughter she adored, a new baby son and a husband who never allowed a single day to pass without letting her know, through word and deed, how much he loved her. And her feelings for him were every bit as strong.

She couldn't ask for anything more than that.

Her heart overflowed with happiness. "I love you, Elias."

"I love you, too." He leaned down to place a kiss on her lips.

Elias's love was one of the many things she gave thanks for each day. They had so much for which to be grateful.

Whatever joys or heartache the future held for their family, they'd face it together, knowing that the Lord would be with them. Always.

* * * * *

LOVE INSPIRED

Stories to uplift and inspire

Fall in love with Love Inspired—
inspirational and uplifting stories of faith
and hope. Find strength and comfort in
the bonds of friendship and community.
Revel in the warmth of possibility and the
promise of new beginnings.

Sign up for the Love Inspired newsletter
at **LoveInspired.com** to be the first
to find out about upcoming titles,
special promotions and exclusive content.

CONNECT WITH US AT:

Facebook.com/LoveInspiredBooks

Twitter.com/LoveInspiredBks

Get 4 FREE REWARDS!

We'll send you 2 FREE Books plus 2 FREE Mystery Gifts.

Love Inspired books feature uplifting stories where faith helps guide you through life's challenges and discover the promise of a new beginning.

FREE Value Over $20

IF YOU ENJOYED THIS BOOK
WE THINK YOU WILL ALSO LOVE

LOVE INSPIRED
INSPIRATIONAL ROMANCE

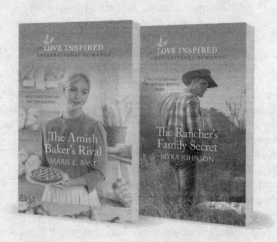

Uplifting stories of faith, forgiveness and hope.

Fall in love with stories where faith helps
guide you through life's challenges, and discover
the promise of a new beginning.

6 NEW BOOKS AVAILABLE EVERY MONTH!

"We need a housekeeper because I can't chase you down every other—" Tucker suddenly remembered they had an audience. "We can talk about this at home."

Nan, spritely at seventy with short silvery hair, grinned big and inclined her head toward the other woman.

"Clara needs a job," she said.

"I don't think so," Clara shot back.

"You need something to do," Nan insisted.

"She doesn't want the job." Tucker winked at the woman and watched her cheeks turn rosy.

Flirting was an art he'd learned late in life, and he still wasn't too accomplished at it. He'd never been a ladies' man.

"No, I really don't," she answered. "I'm only here temporarily."

Should he feel relieved or let down?

"You should introduce us," he told Nan.

"Tucker Church, I'd like you to meet Clara Fisher," Nan said. "She's one of my kids."

One of Nan's foster daughters. She'd had a dozen or more over the years. He held a hand out. "Clara, nice to meet you."

It was a long moment before Clara slid her hand into his. Then she stepped back, putting space between them.

"Nice to meet you, too. But I'm afraid I'm not interested in a job." She gave his niece a genuine smile, then her gaze lifted to meet his. "I think that we probably met in school, but you were a senior and I was just a freshman."

He couldn't imagine forgetting Clara Fisher, with her dark brown eyes that held secrets and a smile that was captivating. He found himself wishing he could make her smile again.

Shay elbowed him. "She doesn't want the job," she whispered. "Can we go home now?"

"Of course she doesn't want to work for us. She's probably heard the stories about you running off two housekeepers." He gave Clara a pleading look.

"Would you take my number? In case you change your mind?"

"I won't change my mind," she insisted.

He had no right to feel disappointed. She was a stranger. And yet, he was.

"Well, we should go," he said as he walked Shay toward the door.

"I bet she can't even clean," Shay said under her breath.

He didn't disagree. But Clara looked like a woman who was trying to put herself back together. He needed someone strong who could stand up to Shay.

The woman who replaced Mrs. Jenkins couldn't have soulful brown eyes and a smile that made him want to take chances.

Don't miss
Her Christmas Dilemma *by Brenda Minton,*
available December 2021 wherever
Love Inspired books and ebooks are sold.

LoveInspired.com

LIEXP1121

**IF YOU ENJOYED THIS BOOK, DON'T MISS NEW
EXTENDED-LENGTH NOVELS FROM LOVE INSPIRED!**

**In addition to the Love Inspired books you know and
love, we're excited to introduce even more uplifting
stories in a longer format, with more inspiring fresh
starts and page-turning thrills!**

LOVE INSPIRED

Stories to uplift and inspire.

Fall in love with Love Inspired—inspirational and uplifting
stories of faith and hope. Find strength and comfort in the bonds
of friendship and community. Revel in the warmth of possibility,
and the promise of new beginnings.

**LOOK FOR THESE LOVE INSPIRED TITLES ONLINE AND IN THE
BOOK DEPARTMENT OF YOUR FAVORITE RETAILER!**

LITRADE0921

**For readers of *Lilac Girls* and
*The Lost Girls of Paris***

Don't miss this captivating novel of resilience following
three generations of women as they battle to save
their family's vineyard during WWII

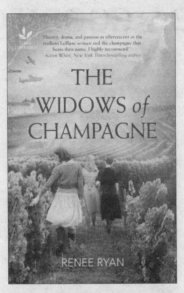

"History, drama, and passion as effervescent as the
resilient LeBlanc women and the champagne that
bears their name. I highly recommend!"
—Karen White, *New York Times* bestselling author

THE
WIDOWS *of*
CHAMPAGNE

RENEE RYAN

"With complex characters and a stunning setting,
The Widows of Champagne will sweep you into a wartime story
of love, greed, and how one should never underestimate the
strength of the women left behind. I couldn't put it down."
—Donna Alward, *New York Times* bestselling author

Coming soon from Love Inspired!

LOVE INSPIRED
LoveInspired.com

LI42707BPA